Black Fair

James Mc Nally

This book is dedicated to my good friend, my work wife, and devoted fan, Debbie Allinger. This marks the first of my work she will not be here to read and that saddens me. A part of Debbie will go into everything I write henceforth. I will miss you.

Streisand fans unite!

Other books by James Mc Nally

Immortal Trilogy
Immortal Coil
Immortal Clash
Immortal Conquest

Keepers of the Forest
The Fortress

The Affected

Short Stories

Still Life Series
Still Life: There's Something Wrong with Dennis
Still Life 2: Hello, My Name is...
Still Life 3: Pay it Backward

In the Details: A short story

Hinterland: A short story of desolation...and magic

Chapter One: Shaina

A brisk morning breeze blew through the open driver's side window, and it felt good on Shaina's face. She inhaled deeply in an attempt to wake herself up. She still had several miles to go before she would arrive home, and after the 48-hour shift at St. Cumberland hospital where Shaina had agreed to assist during a crisis, she needed every trick possible to keep from passing out. The dull scenery wasn't helping matters. There was nothing but tall grass on either side of the road.

Shaina closed her eyes and opened them again quickly, fearing that she had fallen asleep. She slammed on her breaks and stopped short of hitting a man standing in the road in front of her. A jolt of electricity sprinted through her spine, and any sense of exhaustion left her body.

The man, wearing a state police uniform, walked around to her open window. Placing a hand on his gun, he leaned in. "Sorry, Ma'am. We'll need you to go back the way you came. There's been an accident, and this whole area is off-limits."

"An accident?" Shaina glanced at the scene.

Two police cruisers with their lights flashing sat on each side of the road with their noses pointed in, causing a roadblock. Beyond them, some kind of police transport vehicle sat off in the tall grass, tipped on its side. The back door hung open like a slack-jawed mouth. The darkness inside revealed nothing. Shaina turned back to the cop. "Was anyone hurt? I'm a nurse. I can help."

"The driver has pain in his wrist, but other than that everyone is fine."

"I could take a look at it."

The officer contemplated this then opened her door for her. Shaina unbuckled her seatbelt and climbed out of the car.

"I'm Shaina Salvador, by the way, officer..." She read his nameplate "Rosinsky."

"Right this way, Ma'am."

Shaina rolled her eyes when the cop wasn't looking, wondering why she had bothered to introduce herself if he was just going to call her ma'am anyway. She shrugged and followed Officer Rosinsky to the two police cruisers.

The vehicle blocking the right side of the road had its back door open, and she could see a pair of blue slacks and black shoes sticking out. She came around and looked down at the police officer sitting there, cradling his arm.

She read his name tag as well. "Officer Kolter, my name is Shaina. I'm a nurse. Can I take a look at your hand?"

The officer held out his wrist to her, still cradling it in his other hand.

She could see that it was swollen. She knelt to get a closer look but did not touch it. She moved her head to look at it from a different angle. "Can you move the fingers for me?"

The cop wiggled his fingers, wincing.

"I don't think it's broken. Is there a first aid kit?"

Within a matter of seconds, a small white box with a red plus sign on it was shoved in her face. She took it, thanking whoever had handed it to her. She removed the portable ice pack, a white bag with gel inside, and worked it around with both hands, squeezing and massaging the contents. When she could feel the bag getting cold, she handed it to the injured cop.

"Lay this on your wrist to keep the swelling down."

Officer Kolter placed his injured hand on his leg and pulled the other hand free. He took the cold pack from her and put it gently on his wrist, sucking through his teeth as he did so. He took a deep breath. "Thank you, Shaina. It feels better already."

She smiled. "Thank *you* for using my name."

She was about to ask if an ambulance had been called, but just as she turned around, she saw one moving down the road from the direction she had just come. In another second or two, she could hear its siren.

Feeling she had done all she could do, Shaina approached the two cops standing between the cruisers. One man had his head down, clearly showing deference to Officer Rosinsky standing next to him. A fourth policeman stood with his back to her inside the open driver's side door of the second cruiser. He held the mouthpiece of a CB radio a few inches from his lips, talking. Though she hadn't heard all that he was saying, she had heard him identify himself as Bob to the person on the other end of the radio.

Shaina continued toward Officer Rosinsky, who she had placed as the one in charge.

The cop with Rosinsky lowered his head. "She got my gun, Ken."

Ken Rosinsky shushed him. The smaller cop turned away as she approached.

Rosinsky turned to her. "We can handle it from here. Thank you for your help, Miss."

Flippantly, she said. "It's Shaina. And can I please get by now? My home is that way…" She pointed, but the cop wasn't interested in anything she had to say. He brushed past her and stomped over to the policeman holding the CB mouthpiece. He slapped the mic out of his hand, and its spiral cord whipped it onto the seat inside the cruiser. Rosinsky spoke rapidly, shouting a conversation of which Shaina heard only bits and pieces.

"…Gun…stupid asshole…get that piece back."

Bob scrambled into his cruiser and drove away in the direction Shaina herself wanted to go.

Shaina approached Rosinsky again. "Can I go home now?"

"Yeah, Yeah. Get out of here. Just be careful."

"Thank you." Shaina returned to her car. She drove through the gap left by Bob's missing cruiser, relief washing over her as she accelerated toward home.

Though no longer as tired as before the accident scene, Shaina felt herself once again getting lulled into a sense of tranquility. It really was beautiful countryside. She admired the wildflowers growing amidst the tall grass. Clumps of purple and yellow flowers peppered the green sea of grass.

She had traveled no more than two miles from the scene of the accident—she even thought there were flashing lights still pulsating in the rearview mirror—when she saw the shape of something at the edge of the road. As she drew closer, Shaina could tell it was a human. After several more yards, she could see it was a woman.

Shaina's first thought was that the woman was dead. Then she thought that this woman must have somehow been involved in the accident. She amended that thought, because how could the woman be here, and the crash so far away? She considered driving past. The police would come along and find her, and —

But who was she fooling? She couldn't do that any more than she could neglect a patient at the hospital.

She pulled over near the unmoving body.

If she's dead, I'll go back to the accident scene and get one of the officers. If she's just injured, I'll help her to the car and take her back before the ambulance leaves.

As Shaina stepped out of the car and approached the form, another thought crossed her mind: where's the car?

Shaina realized her mistake too late.

The woman sat up abruptly and pointed a gun at her. Shaina froze, staring at the gun, shock and confusion intermingling. She was not a big gun buff, but she did recognize it as a police service revolver.

"Don't move." The woman stood, looked down both directions of the road.

Shaina took an involuntary step backward.

"I said stop."

Shaina stopped, putting her hands out in front of her in a surrendering gesture.

The woman waved the gun at the car. "Get in. Slowly." The woman looked down the road in the direction Shaina had come.

Shaina backed toward to the driver's side of the car, never taking her eyes off the gun.

Before climbing into the car, Shaina said, "I have two small children waiting for me at home." She attempted to keep the tremor out of her voice.

The woman almost smiled.

"I...I'm just saying, I don't want this to end like that Flannery O'Connor story, A Good Man Is Hard to Find." Shaina was referring to the short story where a family comes across a stranger on the side of the road and is murdered.

The stranger with the gun only grunted and climbed into the passenger seat of Shaina's Camry.

Shaina gripped the steering wheel with trembling hands.

"Start the car. You know how it's done."

"I need a second. I'm not used to having a gun in my face." Shaina took a deep, quavering breath, then released it slowly. She started the engine. Shaina put the car into gear—

"wait—"

—and slammed on the break, causing them to lurch forward.

"What?" Shaina's voice was louder than she had expected it to be.

"Don't do anything to draw the attention of the police."

"Really? You cause me to nearly put us both through the windshield to tell me that?" Shaina glared at the woman.

The stranger with the gun shrugged.

Shaina turned and caught a glimpse of her face in the rearview mirror. Black circles dogged her eyes, and her short brown hair was a tangled mess. She did her best to ignore her appearance and turned back to the road, putting on her blinker to make a show of proving that she was using extreme caution. She pulled out and kept her speed at a steady 55 miles per hour.

Several miles passed on the odometer.

The stranger ducked down in the seat, and the car swerved, but Shaina recovered before anyone would have guessed she'd been startled. The gun stayed pointed at her but below the dashboard where no one from outside could see it.

Just as Shaina was about to ask what the woman was doing, a cruiser from the other direction flew past her. In another second, Shaina saw lights flashing from behind her. She froze, unsure of what to do.

"Pull over. They will go by."

Shaina slowed and listed to the dirt. The cruiser went around her and drove off at such a high speed that in seconds Shaina couldn't see anything in front of her.

Shaina's head whipped around. "How did you..."

The woman smiled, sitting up again.

Shaina turned back to the road.

As she began to see orange light in the sky, and houses began to replace open prairies, Shaina contemplated how to get this woman out of her car. She slammed on the breaks. The gun nearly slipped from the woman's hand as it slammed into the dash.

The woman turned an angry stare at Shaina. "What part of 'drive with care' did you not understand?"

"We aren't going any further until I know what you want from me. If I can take you somewhere, I will—"

"I'll tell you why I'm in this car, and why I'm pointing a gun at you. I want you to listen and keep an open mind. Can you do that?"

Shaina nodded and accelerated to the posted speed.

"You heard of the fair that opened up recently near here?"

Shaina nodded again.

"I was being transported to a state facility because I tried to burn that fair to the ground. I'm also being investigated for the disappearance of a young boy."

"Billy Meyers. He's a friend of my son's …or at least, I think he is."

The woman hesitated then continued with her story. "I have nothing to do with that boy, but I did try to burn down the park." The woman stopped talking. When Shaina didn't interrupt again, the woman continued. "I was hired as the resident psychic for the fair. Miss Helen, at your service. I started a few days before the fair opened. I quickly began to detest the place. There is a black fog surrounding the park that only I can see. I call it The Cloud, and I know something hideous is hiding inside it. Something I can't see, but can only sense. Something evil, dangerous. I'm not the monster here. The monster is that…so called amusement park."

Yet, here you are pointing the gun at me right now. Shaina stayed quiet.

"Tommy's not home right now. He's at that fair with your kids."

"No, he's home...wait, how did you know...?"

"Your daughter's name is Susan."

Technically, not wrong. "We call her Susie. Okay, so you're intuitive. That's why you're good at what you do. So what?"

Miss Helen lifted the gun so Shaina could see it more clearly in her peripheral vision.

"This isn't an audition. I'm not trying to impress you, or even convince you. I need to get back to the fair and stop what's happening there." Miss Helen sat back and placed the gun in her lap.

Shaina let a few minutes pass before daring to speak again. "You mentioned Billy. Do you know where he is?"

The woman nodded. "Yes."

"Go to the police. Tell them what you know."

"I did. They didn't believe me. When I was caught trying to burn the park, I was arrested. The cops have been trying to pin the boy's disappearance on me ever since."

"So where is Billy?"

"I can't answer that just yet."

Shaina nearly slammed on the breaks again. "Tell me what's going on here. I will not drive you back to my house."

The woman shrugged. A car behind Shaina honked, spurring her to drive again.

"You truly have no choice but to do as I say. Go home. You'll see that Tommy's not there. It's okay. The house is empty."

"If you're all-knowing, tell me what I'm thinking right now."

"I'm not all-knowing. I don't read minds." Miss Helen paused. "But that said, the police can't help you. Just in case you were thinking to drive us there."

"Lucky guess?" Shaina's voice reeked of sarcasm. She sighed. "Listen, I'm a nurse. I offered to assist with St. Cumberland when they announced they had a code-black emergency. I've been non-stop on the go for the past 48 hours. Sure, I had a catnap here and there, but nothing that would constitute real REM sleep. So, you can imagine, can't you, I'm not in the mood to have a gun pointed in my face?"

"I truly am sorry about that, but you have to understand I'm a desperate woman. I had no choice."

"You do have a choice. You could turn yourself in. And how did you get away from the cops in the first place? Did you cause that accident?"

"No." Miss Helen's voice was sharp, cutting. "I didn't cause the accident. I'm not a witch with magical powers. I'm ...intuitive. When the accident happened, I took advantage of the situation. When the driver spilled the coffee in his lap, I had already gotten my cuffs off. They never expected me to get the upper hand. I grabbed the gun from that cop before he even knew I was free.

"Then the van flipped."

Shaina counted the houses that flipped past her. She was ten minutes from her home and at a loss for a way to get this woman to the police station without causing alarm. Shaina's hands quivered, and her palms began to sweat, making the wheel slippery in her grip.

"You haven't told me where we are going." Shaina chewed on her lower lip.

"To your house, of course."

Shaina shook her head. "I can't do that. I won't be pistol-whipped in front of my kids. I won't take you home."

"No, you're going to take me to your house. Otherwise, I won't be able to help you."

"I don't need your help."

"Oh, but you do. Your kids aren't home, as I've said. They are at the fair, and I assure you they are in danger."

Shaina took a few calming breaths. She gave up on her plan and drove home. She hated the thought of allowing this woman around her kids, but she was oddly curious to see if the kids were there or not.

As she pulled into the driveway, Shaina saw that Tommy's car was gone.

***

Shaina sat in the driver's seat of her car and stared at the darkened interior of her white ranch-style house. If Tommy wasn't there, then she could safely assume the kids weren't, either. If that was the case, Shaina could let this armed woman into her house without fear of putting her kids in danger. Shaina would have to find a way to warn Tommy to keep the kids away until the situation resolved itself. Miss Helen may or may not be a genuine psychic, but she was incredibly intuitive, and the woman had been correct about a great many things. Shaina wondered if the woman would allow the use of a cell phone to call her kids.

"Shall we go inside?"

Shaina turned to her passenger. The gun hung limply in the woman's lap with barely a grip on the thing. She could grab for it, but no. No way that would end well, especially when Shaina had just admitted the woman's powers of deduction were uncanny.

Shaina opened the driver side door and climbed out.

Miss Helen climbed out on her side and came around to the front of the car. She followed Shaina to the front entrance. After unlocking the door, Shaina stepped aside and allowed Miss Helen to enter first. The woman glanced up and down the street before walking into the house. Shaina followed, closing the door behind her.

"I'm famished. Do you have anything to eat?" Miss Helen rubbed her stomach.

"In the fridge. Help yourself."

Shaina took off her shoes in the stone-tiled foyer and scrunched her toes in the plush beige carpet of the living room. The feeling was heavenly after such a long time on her feet. If the woman with the gun hadn't been an issue, Shaina would have plodded down the hall to her bedroom and dropped down dead on the queen-sized mattress and slept for the next twelve hours. Instead, Shaina pointed in the direction of the kitchen. Miss Helen didn't hesitate to go there. Shaina stood in the doorway to the kitchen and watched as Miss Helen placed the gun on the counter and opened the fridge. The woman disappeared behind the refrigerator door, and Shaina's eyes never left the weapon.

So much for intuitive.

Shaina leaped for the gun, snatched it and backed up to the kitchen entrance again. She pointed the gun, holding it in both hands, still unable to control her shaking, and leveled it at the refrigerator.

Miss Helen pulled a package of deli ham, mustard, a head of lettuce and the loaf of bread from the fridge, knocked the door closed with her knee, and placed the items on the counter where the gun had been. She gave Shaina only a cursory glance.

"Some psychic you turned out to be," Shaina said, smirking. "I guess you didn't see this coming, did you?"

Miss Helen began fixing her sandwich.

Shaina's sly smile faded as the only sound in the house was of the woman preparing her lunch. Shaina looked at the gun, wondering if it was even real.

Miss Helen gave Shaina a sidewise glance. "The gun is empty. It's been empty since I got away from the cops. I told you, I'm not the bad guy here."

Shaina stared at the gun. There could have been bullets in it; she had no way of knowing. She pointed the gun at the floor and squeezed the trigger but couldn't make anything happen.

Miss Helen bit into her sandwich, chewed. "You have to pull hard on the trigger. Or cock the hammer back first."

Shaina tossed the gun on the counter. She watched as Miss Helen abandoned her sandwich for the moment, picked up the weapon, popped the cylinder out and spun it to show Shaina there were no bullets in it. A flick of her wrist snapped the barrel back into place. She set the gun back on the counter and returned to her sandwich.

"You lied to me this whole time? How am I supposed to trust you?"

Miss Helen took a bite of her sandwich and shrugged. "Let's call it a magician's misdirection. All part of the show."

"When are you going to tell me what's going on here?" Her words were firm, angry, but a quiver of fear and sadness crept into her voice. "Where is my family?"

Miss Helen's knowing smile faded, and her eyes softened into glistening pools as a calm and caring expression washed over her face. "The answers to your questions have been in front of you the whole time." Miss Helen's eyes focused on the table beyond the island countertop.

Shaina's eyes followed Miss Helen's gaze to the kitchen table, where a white piece of paper lay. She walked over to the note and picked it up. It was Tommy's scrawling script. Large print covered the entire eight by eleven sheet of lined paper ripped from a spiral notebook. The words filled her first with relief, then confusion, and finally with fear as she realized the note's implication.

She glanced up at Miss Helen. She breathed heavily, nearly panting.

"You knew this was here? How could you…?"

Miss Helen placed her sandwich on the counter and made swirling motions with her hands as if she was about to make something materialize from out of thin air.

Then she stopped, picked up her sandwich. "I'm sure you would have noticed it if you weren't so concerned about the gun."

Shaina took her phone from her pocket and dialed her brother's cellphone number. It rang four times, and then the voicemail picked up. She disconnected and called again. It rang but went to voicemail. On the fourth try, the call went straight to voicemail.

Shaina trusted Tommy with her kids—she had no choice really—he was there to watch them while she worked, after all. But his cellphone habits were atrocious. He rarely remembered to charge it, and why wasn't he picking up now?

Shaina glanced back down at the note and reread it.

Hi, Sis. I took the kids to the fair. Be back later tonight.
Love Ya,
Tom

Shaina tossed the note back on the table and looked up at Miss Helen. "You want to go to the fair? Let's go. If that's where my kids are, it's where I'm going, too." She looked down at herself. "But first I'm getting out of these damn scrubs."

Chapter Two: Jeremy

The morning sun beat relentlessly down from the blue sky and wrapped Uncle Tommy's car in a cocoon of bright reflective light and heat. The car's air conditioner blew out a steady stream of cold air that helped to keep the heat at bay. Still, Jeremy absently wiped at a bead of sweat forming on his forehead.

From the back seat of Tommy's Jeep Grand Cherokee, Jeremy heard the soft, scratchy rhythm of an unfamiliar rock song coming from the speakers in the door near his feet. Ignoring it, Jeremy concentrated on his Gameboy and the Pokémon he was in the process of capturing. Next to him, his sister Susie played with her dolly. When she suddenly asked a question, Jeremy looked up from his game.

"Are you going to tell us where we are going now, Uncle Tommy?"

He uttered a conspiratorial laugh that didn't sound half as eerie as Tommy had intended. Jeremy rolled his eyes.

"You'll know when we get there," Uncle Tommy said. "Just know it's going to be Bomb-bastic."

Susie giggled. "That's not a word."

"Yes, it is. It's in the dictionary. Bomb-bastic: adjective. It means da bomb, fantastic, amped up..." Tommy bellowed the last word which echoed in the cab of his vehicle. "Fun."

Susie released a high-pitched, shrieking burst of laughter. Jeremy groaned and returned his attention to his game.

"When will we get there?" she asked.

"Soon."

"You're fun, Uncle Tommy."

"That's high praise. Thank you, Susie."

Uncle Tommy's phone rang. He looked at it but didn't answer it.

"Was that Mommy?" Susie asked.

"Don't worry." Uncle Tommy hit a button on the side, and the phone powered down. He turned his head to look at them. "I left her a note so she'll join us a little later. Right now, she needs to rest after working all night."

Susie turned her attention back to her dolly, swinging its arms, and moving its legs back and forth. "I'm going to marry Uncle Tommy when I get older, Dolly, and you're invited to the wedding." She mimicked the dolly jumping up and down in her lap. "Yay."

"You can't marry Uncle Tommy, dummy. That's *insects.*"

Susie dropped her dolly in her lap and turned to Jeremy. "I can so marry him. And that doesn't give me bugs."

"Not that kind of insects." Jeremy rolled his eyes at his dumb sister. "The kind where you have kids with your relative. Your kids come out..." He lolled his tongue from the side of his mouth and twitched in his seat.

Susie turned away from her brother. "We don't need kids. We have Dolly."

Uncle Tommy peered at the two in the back seat through the rearview mirror. "I'll marry you, Cupcake. Sounds like a fun time, and I'm always up for that. Jeremy will be the best man. Dolly will be the flower girl."

"Who will give you away?" Jeremy asked his sister. "Dad is dead."

The car lurched, and Jeremy dropped his Gameboy. The headphone plug came loose, filling the cab with the high-pitched dinging music that was somehow off-key.

"That was unnecessary, young man."

Jeremy caught a glimpse of Uncle Tommy's angry scowling face in the mirror and dropped his gaze to his hands. He reached down and collected his game, using the moment to hide his burning face from his uncle. He clicked the Gameboy off and tossed it on the seat next to him, peering out the window though there was nothing outside he wanted to see, either.

When he dared to glance over at Susie, he saw she had moved on to other activities to occupy her time.

Susie lowered her dolly to her lap. "Are we there yet?"

Uncle Tommy didn't respond.

Jeremy stared at the reflection of Uncle Tommy's face in the rearview mirror. The man's smile had not returned. Jeremy's chest felt suddenly heavy. "He'll tell us when we get there." He pointed to the doll. "What's your dolly's name?"

Susie held her up in front of her. "Dolly."

"Your dolly's name is Dolly? That would be like naming your kitten Kitty."

"We're getting a kitty?"

"No, that's not..." Jeremy squirmed. "I was just saying you should name her something other than what she is."

"Why can't I call her Dolly, Jamie?"

Jeremy shrugged. "I guess you can. But you know how to say my name right. Stop calling me Jamie."

"I don't want to." Susie turned her attention to Dolly.

Jeremy shook his head and looked out the window.

After another couple of minutes, the silence was replaced with Susie and Uncle Tommy singing The Ants Go Marching In. Jeremy couldn't help himself; he sang along, too.

The surroundings outside the car changed from open fields to lines of cars going in both directions. Tommy's driving slowed. He heard the sound of a lot of people talking at once. The car had slowed down as well. All this told Jeremy their destination approached. When Jeremy looked out the window, he saw parked cars everywhere. They were in a parking lot. The singing stopped when the car stopped.

Uncle Tommy turned in his seat to peer back at them. He smiled. His eyes flicked from Susie to Jeremy and then again at Susie. "We're there."

"Yay," Susie said. "Where?"

Uncle Tommy climbed out of the car and walked around to Susie's side of the vehicle. He opened her door and helped her with the seatbelt.

Jeremy unbuckled himself and climbed from the car to meet his sister and uncle on the other side of the vehicle. Uncle Tommy took Susie by the hand and led her through the parking lot. After a few turns, Tommy stopped and picked Susie off the ground, placing her on his shoulders. He pointed off at something Jeremy couldn't see yet. It wasn't until they made it out of the parking lot that he finally saw where they were going.

Jeremy's legs refused to move. Time stood still. There was no sound as if his ears stopped working entirely. He only realized Tommy had stopped walking when his uncle's steady hand shook Jeremy's shoulder.

He turned slowly toward his uncle's concerned face.

"Jeremy," his uncle said, and he could hear the world again. "Buddy, what's wrong? You look like you've seen a ghost."

Ghost? No, it was worse than that.

Jeremy watched colorful swirling rides move up and down and around, lights blinked and steel glinted. People laughed and rushed around, stood in line at the ticket booth and waited for rides to end and allow them their turn at the fun. The sound of pinging and dinging suggested someone had won a game of chance. The smell of popcorn and cotton candy made Jeremy want to throw up. His hands shook, and his lip quivered. The fair caused a crippling fear to rip through his limbs. Susie sat on Tommy's shoulders, staring at Jeremy. Tommy shook Jeremy again and forced the boy to look at the man. Jeremy felt the hot sting of tears in his eyes.

"What's wrong with you, Kiddo? It's just an amusement park. What has you so scared?"

Jeremy looked up at his uncle and opened his mouth to speak, to say what had him so worried.

But he couldn't do it. Jeremy couldn't admit to the dark secret he had been keeping for the last several days, of where Billy Meyers had gone.

Jeremy looked down at his shaking hands.

Jeremy breathed in deeply and let it out slowly. He controlled the shaking in his limbs by closing his eyes and letting go of the memory. There would be a moment when Jeremy would have to deal with Billy, but that time wasn't now. Maybe when he was home again and safe in bed with his mother, he would tell her what he knew. Right now, Uncle Tommy and Susie depended on him to pull it together and enter the fair.

"I'm okay now," he said.

Uncle Tommy gave him a stern look. "Are you sure? Don't be brave on my account. If you're not up for this…"

"I want to," Jeremy said. "Really. Let's do it."

Jeremy took Susie by the hand and pushed past Uncle Tommy.

Tommy paid for their tickets and they each, in turn, walked through the turnstile.

Susie pulled Jeremy through the crowd of people to the spinning teacups. "I want to go on that ride."

Jeremy held onto her hand and nudged people out of his way to keep up with her. He tried to apologize, but he was moving too fast, and he doubted anyone heard him. He couldn't stop until she did.

Susie stood at the fencing surrounding the ride and watched in wide-eyed wonder as the cups spun faster and faster. Kids laughed, their hair blowing around their delighted faces. Susie inched her way to the entrance.

After a few minutes, Uncle Tommy showed up with a fist full of tickets. "Had to buy these or no one is doing anything." He held up the tokens for the kids to see.

When the ride stopped, and all the kids disembarked, Susie was the third in line to get on the amusement ride. She ran into the loading area before anyone could stop her.

"You should go with her." Tommy nudged the boy through the gate.

"I don't want to go on a baby ride." Jeremy tried to push back.

"No choice, Bud. She can't go on alone, and I'll break the thing."

Jeremy scuffed his feet, but he gave the man his ticket and joined his sister inside the teacup. Uncle Tommy waved to Jeremy, but the boy didn't wave back.

The ride started up, and Susie squealed with delight. Jeremy held the bar and kept his sister back with his body as the force of movement pushed her against him. Susie laughed. Jeremy thought it was fun, too, but he wasn't about to show it. When the ride ended, he led Susie to the exit, where Uncle Tommy waited.

"Let's go on the train next." Susie led them to the child-sized train and once again, Jeremy had to join her. Smoke puffed from the engine's pipes and the train chugged around the track.

Once the train ride ended, Susie and Jeremy rode the carousel. She climbed onto the back of a pink unicorn, and Jeremy took the brown stallion next to her. He had to keep reminding her to grab the bar.

"If you don't hold on, I'll make you sit in one of the benches instead of a horse." Jeremy had to talk loudly to speak over the pipe organ.

"Boo," Susie said, frowning.

But the threat worked.

As they stepped off the carousel, Uncle Tommy met them at the exit.

"Let's walk around for a little while and see the sights. We can go on more rides a little later. Is that okay with you two?" Though Tommy was speaking to both of them, he was looking at Susie.

The girl thought this over then nodded. "Okay, we can do that."

"Hey, so she's in charge now?" Jeremy didn't think he liked that idea.

"Yes." Uncle Tommy smiled at Susie. She giggled.

Susie ran up to the sledgehammer game. "Uncle Tommy, show us how strong you are."

Tommy took her hand and tried to lead her away from the attraction.

The man wearing a change apron over his jeans, and a muscle shirt that exposed huge biceps picked up the hammer and held it out. "Come on Uncle Tommy, let's see what you can do."

Uncle Tommy stopped trying to pull her away — she wasn't budging anyway — and stared at the man holding the hammer. His eyes narrowed, but the man only laughed.

"Fifty cents a swing."

Uncle Tommy released Susie's hand and took the hammer. He pulled two dollars from his pocket and handed the money to the man. The man slipped the bills into one of the pockets of his apron. Tommy took the hammer's handle in both hands, holding it as far back on the shaft as he could without losing a grip on it, and spread his legs apart. He lifted the hammer over his head and dropped it down on the striker. The pellet shot only a quarter of the way up and came back down.

The barker turned to the kids and put a hand to his mouth, feigning secrecy even though Tommy could hear him. "You should call him Uncle Wimp."

Uncle Tommy ignored the man and prepared to hit the striker again. This time the pellet flew up halfway before coming back down.

"He's up to Uncle Grandpa, kids."

Susie giggled.

Jeremy thought to tell his uncle he didn't have to prove anything, but Tommy was too focused. The hammer came down, and the pellet went up, then came back down after just missing the bell.

Jeremy stepped forward. "That was a good one, Uncle Tommy."

"I have one more try. I can do this." Sweat dripped from Tommy's temple and ran down his face.

Tommy spread his feet farther apart, he went up on his toes and lifted the hammer high over his head. With a grunt, he brought the hammer down on the striker. The pellet went up, up…

The bell dinged, and the bullet came back down.

Uncle Tommy dropped the hammer. He smiled and looked back at the kids. "I…did…it," he said, panting between words.

"Good show, young man." The game attendant pointed to a series of cubbies with prizes in them. "Your pick of a reward for all your hard work."

Uncle Tommy pulled a pink teddy bear from one of the slots and handed it to Susie. She snatched it up and held it tightly to her chest.

"Thank you, Uncle Tommy," she said as she rocked it, cradled in her arms.

He walked away from the game, and the children followed closely behind.

"What are we going to do now?" Jeremy asked.

"No more games," Tommy said. "Let's see if there are other attractions here besides games and rides."

Jeremy glanced around and saw something that interested him. He pointed. "What's that?"

Tommy looked in the direction of Jeremy's finger. "A freak show? That might be a bit too much for Susie. It might frighten her."

As they walked by, the barker directed his spiel toward Tommy and the kids.

"Come in and see some of the most spectacular sights on the planet." The man's eyes flicked to Susie. "We have the wolf boy, Jake. Meet the tallest man in all of New York State." The man turned to his companion. At first, Jeremy thought this was a fat man, but at a second glance, the boy realized he was looking at a bearded woman. She smiled at Jeremy, waved at him, and he reluctantly waved back.

"There's a funhouse. That looks harmless enough." Tommy pulled the kids closer to him as they moved away from the freak show.

As Tommy led the kids to the funhouse and paid for their tickets, Jeremy watched the couple in front of them--a girl with a boy holding her by the waist, giggled and squealed. Jeremy took Susie's hand. She tried to squirm out of his grip, but he held fast.

"You don't want to get lost, do you?"

"I want to hold Teddy."

"Just hold him with the other hand."

Teddy dangled from her left hand, and Jeremy held tight to her right hand. Uncle Tommy followed the kids, but Jeremy turned to keep his uncle in sight. Tommy smiled at him. They entered the building.

They walked into what looked like a hallway painted several bright colors. The first color was lime green. That gave way to yellow as they walked further down the hall. The next color was orange. At the orange walls, Jeremy began to realize something was happening.

The next color was red. After moving farther down the hall, all the colors seemed to turn and swirl.

Jeremy bumped his head on the ceiling. He turned and watched Uncle Tommy hunch over to get through the hall. Nervously, Jeremy considered turning around but saw that an elderly couple entered behind them, pinning them in.

When they reached the end of the hall, he spotted a shiny gold doorknob in the wall. He turned it, and the wall opened. They stepped into a regular-sized room. Once Uncle Tommy was through, they closed the door and continued through the dull white room to an open entryway. They stepped through to the room beyond.

The sight was at once spectacular and startling. Jeremy looked around the room at himself, repeated over and over, getting smaller as the images grew farther away. He was in a hall of mirrors, he knew, but it was so hard to see where reality ended, and the reflection started. Susie dropped his hand and ran up to a mirror. She giggled at the many layers of herself in the glass.

Jeremy took Susie's hand and guided her through the mirrors.

At the other end of this room, they entered yet another room. This room was dark and got eerier the deeper in the group went. The walls closed in, and they had to feel their way through the narrow passageway. The passage forward ended abruptly, causing them to bump into each other, and they had to turn and find another direction.

When Jeremy bumped into the wall again, his mind brought up an image of Billy in the passage behind him. The missing kid had green skin and milky eyes. Dead, clutching hands reached through the darkness for Jeremy.

The boy's voice lifted between the screams from frightened girls and their prankster boyfriends.

"Jerrremmmeee..." Billy said inside Jeremy's head. "You left me behind, and I died. You killed me, Jeremy."

"Ow. You're hurting my hand, Jamie." Susie tried to tug her hand free.

Jeremy's attention drew back to reality. "Sorry." He loosened his grip but didn't let her go free. "Keep holding my hand so you don't get lost in the darkness."

When a hand touched Jeremy's shoulder, he flinched.

"It's just me," Uncle Tommy said. "No need to be scared."

"I'm not scared." Susie and Jeremy spoke in unison.

Uncle Tommy chuckled. "Good to know." He kept his hand on Jeremy's shoulder and led the children through the inky blackness.

Jeremy felt comfort in the touch of Uncle Tommy's hand. His hand not clinging to Susie was splayed out in front of him as he shuffled forward. A wall in front of him forced him to turn right and continue. He lost all sense of direction. After another turn, to the left this time, the floor beneath Jeremy shifted. He lost his grip on Susie's hand, and Uncle Tommy's hand disappeared.

"Jamie." Susie's voice was a hoarse whisper. "Where did you go?"

"I'm right here, Sissy." Jeremy groped through the dark until he found her, and he hugged her to him this time.

"I'm here, too," Uncle Tommy said. The robust and reassuring hand was back on Jeremy's shoulder.

The floor leveled out again.

"That was interesting," Uncle Tommy said.

"Are we near the end yet?" Susie asked.

"Soon." Jeremy took Susie's hand. He heard the door opening but didn't see any light. After a few moments, he understood why. The next part of the passage caused the group to move to the left, move directly forward only one or two steps, and then turn right. The turns continued for the next several steps until finally, Jeremy's hand touched the door.

Jeremy pushed, and a spring-loaded door flapped forward. Bright, late-morning light blasted his corneas. He stumbled out of the darkness. He pulled Susie along after him, and Uncle Tommy came out last.

"Finally." Susie pulled her hand free of Jeremy's and wiped her palm on her shorts. "Jamie's hand was all sweaty, yuck."

"That was different, wasn't it?" Uncle Tommy squinted at the sunlight.

"Let's go again," Susie said and giggled.

"No." Jeremy answered much too quickly.

Uncle Tommy gave him a knowing smirk, and Jeremy looked away, face heating.

"I think we need to find something else," Tommy said. "We can go through again when your mom joins us."

Chapter Three: Cary Lynn

As the line to the funhouse moved up, Cary Lynn Javes smiled and waved at the little blonde girl in front of her. Cary Lynn nudged her husband Clifford, and nodded at the girl. "Isn't she just a little darling?"

Clifford glanced but only grunted his agreement.

The little girl turned back toward her family and let the older boy—her brother, perhaps? -lead her closer to the exhibit's entrance.

"Positive you want to go in there," Clifford said to his wife, drawing her attention away from the family in front of them. "Might be too scary for you. You might have a heart attack."

"Shut your mouth." Cary Lynn turned away from her husband to shut out the sight of him. She knew he was chuckling at her childish reaction, but she didn't care.

The line moved up again, and Clifford nudged Cary Lynn. She took a step forward. The little girl looked back again. When Cary Lynn waved this time, the girl turned and hid her face against her brother's arm. The man (their dad? Cary Lynn didn't think so) went on about his business, oblivious to the children. If they ran off, would he even notice? Cary Lynn didn't think so.

Cary Lynn concluded that the man was not their father. He might have been an uncle, or some other relative—definitely related to the kids—but not the father. Cary Lynn came to this conclusion because this man did not show a paternal connection to the children.

The line moved up.

Cary Lynn hummed a tune she enjoyed as a young woman. Now and then she threw in some of the lyrics she remembered.

"...In the year..." Humming. "2525." Humming. "4545."

The line moved.

Cary Lynn watched the young couple in front of the little girl and her family enter the funhouse doors.

"Thank God you stopped with that infernal humming. Hurts my ears."

"Shut your mouth, mean old man."

After the man and the two children entered the Funhouse, Clifford paid for Cary Lynn, and his entrance and they waited for the attendant to announce their turn. Cary Lynn slipped her hand into her husband's hand and pulled him closer. He glanced down at her.

"It's too late to back out now," he said. "I already paid."

"I'm not backing out." She squeezed his hand. "Just getting a little excited, is all. I'm looking forward to the adventure."

The attendant opened the little gate indicating it was Cary Lynn and Clifford's turn to enter the doorway with the Jokerman letters spelling out Funhouse in multiple colors.

Cary Lynn shuddered when the door sealed shut behind her. She clung to Clifford's arm as they shuffled through the darkness. When they bumped into the wall, Clifford reached out and pushed, and the wall gave.

"It's a door," he said.

They entered a room that looked like a funnel of colors. As they moved through the hallway, the swirling colors gave the illusion the walls—and even the floor—were moving. Cary Lynn lost her footing, and Clifford caught her. She giggled at having fallen for the magic.

"It's tricky in here." She kissed her husband's scruffy, wrinkled cheek. "Thank you for keeping me from going topsy-turvy."

Clifford smiled at her. "I'll always take care of my girl. You know that."

They strode hand in hand to the end of the hall of color, crouching as they went. The door out led them to a room full of mirrors. They stopped and turned around, staring at themselves on repeating patterns.

"We lost them." Cary Lynn stared at her frowning face in the mirror directly in front of her.

"Lost who?"

She turned to face her husband. "The family we were following."

"I wasn't following anyone."

Cary Lynn grunted. "We weren't following them on purpose. They were just in front of us, that's all. I wanted to keep sight of them, so we didn't get lost."

"We won't get lost, my love. They design these things so you naturally find your way out."

Clifford led the way, and Cary Lynn trusted him to get them out of the mirror maze. She continued to hold onto his hand as he led them down one way, and then another. They had to double back on occasion, but Clifford always assured her they were nearing the end. When Clifford failed to find a door out of the maze, she started to worry. When she heard the sound of other fairgoers giggling and passing them by, she began to panic.

"We're lost. I knew it."

"Don't freak out on me, we're almost there."

Cary Lynn heard the voice of a young girl talking to someone in a nearby pathway.

"Can you help us?" Cary Lynn asked in as loud a voice as she could manage. "We're lost."

"We're not lost," Clifford said.

"Shut your mouth." Cary Lynn pleaded again. "Please, we can't find our way through this god-forsaken maze. Please help us."

Cary Lynn heard the same girl speak again.

"Follow the sound of my voice. You'll find your way out." The girl giggled. Her voice moved away.

"Where was her voice coming from? I think it was over here." Cary Lynn began dragging Clifford through the maze.

The turned several corners, but the voices had disappeared. When Cary Lynn turned and walked back the way she had come, she met a wall of mirrors where she had been sure there was an opening just a moment ago.

"The walls are changing." Her voice was a terrified whisper.

"What? No, you're just getting yourself turned around." Clifford tugged on her hand. "Look, there's a path just over here."

Cary Lynn tried to pull away. "No, this wasn't open a moment again. The walls are changing."

"This place isn't as elaborate as all that. I'm sure you're mistaken. Come on now. Don't freak out on me just yet. There has to be a door around here somewhere." He pointed to a dark gap between two mirrors. "I'll bet the door is in there."

Clifford pulled Cary Lynn into the darkness between the mirrors. They felt along the wall, looking for a door. Cary Lynn felt the wall in front of her give, and suddenly she stumbled down a steep incline, pulling Clifford along with her. She felt herself tumble off a ledge, landing in a heap on a cold stone floor.

Cary Lynn rolled first one way, and then the other. With a grunt, she stood and dusted herself off. She felt around in the darkness for her husband. She found him and struggled to help him stand.

"Will you at least help me help you?"

Eventually, Cary Lynn got Clifford to his feet.

"Where in the hell are we?" Clifford said.

Staying close together, they searched for a doorway, but they could only feel stone walls everywhere around them. The Funhouse had swallowed them up. She felt Clifford groping for her in the inky darkness, and she clasped his hand, pulled him closer to her.

"How about now?" Cary Lynn asked. "Is this a good time to freak out?"

Chapter Four: Larry

Gina Hathaway smiled and accepted the second of the two tickets Larry Masters purchased. Their hands touched, and Larry watched as she shyly turned away. Her auburn, shoulder-length hair covered her eyes.

She is so pretty. Larry kept his eyes on her, enjoying her uncomfortable stance. "You should wear your hair back."

"Why?" Gina said.

"So you're not ever hiding your beautiful face."

He reached out toward her head, but Gina pulled away from his touch and tucked her hair behind her ear.

She giggled, covering her mouth.

Larry found her hand and led her into the midway. The first thing he spotted was the strongman competition. He dragged her to the attraction and released her hand. The price was fifty cents a swing, and a chart explained what level of prizes were available to win. Larry handed the attendant a five-dollar bill. To win the giant green blow-up alien, Larry would need to ring the bell ten times in a row. He took the hammer in his hand and lifted it over his head. In one swift motion, he brought the hammer down and hit the striker. The pellet rose and hit the bell.

He hit the striker and once again the bell went off. He swung the hammer, ringing the bell on his third, fourth, and fifth attempts. He rung the gong eight times. On his ninth try, he sounded the toll again, but only barely. His muscles screamed--at the outer limits of their endurance. Sweat beaded on his forehead and dripped into his eyes. He wiped at the perspiration on his face and dried his hands on the fabric of his shorts. He blew on his palms then picked up the hammer once again. One more strike of the bell and Gina would have her glowing alien.

Larry lifted the mallet and slammed it down. He felt the handle slip even before the head of the hammer hit the striker. The pellet rose two-thirds of the way and came back down.

No bell sounded.

"So close," the attendant said. "But I'll be honest with you; the tension on this thing is set so high to be nearly impossible to hit the bell enough times to win that grand prize. Sir, you did an amazing job, and you now have a choice of prizes."

Panting, Larry dropped the hammer and turned away from the attendant. The heat in his face caused more sweat to pour off him. He gripped Gina's hand and held tightly when she tried to squirm free. He ignored her cries, dragging her away from the game, from the insults being hurled at him.

When Gina finally pulled free, she stopped, and Larry turned to face her, but he kept his head lowered. He didn't dare meet her eyes.

"What's the matter with you? You did an amazing job back there. So what if you missed the last bell. You won a prize. I want my prize."

Larry glanced up at her. "I'll win you a better one."

Gina's smile made Larry's heart race, and this time, it wasn't from struggling to lift a hammer. Dare he call it love? He smiled. *Thank God for banana smoothies.*

Larry met Gina at the mall while working at the smoothie bar. He asked for a banana smoothie because it was the first thing you noticed on the menu. Larry struck up a conversation with her, and before long, had asked if she would go to the fair with him. He felt weightless when she said yes. She was so pretty that Larry was afraid that his pockmarked face would scare her away, but she must have thought he was attractive. Larry took her attention as a sign of attraction and used it to encourage himself to keep the conversation going.

Larry reached over and kissed Gina on the cheek. As she pulled away, she placed a hand on the spot where he kissed her. Her face reddened. The urge to lean over and kiss her on the lips overwhelmed him, but he resisted.

"There's more where that came from." He pointed at the glowing green alien hanging at the apex of the prize shelf behind them. "Fuck that. I'm going to overwhelm you with all kinds of prizes. Do you like prizes?"

"I guess so." Gina walked away from Larry, and he didn't realize she was moving away from him until a group of people passed between them, breaking his trance. He rushed through the crowd, shoving people away, returning to Gina's side. His sweating, shaking hand gripped hers, and she turned to face him. The sight of Gina's frown made Larry's lips quivered. *I'm showing weakness, and I can't do that, not in front of her. Not in front of Gina.*

That weakness was his mother's fault.

***

Larry's father died when Larry was young. For his entire life, as long as he could remember anyway, it had been just Momma and him. She went to bingo every night, so things like dinner—and bedtimes—were at Larry's discretion. And, unless there was a big win that night (and there rarely ever was), groceries fell to the wayside. Most times, the only thing to eat in the house was boloney.

Larry made his own lunches. A hot item was peanut butter and baloney sandwiches. He ate his one sandwich in the corner of the lunchroom, chewing slowly and making it last. He minded his own business, but one day he noticed a girl staring at him. The girl turned to the female teacher nearby and motioned for the teacher's attention. The adult leaned over, and the girl whispered into the teacher's ear.

Larry heard every word.

"That boy over there only has one sandwich for lunch." The girl stared at Larry, feeling sorry for him. That look had stuck with him. The rest of that day, he felt that same sandwich rolling around in his stomach. By the end of the day, he threw it up.

The following day the same teacher looked at Larry with a mix of disgust and pity, turned away, and shuffled into the classroom. Feeling like a rejected orphan, Larry slunk into the room. He went to his usual seat in the back and didn't look at anyone.

His home life was no better.

Momma was a big woman. She had a big voice. When Larry stomped down the stairs, loud and fast, he accidentally broke a lamp and learned just how loud she could be. Momma demanded he go out to the willow tree in the back yard and pull a switch. She then proceeded to hit him on the back, the buttocks and legs with the switch. Larry screamed in pain, frustration, and anger.

Larry stumbled through the next ten years.

When Larry turned eighteen, his mother learned of her breast cancer. He had been very intimately acquainted with those breasts. She walked around the house wearing only the skid-marked, blood-stained giant bloomers. Her exposed breasts dangled down like two empty hot water bottles, flat and drooping. He had gotten so used to the sight that he thought nothing of them. They might as well have been her ears.

But his real exposure to breasts came when he was fourteen years old. He managed to obtain a friend named Mark Folio. Mark invited Larry over to play and have dinner. Larry had been in the parlor playing video games with Mark when the urge to urinate hit. Larry stood and looked around, realizing he didn't know where the bathroom was.

"I need to pee," he said.

Mark waved a hand. "Top of the stairs, second door on the left."

Larry shot up the stairs, holding himself. He'd let a little bit slip out by accident. After reaching the top, he headed down the hall to the second set of doors but had forgotten which direction to turn. Larry went right.

He pushed the door open and stood in the doorway. He couldn't pull his eyes away from the scene in front of him.

Mark's sixteen-year-old sister stood in front of the mirror, singing a Britney Spears song into a hairbrush.

She wasn't wearing a shirt.

Larry stared at her small, perky breasts and wanted to touch them. He stumbled into the room.

Mark's sister turned.

She screamed.

"Pervert. Get out. Get. Out." She threw the hairbrush at him. It hit the wall near his head and bounced off.

Larry turned and rushed through the door across the hall. He leaned against the door, heart racing. The girl's body had been so beautiful. He never knew the female form could be so tempting. He peed and returned to the parlor. As Mark's sister and mother discussed the incident in the kitchen, Mark continued to play, oblivious to the commotion Larry had caused.

Mark was confused when his mother stormed into the room. "I think your friend needs to go home."

"Why?" Mark stood and crossed his arms.

"Your friend was peeping in on her, scaring her half to death. She's not comfortable with him here. He has to go."

Larry left without a fuss, but he never forgot those round, supple breasts. He went home to his mother that night and watched as she slowly rotted away from cancer. When she died, he was so happy to be free of those horrid, sagging breasts.

Now here was Gina, with her perky breasts poking through a silk blouse, agreeing to go with him to the fair.

***

Larry blinked away tears and smiled. "You should play a game, too."

Gina shrugged and glanced around. "I'm good at game where you shoot water into the clown's mouth, I guess."

He followed Gina to the row of squirt guns as she took a chair. Larry stood behind her, staring at the exposed nape of her neck and upper back. When the rest of the seats filled up, the attendant spoke into a mic.

"Okay, folks, the game is about to begin. Place your money on the counter, and we'll begin."

Larry offered to pay for Gina's game, but she insisted on paying her own way.

"On your mark."

The seated people aimed their little plastic squirt guns at their targets.

"Get set."

A pump started up somewhere behind the booth, and water filled the hoses attached to the guns.

"Go."

Gina sprayed her water gun perfectly into the clown's mouth, and her dancing clown started up the pole. Larry tried to concentrate on Gina's performance but was too distracted by her pale, silky skin. *She smells so nice like she rubbed herself in rose petals before she got dressed.*

His attention shifted from Gina to the game after hearing the bell that signaled someone had won.

Larry studied all the clowns in the row. Gina's clown was the only one to reach the top.

"And the little lady at the end is our winner."

The attendant handed her a pink, oversized whistle on a green lanyard. She held it out to Larry with a smile. "Now I won a prize for you."

"No, keep it. You were outstanding back there." *Besides, sweet Gina, you are my prize.*

"I'm in the mood for cotton candy." She sauntered over to the food stand and stood in line.

Larry reached down into his pocket and pulled out a wad of bills. When it was their turn, he once again tried to pay for her order, but still, she refused to let him. Grinding his teeth, Larry crammed the wad of bills back into his pocket.

Gina pulled off small pieces of the cottony treat and placed it on her tongue. He watched as the candy dissolved on her tongue and turned her mouth blue.

He glanced down and up again then let his eyes sweep over her face. Contented with eating her candy, Gina closed her eyes and smiled. She placed another bit of the cotton candy into her mouth and let it dissolve. When she opened her eyes again, she spotted him looking at her.

"What?" She wiped at her mouth. "Did I get some on my face?"

Larry laughed, feeling a bit of his charm returning. "No, but your teeth and tongue are all blue. It's cute."

She tore off another chunk and crammed it into her mouth. "Do you want some?"

She held out what candy still clinging to the paper cone, but Larry went after the piece she had placed in her mouth, taking it off her lips and eating it.

He raised his eyebrows. "Mmmm."

Licking his fingers, he glanced up to see Gina staring at him wide-eyed, and maybe even a little scared. He pretended to chew and after a few minutes, took her hand holding the candy and crammed it into her face. The cone fell from her grip and dropped to the ground.

"What the hell?" Gina wiped at the sticky mess on her face.

"Sorry." Larry reached down and picked up the remnants of the candy then tossed it in the nearby trash can. "I'll buy you another one."

"No, that's okay. I had enough."

"Are you sure?"

"I need to find a bathroom." Gina's eyes scanned their surroundings. When she spotted the closest bathroom, she headed in that direction.

Larry followed her. She disappeared through the doorway with a silhouette of a person wearing a dress, and Larry punched his hands into his pockets, kicking at the dirt. He spat into the cloud of dust.

What were you thinking, you idiot? Gina's a classy girl. She's not playful, like us. She's a good girl.

Then: *She's a slut. Hi, Gina, you slut.*

"Hi, Gina, you son-of-a-slut."

"What?"

Larry glanced up as Gina exited the bathroom and approached him.

"I thought I heard you say something."

"Oh, nothing." He hadn't been aware that he had spoken out loud.

They walked along the midway side by side as dinging, pinging and ringing bells reverberated around them. The smell of popcorn and candy apples wafted on the air. He heard the sound of cheering crowds off in the distance and wondered what beautiful thing had happened to cause such jubilation. He wished some of that delight would infect his girlfriend. He had tried everything, but still, she showed no real interest in him. She kept her distance and pulled her hand away when he tried to hold it. His face burned, and his eyes grew watery.

Larry glanced over at his date. The silence between them grew uncomfortable and awkward with every minute that passed. He tried to think of something he could say to break the silence, but somehow, Larry doubted they would be the right words, so he walked beside her. Ahead, he saw a man standing on a platform. This man spoke in a soft but commanding voice that caused Larry to move toward him. As he grew closer, he could hear the words the man was saying.

"...So, come along inside and see the two-headed snake and other creatures with similar oddities. Enter here and meet the most amazing people on earth. Watch with your own eyes as the geeks and freaks perform stunts you'll never imagine a human being can do. And I assure you that these monstrosities are every bit as human as you and me, only the folks inside were blessed with gifts you could only dream of having. Pay the ticket and step inside to begin a journey that will lead you into a part of this world you never knew existed. Just be warned the show is not for the faint-hearted or those with weak bellies."

Larry touched Gina's lower back. "Let's go inside and take a look."

Gina pulled away from Larry slightly, but he did not let her go.

"I don't know," she said. "I think I might be that faint-hearted and weak bellied person he warned not to go inside."

"Don't be such a baby." Larry's tone was a little angrier than he meant to sound, so he smiled and grabbed her hand and pulled her toward the freak show entrance. "It will be fun, and besides, I'll be there to protect you."

Gina reluctantly let Larry pull her to the show.

Larry paid for their tickets before Gina could protest and they walked through the threshold into the dimmer, quieter interior of the freak show's tent.

As they walked along the corridor, with walls made of cloth, Gina stepped up closer to the postcards pinned to the thick fabric.

Larry read the sign above their heads: Pitch cards of a gone-by era.

He stepped closer to look at what had captured Gina's attention.

The pitch cards were brown and white images, of which, one had extremely tall people standing next to extremely short people. There were conjoined twins and people with missing limbs. At the sight of some of the more gruesome-looking photos, Gina turned away and hid her face against Larry's arm. He guided her away from the pitch cards, leading her by the hand, moving deeper into the tent.

The first room had a color sign above the entrance stating this room held the world's shortest bee wrangler.

They stepped through the door and took a seat in the third row from the empty stage. Larry glanced around at the 20 or 30 other people waiting for the show to begin. He noticed the couples clinging to each other in anticipation of the show. Larry tried to move closer to Gina, but she showed no interest in being closer to him. He decided to retake her hand, but she quickly slipped from his sweaty grip.

Five minutes after Gina and Larry took their seat, the first curtain slid back, and a man on the stage waved to the crowd. The audience clapped respectfully.

"Hello, ladies and gentlemen. Thank you for being with us today. I'm about to introduce you to Wanda Wells. Though Wanda stands a mere 3 feet 7 inches in height, she's a giant when it comes to entertainment. This little lady is going to amaze you with her gift of speaking to bees. Watch how they do her bidding. But don't be afraid. There will be glass between you and Wanda with her bees. So, feel free to stay on the edge of your seat and enjoy the show."

The man threw his left hand over his shoulder as he walked backward toward the right side of the stage. The curtain behind him parted. The patrons clapped, but all Larry saw was an empty glass tube. As the applause died down, and nothing seemed to be happening, Larry began to fidget in his seat. He had been hoping for a gruesome show that would send Gina into his arms, cringing and scared. After another minute of no movement on the stage, Larry contemplated moving on to the next show. Just as he had resolved to stand, something began to descend inside the glass tube. A short-statured woman wearing a blue leotard came down on a trapeze. She stepped off, and the trapeze rose out of sight.

The small woman raised her hands, and the crowd cheered.

The woman had an amulet around her neck. It was unassuming, but it was the only jewelry showing on her person. It was large, gaudy. At her mouth was the most delicate microphone and earpiece Larry had ever seen. When she spoke, her voice boomed from the speakers around the room. Larry flinched as the sound accosted his ears.

"Good day, nice people. Thank you for coming to see me. I'm Wanda, and I'm here to show you what I can do. Some of you might have noticed this big silver necklace, but it's not a fashion statement. The locket holds the pheromones of my hive's queen. I use this to control my bees. What you're about to see will scare some, astonish others, but I assure you, I am in no danger. And though I'm confident that you would be safe, too, I have included this glass cage so you can feel 100 percent safe. Now, without further ado, let's get this show on the road."

The woman pointed one of her stubby fingers toward the ceiling. After a few seconds, a dark cloud started to descend toward her. As Larry watched, he realized the fog was bees. They swirled around her and slowly began to settle on her body. Within minutes, her chest was swallowed up by the dark crust of bees. Soon, they began to settle on her neck and face, even on her head. When she moved her arms to the left, the remaining bees in the air swayed to the left. When she moved to the right, the bees followed her. She moved her hand in a circular motion, and the bees followed. The crowd responded with gasps and sounds of awe.

Gina looped her arm around Larry's and moved closer to him. "It's beautiful." She looked up at his face.

"Yes," he said as he peered into her eyes. He leaned down and kissed her on the lips. Her reaction was hesitant at first, but then she kissed him back. When he moved his hands to her body, she pulled back. Larry turned, trying to concentrate on the show and drive his urges away.

Wanda continued to explain the details of her act. Her voice was still loud, but she spoke softly, not wanting to disrupt the bees' natural order.

"I carry the scent of their queen on me, so the workers are not doing what I do, but are simply following her scent."

Wanda was nearly completely covered now.

"How does she breathe through all those bees?" The older woman sitting next to Larry asked a companion.

As Wanda's show ended, and the curtain closed on her, the audience stood, clapping wildly. As the applause died down, the people began filing out through a second door at the other end of the canvas wall.

Larry led Gina out to the hallway and down to the next room in the tent.

Here was another stage, another curtain. The crowd took their seats and waited for this show to begin. This one started with less fanfare and with only the performer there to introduce himself. There was no doubt in Larry's mind that Wanda was the star of the show. Everyone else would be simple street performers.

The man on the stage stepped forward holding a mic. There was a bit of squelch as he spoke to the crowd.

"Thanks, everybody, for coming. My name is Dylan Moyer, and I'm going to do some stuff that I hope will shock and amaze you. I'm the reason for the disclaimer that people with weak stomachs should reconsider their decision to enter the show. At this time, I'll give everyone a chance to leave. If you want your money back, we'll hand it over, but know that if you stay and decide my act is too shocking to see, you won't get your money back after you see what I do."

The man on the stage paused and waited for people to leave. Larry gripped Gina's hand tighter. He brought her here for this reaction; he wasn't about to let her go now. He glanced around, but no one stood to leave.

"Okay, then. Let's get on with it...oh, and folks, don't try this at home."

Dylan wore a pair of sweatpants and a sleeveless tee-shirt. His muscles glistened with sweat or oil, but Larry wasn't sure which. He could see that the man had an impressive pair of guns. Larry glanced at Gina and studied her as she studied the man on the stage. When she noticed he was looking at her, she turned away with a shy smile.

"You think he's hot?" Larry asked.

Gina shrugged.

The man on the stage pushed a tray forward and lifted a towel covering the instruments it held. Dylan lifted a knife from the table and showed it to the audience. He spoke as he worked, explaining his actions. Setting the mic down, Dylan picked up a piece of paper. He ran the knife-edge over the paper, and the article tore in half, the cut piece drifting to the floor.

He held the knife up and showed it to the audience once again.

Without warning, Dylan shoved the knife through his forearm.

People in the audience, men and women alike, screamed.

Dylan picked up another knife, identical to the first, and drove this one through his arm with the first. The blades of both knives jutted from the other side of his arm. Dylan held his arm up for the audience to see, but Gina hid her face in Larry's chest. He wrapped an arm around her shoulder, pulling her closer. She wasn't looking when Dylan picked up a third knife and drove it into his other arm.

Larry was impressed. There was very little blood.

But what came next shocked even Larry.

"I'm going to call for someone in the audience to come up here and confirm that I have, indeed, stabbed myself. Do I have any takers?"

Larry's hand went up before he was aware of the movement.

Larry looked around. He was the only volunteer.

"Okay, sir. Thanks a lot for being my assistant. If you would, please come up here on the stage."

Larry stood and worked his way to the aisle. He walked down to the stage in a fog, wondering what had possessed him to volunteer. If this man was willing to stab himself, he could be prepared to stick a sucker like Larry.

"Thank you, sir. What's your name?"

Larry leaned into the mic and said his name.

"Well, Larry, do you think you can pull these knives out of my arms?"

Larry leaned toward the mic again. "I can try."

Dylan laughed. "That's the spirit. Now, folks, I called Larry up here so you can see firsthand that this is not a trick. I truly did impale myself, and good Larry here will be able to attest this is not a trick. Ready Larry?"

Larry nodded.

Dylan held out his arm to Larry. The three daggers protruded from the arm like slot machine levers.

Larry glanced out at Gina. She watched intently, eyes wide and glistening.

Larry gripped the handle of the first knife and pulled. The arm it was embedded in moved with the tug. Larry gripped Dylan's arm with one hand and the blade with the other. He pulled again. This time the knife came free. Larry held it in front of his face, staring at it. Dylan took it from Larry and placed it on the table.

"Can you do that two more times, Larry?"

Larry didn't answer. Instead, he gripped the second knife and pulled hard. The knife came out of the arm with a squishy slurp. Larry tossed the knife on the table and removed the last blade. After discarding the knife, Larry gripped Dylan by the wrist. He held out the man's arm and ran fingers of his other hand over the spot where the blades had been.

There was blood, but no wounds.

Larry studied the blood on his fingers, lifting his hand to his lips.

Dylan frowned. "Don't do that." He prevented Larry from tasting the blood.

Larry shrugged and wiped his fingers on his pants. "How did you do that?"

"I heal fast. But you agree that the blades were in my skin?"

"Yes, I pulled the knives from your flesh, for sure, but..."

"Thank you, Larry. You can return to your seat now."

Larry leaned into Dylan and spoke in a whisper. "Does it hurt?"

Dylan whispered back. "Like a bitch."

Larry stepped off the stage and returned to his seat next to Gina.

For Dylan's next trick, he drove long, thin needles into his body. He placed several in his arms, through his biceps. He pressed them into his thighs. He walked around so people could see that the needles had come out on the other side. He drove needles into his stomach. He thrust needles into his cheek, through his mouth, and out the other cheek.

He drove a needle through his neck.

The audience watched, enthralled. No one gasped; no one screamed. No one said a word but merely watched.

Dylan, looking like a human pincushion, picked up an object that looked like a giant fish hook. He held it out to the audience. Some people turned away, afraid to know what Dylan planned to do with it, but not Larry. He watched. When Gina buried her face in the crook of his arm, he let her.

Larry watched as Dylan wove the tip of the hook into his nose. The hook then curled around inside his mouth and encircled the pin that had passed between his cheeks. He clicked them together with a soft metallic chime.

Dylan held out his empty hands, and the audience roared.

Larry clapped so hard his hands hurt.

"This was awful," Gina said. "Gross."

Dylan systematically removed the hook.

"And now, great people of the audience..." Dylan bowed. "Here comes the most interactive part of the show." He lifted a staple gun from the table and held it out for the audience to see. "If you have a dollar, I'll let you staple it to my arm. Staple a five to my torso, or a ten to my head. Staple a fifty to my ass. For a Benjamin, I'll drop my trousers so you can staple it to my..." He indicated below his waist.

Gina had rubbed up against Larry at every cringe-worthy moment, causing him to become aroused. Larry held her tightly, smiling widely. As the freak show came to an end, Larry suggested they leave, and Gina was more than willing to go.

Chapter Five: Shaina

The sun shone through the windows of her kitchen nook and heated Shaina's face as she sat at the table sipping coffee and looking at the woman sitting across from her. Shaina placed her cup on the table and dropped her hands in her lap.

Miss Helen had raided Shaina's closet and traded in her prison clothes for loose-fitting pants and a flowery blouse.

Shaina cleared her throat before speaking. "What is the game plan? What do we do now?"

Miss Helen sipped her cup of coffee before answering. "Now we go to the fair." She placed her cup on the table.

Shaina gaped.

Miss Helen smiled.

"You can't be serious," Shaina said when she could finally find her voice. "You must know there will be a strong police presence there. They'll be looking for you there. You can't possibly think..."

"I appreciate your concern, but I'll be fine. I'll wear a disguise."

"I think you should turn yourself in. I'll vouch for you. I know you didn't hurt that boy. I don't know why you attempted to burn down the fair, but even that seems like it was only a half-hearted attempt."

"You're right. I wouldn't have risked the lives of those who live at the fairgrounds. I was merely trying to draw them out. I wanted them to evacuate the grounds. They are in more danger there than I could ever be."

"Tell the police that."

"Don't you think I did? No, I have to see this through. I have to solve this mystery, and then I'll turn myself in."

"You're willing to go into the lion's den?"

"I am." Miss Helen let a sly smile slip at the corner of her mouth.

They placed their empty cups in the dishwasher.

Miss Helen opened a closet door. Shaina watched. The other woman pulled out a large white sunhat with a vast, floppy rim and put it on her head. She took a lacy black scarf and wrapped it around her neck, covering the lower part of her face. She then donned a large pair of Louis Vuitton soupcons. The sunglasses covered the rest of her face.

"How do I look?"

Shaina shrugged. "I don't think you'll fool anyone. I think you'll be spotted five minutes after walking through the gates."

"I'm willing to take that chance. Ready to go? No sense wasting any more time. Besides, your family is waiting for you there."

Shaina did want to see her kids. They were at the fair, and she would find them there. Shaina wished to be rid of this woman as well. She felt dead on her feet, but until her reunion with her family, she could not sleep. Shaina followed the overdressed woman to the car, and once again climbed behind the wheel as Miss Helen took the passenger seat beside her. After backing out of the driveway, Shaina headed toward the outskirts of town. As the houses became more and more sparse, and the fields of wheat and corn replaced them, Shaina began to wonder if she was doing the right thing. After all, the police station was only a couple of blocks away from her house. Miss Helen was no longer holding a gun to her head.

But that wasn't true, was it?

Shaina had driven away from the police station and was on her way to the fair because no matter what Miss Helen said, she was correct about one thing. Her kids were at the festival, and right now, that was all that mattered to her. She would go to the fair and get her kids. Once back with her kids, Shaina could rid herself of this woman sitting next to her. She didn't care if the police presence resulted in the apprehension of Miss Helen.

Shaina turned and eyed her passenger. "How did you try to burn down the fair, and why didn't you succeed?"

Miss Helen turned in Shaina's direction slightly then turned away again. "I used a candle to light the curtains in my hut on fire. The only thing that burned was the hut. The police held me for questioning until the boy came up missing, and of course, they wanted to pin that on me. You should understand that they haven't convicted me of anything. I was en route from the prison to the local jail. I'm due to appear in court tomorrow for arraignment. The state has no evidence against me and will probably have to drop the charges. Shaina, I didn't have anything to do with the boy's disappearance. They hope I will admit to it."

"If you believe they were going to release you, why would you escape the day before becoming a free woman?"

"That's because time is of the essence. By tomorrow everything will be over, and many people will be dead. My guilt or innocence is irrelevant in the face of the violence that I plan to stop tonight."

Shaina didn't know what to say. She gaped at the woman until she was forced to look back at the road. Something this woman said rang true with Shaina, yet she didn't want to believe. If what Miss Helen said was true, her kids were in grave danger. Disregarding the warning made her feel like a bad parent. If she believed Miss Helen, would that make Shaina just as crazy?

Shaina's mind kept returning to Billy. Where was that little trouble maker? To say Jeremy and Billy were "friends" was to play fast and loose with the word. Billy coerced her son into doing things Jeremy would never do on his own. She knew this to be true because she had seen it. She watched as Billy talked Jeremy into stealing money from her purse when the bully didn't know Shaina was watching them. Thankfully, Jeremy had backed out of the plan before actually going through with it. She was proud of Jeremy that day. Billy verbally abused her son for doing the right thing, but Jeremy took the castigation like an army recruit in basic training. She had considered refusing to let Jeremy hang out with Billy, but in the end, she kept her silence. She supposed her thinking was that Jeremy would be a better influence on Billy than the other way around.

Shaina tried not to look down Front Street as they passed by. She had been tempted to turn down that way, head toward the courthouse and the police station. Without the gun, Miss Helen would be helpless to stop her. But she continued on the route specified and drove toward the fair. She wouldn't do anything that might jeopardize her family.

If this woman said the fair was dangerous, she had no choice but to believe it. If the woman wanted to go to the show, Shaina would take her. Once her family was safe, Shaina would think about helping Miss Helen clear her name.

She gave the woman a sideways glance. Miss Helen was turned toward the window, looking out at the scenery floating by. She seemed harmless enough, but Shaina was a nurse and knew looks could be deceiving.

As Shaina reached the parking lot of the fairgrounds, she found the closest space to the entrance and stopped the car. With a glassy-eyed stare, she watched out the windshield as the large amusement rides spun and myriad colors danced across her eyes. Muffled screams of delight drifted through the distance of some eight hundred yards.

Miss Helen cleared her throat.

Shaina glanced at the woman with the thought: *what's your hurry?* She said nothing, however.

"We going in or what?"

Shaina took a breath and exhaled. "Just collecting my thoughts. Do we have a game plan?"

"Yes. We buy tickets and go into the fair."

"Am I expected to find my family in all those people? We could wander around 'til closing and never run into them."

Miss Helen placed her hands on the hat in her lap. "I've thought of that. I think you should go to the main office and ask for Dashiell Pearson. Tell him that you need help finding your family. He'll be able to help, and you wouldn't even need to leave his office."

"Won't he be a little upset with you when he sees you?"

"Oh, I'm not going with you. You're on your own. I think Dash is going to take one look at you and bend over backward to help."

"You think he'll find me attractive? Really?" Shaina gave her face a cursory glance in the rearview mirror. "I have bags of sleep deprivation under my eyes, my hair is a mess, and I'm wearing no make-up. I look like hell."

"You have natural beauty." Miss Helen smiled. "If you need to, mention that I came here with you. But only mention me if he's not inclined to help you."

When Shaina opened her door, Miss Helen did the same. Miss Helen exited the car and donned her large hat and glasses. Inside the vehicle had been hot—even with the air conditioner running—but being directly under the late-morning sun was warmer.

Shaina locked her doors with the fob and followed Miss Helen through the parking lot to the front entrance. As they lined up to buy tickets, Shaina felt exposed, guilty. Miss Helen smiled and chatted with everyone who passed by.

"You don't know how to keep a low profile, do you?" Shaina asked.

Miss Helen laughed as if Shaina had told a joke.

As they reached the ticket window, Miss Helen placed a hand on Shaina's arm. "I have this, Sweetie." The older woman padded her pockets then stared at

Shaina with an abashed grin. She let out a girlish giggle. "Then again, maybe not."

Shaina reached into her pocketbook and paid for both tickets. The girl behind the glass stared at the money for a hot minute before tweezing it between two fingers and dropping it into the drawer. She then handed over the change with the tickets.

Shaina studied the girl. If she recognized Helen, she hid it well. The girl showed no more interest in Miss Helen than she would show a stew bum in the gutter. The girl's bored expression never changed.

Shaina proffered Miss Helen a ticket and turned to the line of patrons waiting to go in. The woman's smile never faltered.

The fat man on the stool took Miss Helen's ticket and tore it in half. She moved through the turnstile. As Shaina relinquished her card to the fat man, his hand lingered on hers, and his eyes remained on a location just south of her eyes. After sweeping a glance down the length of her, and back up again, he took the ticket and ripped it without taking his eyes off Shaina's chest. The two halves went into a basket at his feet.

Shaina moved through the turnstile, self-consciously rubbing at the hand the greasy ticket taker had touched. *I need to wash my hands as soon as possible.*

"There's a bathroom over there if you want to wash your hands."

Shaina's eyes flicked up quickly to Miss Helen's face. The woman's smile had turned into a knowing smirk. For a brief moment, Shaina had wondered if the woman read her thoughts, but the idea flitted away when she realized anyone could have guessed what was on her mind from her body language.

After using the washroom, Shaina scanned the midway, but couldn't see Miss Helen. The woman had to wave her over.

She does blend into the crowd.

As Shaina reached her, Miss Helen pointed to a set of wooden stairs leading up to a room with windows on all sides. "Go there."

Shaina stared up at the control room then turned and studied Miss Helen's face. "Where are you going to be?"

Miss Helen shrugged. "I'll be around."

After a moment of hesitation, Shaina walked over to the steps and started up. When she reached the door, she knocked. She waited and was about to hit again when the door opened. A guard stood in the doorway.

Shaina cleared her throat. "Could I please speak to Dashiell?"

The guard shifted his weight. "What's this about?"

"It's a bit of an emergency. If you would please, I'd like to talk directly to Mr. Pearson."

"Ain't happening."

"Please, if you don't mind, I must talk to Mr. Pearson." Shaina stiffened her arms, preparing for a scuffle.

"He's not seeing guests at the moment. Come back another time or tell me what this relates to."

Shaina said nothing. The guard puffed out his chest and smirked. His chin lifted, and he slowly closed the door.

"I'm here with Miss Helen."

The door swung open, and the guard stepped out. He peered down the stairs, past Shaina. All hints of a smug look gone.

"Where is she?" The guard continued to scan the area around the steps for the elusive woman.

"If you would please let me in and speak to Mr. Pearson, I can tell everyone at the same time."

The guard stepped aside and allowed Shaina to enter.

"Have a seat, and I'll let him know you're here."

Shaina was glad to be done with the guard. She took a seat in a padded chair with a lumbar back. The chair seemed to cradle her body, and as Shaina settled into the comfort of the chair, she suddenly realized just how long she had been awake. She almost closed her eyes and fell asleep sitting there, but just as her mind drifted off, the guard returned.

"I'll get you something while you wait? We have coffee or water…"

"Coffee, please. Black, two sugars."

The guard walked over to a counter with an industrial-sized coffee pot. He flicked the little lever, and black liquid poured from the spout into a white Styrofoam mug. He dumped two packets of sugar into the cup and used a red stirring-stick to mix it in. He handed her the mug with the stir-stick still in the coffee. She removed it and tossed it into the wastebasket near her chair.

She took a sip of the robust, hot coffee then closed her eyes and savored it. When she opened them again, a handsome man stood next to the guard. The surprise must have shown on her face because he smiled at her.

"I didn't mean to startle you. You have news of our infamous Miss Helen?"

Shaina took a moment to pull herself away from his blue eyes, and the curl of light brown hair that laid across his forehead. She studied how his lips curled into a fine line across his face as he smiled. She thought: *he's beautiful.*

"Ma'am, are you okay? You look —"

She cut him off. "Tired. I know. That's because I am. I've been up since six o'clock yesterday morning. I was kidnapped at gunpoint by your psychic coming home from work this morning, and now she tells me your fair is the real danger. She sent me here to talk to you. She said you could help me locate my kids."

"We'll certainly try, Ma'am."

"Don't call me that. My name is Shaina, and I'm only a couple of years older than you. I'm not a Ma'am. Not yet, anyway."

Dashiell smiled. "I'm sorry. Shaina. We'll help any way we can." His smile faded. "Are you telling me Miss Helen came here with you, to the fair?"

She nodded.

Dashiell pounded a fist into his open palm. "Hot damn, we'll surely get her now."

When Dashiell and the guard moved to the windows overlooking the fair, Shaina joined them. Shaina located the place she had last seen the psychic, but only strangers passed by the place where she pointed. She studied the crowd below and couldn't spot her.

"She was right there, next to the ring toss game."

Dashiell turned away from the windows. We'll find her, too. If she's still here."

"Is my family in any danger from her?"

Dashiell stopped and turned to face Shaina. His eyes were the deep blue of the sea. She tried not to get swallowed up in them. As she studied his eyes, she saw a depth of compassion there that she had never seen in a stranger's eyes before, not for her or her family. He showed a genuine interest in her concerns, and that, in turn, caused a swelling in her chest that caused her to take in a sudden, deep breath.

No, it's just that I'm so damn tired.

When he reached out and placed his fingers on her arm, Shaina tried to ignore the tingling sensation caused by his touch. She swam in his eyes again.

He spoke in a soothing voice. "Shaina, I give you my word that your family is in no danger here. I want you to believe that."

Shaina shook off Dashiell's hand and stepped away.

"That woman held a gun on me this morning. What kind of people do you hire to work here? If she finds my kids before we do, what will she do?" She didn't mention that the gun was empty. "I need to find my brother and two kids."

"What's your brother's name?" Dashiell asked.

Shaina told him.

"I assure you she's not as dangerous as it may originally seem. In a way, I believe her when she says there is something odd about the fair, but not for the reasons she believes. My uncle closed the fair down in the seventies when his son, my cousin, Owen Jr, contracted a fatal disease. The circumstances surrounding my cousin's death are very sketchy, but what I do know is that my uncle Owen became a recluse ever since his son died. He was a recluse up until the day of his death."

Shaina frowned. "I need to..." She staggered and almost fell.

Dashiell stepped forward once again and caught her. He helped her to a chair. "You are exhausted, aren't you?"

She peered into his empathetic eyes again. Remotely, she nodded.

The door opened, and two policemen walked into the control room. Dashiell must have seen the confusion on Shaina's face because he explained their presence to her.

"I called them from the office before I met with you."

Shaina turned to look at Dashiell, who smiled, but Shaina's confusion only intensified when she realized she was afraid of the police.

Their presence made the danger feel more *real.*

The taller policeman stood slightly closer to her than his shorter partner, holding a small pad in one hand and a pencil with a menacingly sharp point in the other. He spoke without looking at Shaina.

"We have just a few short questions to ask and then we'll be out of your hair."

"Okay," she said. "But shouldn't you be out looking for my family, and Miss Helen?"

The cop looked at her for the first time since entering the compound. The cop's intense stare caused a bead of sweat to form on her hairline, but she refused to look away from this man.

"Ma'am, we have…"

Dashiell interrupted. "Don't call her ma'am …she hates that. Her name's Shaina."

The cop diverted his razor-sharp gaze away from her and pointed it at Dashiell, who shrugged, chagrined. Without saying anything to Dashiell, the police turned back to Shaina, and his gaze was softer now.

"We have a police presence on the grounds looking for the suspect. Tell me about what happened this morning."

Shaina took a deep breath and let it out slowly. She kept her eyes on the cop, not wanting him to think she was lying. Shaina told him about the long shift. She spoke of the accident, and how she assisted in the care of the officers.

"After leaving the scene, I saw a form on the side of the road. I wasn't thinking about the accident. I stopped the car and approached. That was when Miss Helen pointed the gun at me. The gun she swiped from one of your men."

The cop cleared his throat. "That incident is being investigated."

"Tell me something. Did Helen cause the accident?"

The cop scribbled something on his pad. Once again, he spoke without looking at Shaina.

"The incident is still under investigation, but no. There is no evidence that the subject caused the accident."

She finished telling the officers about her trip home with the gun pointed at her head. She did mention to the officers that Miss Helen confirmed the gun was empty, and that it had been the entire time.

"Do you know for sure the gun was empty?"

"Yes. Helen showed me the empty chamber and even fired the gun to prove it. The gun just clicked."

"There wasn't a scuffle of any kind? No trouble where the gun had discharged accidentally? You can be frank with us."

"No." Shaina's face heated. "Nothing like that. She was very civil and even apologized for the discomfort she'd caused. She wanted to get back to the fair, that's all."

"Knowing that the gun was empty, you still assisted her in coming here?"

And there it was. *The police want to pin me as an accomplice.*

"I drove Miss Helen here because she insisted on coming, and my family was already in the park. My only intention was to get to my kids. She believes everyone here is in danger. She came here to uncover the truth about this place." She was aware that her voice had gone up an octave, and that she was talking fast.

"And what truth would that be?"

Shaina groaned. *I'm too tired to do their job.* "I don't know...that this place is dangerous, I guess. Ask her when you find her."

"Did she mention the missing boy?"

Shaina kept her involvement with Billy away from this dog-with-a-bone cop. "Only that she had no involvement in his disappearance."

"And you believed her?"

"I don't know what I believe." Shaina struggled not to yawn.

Dashiell stepped forward. "I believe she gave you everything she knows. Let her look for her kids."

The cop shoved the small pad into the breast pocket of his shirt and slid the pencil in beside it then his hands dangled at his sides. "There's no need to be defensive. We aren't making any assumptions about your part in this incident, Ma'am — or Ms. Salvador. We know that you are an innocent bystander that was in the wrong place at the wrong time."

Shaina didn't feel any more at ease. The cop's words were soothing, but his tone implied something else. Shaina heard: *we believe you. For now.*

"I guess that's all we need from you at this point. I trust you will be close by if we need more information?"

Shaina tried and failed to keep the sarcasm out of her voice. "I'll be around until I find my family. After that, you'll have to look for me at my house. Is that okay with you?" She waited for him to contradict her.

The cop tilted his head slightly, smiled, and hooked his thumbs into his belt. "That sounds fine. We have your address?"

She leveled a gaze at the officer that would have melted ice. "I'll make sure you have it." She turned to Dashiell. "Can we now get back to the task of finding my brother and kids? How do you propose we go about it?"

Dashiell led her to the row of monitors. There were twelve in all, and each one showed a different view of the fair. She stared at the twelve small movies playing out in front of her.

"This is going to take forever." She plopped into another soft chair with lumbar support. She rolled up to the monitors and scrutinized the blurry faces. "The quality is horrible. I can barely recognize these blobs as human. I'd be better off going out and searching close up."

"We are in communication with the individual attractions, and we have them looking for any groups with a young man and two small children, a boy and a girl. They've been instructed to ask the man if he's Tommy Roberts. I didn't include the names of the kids for their protection."

She nodded her approval, but she still let out an exasperated sigh. "This is still going to take way too long. I feel like I should be doing something more."

"Tell you what, let us do what we can first. If we fail, you can go from one end of the grounds to the other if you want. In the meantime, I have a cot in the backroom that I use for naps. Why don't you go lay down and rest? If there's any news, I promise to wake you. Right now, we're doing everything possible."

She couldn't argue. She stood and followed Dashiell to the back office.

The minute her eyes saw the small cot and the pillow, she knew she needed this. Dashiell handed her a blanket and exited the room. Sitting on the bed, Shaina wasn't sure if taking a nap now was the best idea for her, but it sure did *sound* like it was. She sat down on the cot and stared at the walls. There were pictures of the fair in all its glory back in the day. As tired as she was, her mind would not release her to sleep just yet. She stood and walked around the room, looking at the different pictures. She found a weathered picture of a man holding his son. A twinge in her chest caused her heart to flutter. A lump formed in her throat and she suddenly thought of her kids and her lost husband. She wanted to see them now more than ever.

She moved on to other pictures — some of freak show oddities, some showed people doing ordinary things — until she finally worked her way back to the cot. She felt antsy like she should be doing something more. She couldn't possibly think about sleeping now.

Her mind turned back to Miss Helen. Was the woman as dangerous as everyone seemed to think she was? She didn't think so. She did do some very bizarre things, but she doubted the eccentric woman could hurt anyone.

She tied to call him again, but still, there was no answer. Tommy wasn't much for talking on phones, but damn it, this was important. Important to her, perhaps, but he didn't know about Miss Helen. He didn't realize how stressed out she was at that moment. If history served, Tommy would expect Shaina to come home from work, sleep, and then deal with him. Tommy liked his time alone with her kids. Tommy always accused her of coming between him and the kids. She smiled. As angry she was at that moment, she loved how much he cherished her kids. They would be safe with him.

She inhaled and closed her eyes until her racing heart slowed. She found that the longer she kept her eyes closed, the more she didn't want to open them. She leaned over and laid her head on the pillow. It smelled clean, and the bed was soft. Her heartbeat slowed even more, and her breathing became measured and shallow. Her kids swam in and out of focus in her mind. They appeared happy, innocent. She slipped further into the warm, pervasive pool of sleep. She had the sense of someone moving around her, but it wasn't invasive enough to pull her back up from the shallows. She dimly perceived someone placing a blanket over her.

She moaned. "Mm mm, thank you."

A voice soft and warm in her ear responded. "You're welcome. Sleep well, and when you wake up, your kids will be with you again."

Shaina shifted on the bed. "You promise?" Her voice was soft and low, and somewhat childlike.

The voice came again. "I promise."

She fell asleep with the promise on her mind.

Though Shaina did not dream as she slept, she couldn't know the real nightmare waited to begin when she awoke.

Chapter Six: Rachael

She didn't come to the fair to have fun.

Rachael McManus paid for her hotdog and stood to the side as she waited for the vendor to pass it out the window. She took it, gently cradling its paper boat, and carried it to the condiment station. Rachael slathered it in mustard and ketchup. She had it nearly gone by the time she found a spot to sit at the picnic tables. She finished off the hotdog as she glared out at the real reason she had come to the fair.

Alan and the Bimbo stood in line at the Ferris Wheel, giggling and jostling each other. The Bimbo bumped into the man behind her, and she turned and placed a hand on his shoulder. Rachael was too far away to hear what they were saying, but the body language said it all.

"I'm sorry, but here—take a look at my ample bosom to make up for my clumsiness." Rachael mumbled the words under her breath even as she imagined the conversation.

Alan turned his new woman around, a fierce protectiveness (jealousy?) etched into his face.

The Bimbo's name was April, but Rachael preferred to call her Bimbo. Rachael learned the woman's name at the same time she learned she had been replaced.

Rachael and Alan had been together for three years. Sure, it was a rocky three years, but they were in love. At least, Rachael believed what she and Alan shared was love. Rachael had moved into Alan's apartment a year ago. About six months ago, Alan began to grow more and more distant until five weeks ago when he demanded Rachael should move out. It was over between them, Alan had said. He wanted her out of his life. He gave Rachael no reason.

Was it another woman? Rachael had asked. And after a pause, he said no. He just wanted her gone.

It was a lie.

Rachael turned in her key, but she had long ago created a duplicate. She continually forgot her key, and she wanted to ensure she could always get into the apartment, so she made a spare and hid it under the welcome mat outside the apartment door. She never told Alan about the key because she didn't want him using it and forgetting to put it back.

After removing her stuff, and finding a new place to live, Rachael returned to the apartment and used her hidden gem to enter.

At first, she had believed him when he said he was alone. But that all changed when she found luffas in the shower, perfumes on the dresser...

And dresses in the closet.

She almost wanted to believe he was gay or had become a cross-dresser, but when she found the love letter signed by someone named April, Rachael's bubble of hope popped.

After a little more digging, Rachael learned that April was a loan manager at KeyBank. Rachael met her there, using the fake name Ramona. Rachael had been tentative at first. She didn't know if Alan had mentioned her, or had shown April a picture of her. She had nothing to worry about.

The Bimbo had no idea Rachael existed.

Rachael broke into the apartment several times after that and learned of Alan and April's plans to come to the fair. The tickets were on the stand under the calendar with the date they planned to attend circled.

So, Rachael followed them.

As they stood in line for the ride, April fixed her hair. Alan crammed a hand in one of her back pockets, cupping the Bimbo's ass. When it was their turn to get into a carriage, Alan helped his sweetheart up the step to the seat. The wheel moved on and they were lifted into the air, one carriage at a time, until the ride was full. As Alan and the Bimbo reached the apex of the ride, he rocked the seat. April screamed and gripped his arm. She socked him playfully as the ride settled down. He laughed as she pouted, but it was a ruse. The Bimbo loved every minute of the interaction and cuddled up to Alan as the ride made its rounds.

When the ride ended, Rachael followed them further into the fairgrounds. She watched as Alan tried — and failed — to win his Bimbo a prize at the basketball shoot. He managed to win a small reward for his girl on the ring toss. Rachael believed it was a little pink teddy bear. Very small. The Bimbo hugged him and gave him a kiss on the cheek. He smiled, running his hand through his blond hair, and Rachael felt a twinge of pain in her chest. She choked back a sob.

Flexing and unflexing her fingers into fists helped drive away the creeping sense of loss that threatened to cripple her. The moment passed, replaced by a love for Alan that ebbed Rachael's hatred of the Bimbo. She planned her moment of confrontation that would mar their perfect day together.

As Alan walked toward a concession stand, the Bimbo stood patiently by the ticket booth.

Rachael strode over to hover at the far side of the concession stand, putting Alan between the Bimbo and herself. He glanced up at her with a smile. Instantly, his head swiveled back around in a double-take, the smile replaced with a look of confusion that quickly morphed into a look of anger.

Rachael laughed.

His lip curled into a snarl. "What are you doing here?"

"Good to see you, too."

Alan glanced at the Bimbo. He smiled and waved. He turned back to Rachael and just that fast his expression changed from jovial to hateful. His scowl only fueled Rachael's good mood.

"I take it you didn't tell her about me?"

"Why would I?" Alan moved up to the concession window as the couple in front of him moved away. "Could I get two cokes, please?"

"Make that three." Rachael leaned into the window at the pimple-faced teen boy inside the small building.

The boy stared at her for a moment, then turned to Alan. Rachael leaned against the side of the building.

Alan shrugged, "Three drinks."

Once the three beverages were delivered, Alan took two of the cups and walked to the straw dispenser. Rachael followed him with her refreshment.

Alan stared at Rachael as she sipped at her drink. "Do you plan on telling her who you are?"

Rachael pulled the straw from her mouth. "Why would that matter?"

Alan looked up, then down at his feet. He glanced sheepishly at Rachael. "I love her. Don't ruin this for me."

"Like you ruined us? What makes her so special?"

He didn't answer, and she didn't want him to. He didn't need to. Alan and Rachael had never been in love, and she knew that. Still, what they had had been exceptional, right?

"I love you." Her eyes filled with tears.

"No, you don't. You never did. You put me down constantly. You mocked every decision I made. I was property in your eyes—something you owned—and not something you took particularly good care of." He paused, and Rachael could see he was trying to stifle an anger toward her that had been building for a long time. She didn't want to hear anymore, but he continued. "April loves me, and she shows me every day with the little things she does."

As he continued to talk, Rachael allowed no emotion to show on her face. *If he goes into detail about their love-making, I'm going to puke on his shoes.*

"She's the best thing that's ever happened to me. If you really love me, leave me alone and let me have this."

"Stop worrying. I'm not going to interfere." Rachael lifted her chin. "Besides, she and I have already met."

Alan's tanned face turned as white as chalk dust. "What are you talking about?"

"I went to the bank where she works. Don't worry, I didn't tell her who I am. I just wanted to meet her. She's pretty."

Alan eyed her with a suspicious glare. Then his expression changed to one of confusion. "How did you even know who she is?"

Rachael didn't respond. She didn't want him to know she had a key to his apartment—she might need it again.

"I'd appreciate it if you would stop following us around now. Go live your life and let us live ours."

Rachael's face heated. "You want me to just fade away into the mist? After how you ended things, you think I can just disappear? No, I'm going to be the nasty, mean, evil thing you made me out to be. We could have been happy together, but you and your wandering eye had different plans. How long have you been cheating on me with that Bimbo? I never cheated, that's on you."

"I never cheated, either." His voice sounded weak as if even he didn't believe it. "I broke up with you as soon as I realized I had feelings for April."

"You might not have slept with her yet, but you cheated. You cheated in your mind."

Alan didn't deny it.

"I'm sorry if breathing the same air offends you, but I have every right to be here, too."

"I don't care. Just stay away."

Alan turned and walked away before Rachael could say anything more. He returned to the Bimbo and handed her a drink. She didn't seem to know—or care—why Alan had taken so long to return. She sipped her Coke and giggled when Alan said something, presumably something funny, but Rachael thought the laugh sounded fake, forced.

Alan bought tickets and they walked away from the booth. Rachael followed.

He didn't seem to care that Rachael was following them, though he must have known, even if he didn't look back at her. They took a seat on a bench. Rachael stood by a tree growing in the center of the midway. Red mulch encircled the base of the tree. She watched as they sat looking at each other. Alan talked, and the Bimbo occasionally nodded, as if agreeing with what he was saying.

Such a severe talk for a couple who only moments ago was joking and laughing. *What's he saying?* They didn't look over at her—and if he were telling her Rachael was there, the Bimbo would have looked by now, wouldn't she have? No, he wasn't talking about Rachael.

When he finished speaking, they turned their heads away from Rachael and looked out at the rest of the midway. They finished their drinks. The Bimbo stood and walked their empty cups to the trash can.

Rachael studied Alan. She waited for him to turn and look at her, but he didn't. His back was to her, so she couldn't see his face, and that made her stomach churn. *Turn and look at me. Tell me what you're thinking.*

Rachael looked toward the trash can, but the Bimbo wasn't there. Where did she...

"He told me everything, you know."

The voice had come from behind her, and Rachael turned to see who was standing there.

The Bimbo stood with her arms crossed in front of her chest. "I'm not afraid of you. I don't care if he didn't tell me about you. I know about you now, and if you don't leave us alone, I'll take legal action."

Rachael struggled to find her voice. Finally, she did. "It's a free country, and I can go anywhere I wish."

"Yeah? Well, harassment isn't legal, and I'll have you arrested if you keep following us. I have some pretty influential friends. We can make life very difficult for you."

Rachael huffed, incredulous.

"Don't believe me? Wait till you try to use your ATM card and find your assets are frozen."

"You ca..." Rachael cleared her throat. "Can't do that."

The Bimbo chuckled, shrugged.

Rachael opened her mouth to speak, but no words would come. The Bimbo raised her chin and brushed past Rachael, returning to the bench where Alan waited patiently for her return. The Bimbo took his hand, and they walked away.

Rachael continued to follow them, showing no fear of the threats. They ignored her for the most part but once in a while, Alan would look her way. Once, Rachael locked eyes with him, and he smiled. Alan was saying *I like having you in my life.*

Rachael's heart raced in her chest, and her breathing quickened. *He still loves me.*

It was the Bimbo. She had him under a spell. Remove her, and Rachael could be back with Alan.

She watched them as they played together, frolicking like schoolkids. They went on rides and walked hand in hand as they traveled through the midway, moving from one attraction to the next. Alan never looked at Rachael again, and that had her nervous. Why was he torturing her like this?

When they stopped at the line leading into the funhouse, Rachael took a seat and studied them as they stood in line. In front of them, a red-haired girl with a braid running down her back danced to music Rachael couldn't hear—and probably didn't exist—as the couple behind Alan and the Bimbo laughed and pointed at the red-haired girl.

As the lined moved inexorably forward, people poured out of the exit door at the other end of the attraction. In front of Alan, a redhaired girl and her boyfriend (or brother?) handed over their tickets. Rachael stared as Alan and the Bimbo entered the funhouse, then stopped watching the entrance and concentrated on the exit. She focused on the people coming out, anticipating when Alan and the Bimbo would emerge. After about five minutes had passed, the redhaired girl and her boy exited the attraction. She giggled and threw herself at the boy. She kissed him on the lips, and Rachael no longer thought it was her brother.

Alan and the Bimbo did not emerge. Sixty seconds passed, then eighty. Rachael stood and looked around. She was sure she hadn't missed them. They hadn't come out, she was sure of it.

She walked over to the fence surrounding the funhouse and stood at the gate. She glanced toward the ticket-taker, but the man wasn't looking. She entered the gate and stood next to the door. There was no way to open the door from the outside, but when the next group of people came out, she grabbed the door. They eyed her suspiciously but did nothing to stop her.

Rachael entered the funhouse through the exit.

Strobe lights lit her way, but their effect was disorienting. She struggled through the strobes until she came to a door. She passed through the door, and it sprung shut, pushing her into the room beyond. People going the other way passed by, paying her no mind. She worked her way through the darkness. A girl screamed when Rachael touched her, then laughed and moved on. Rachael continued her slow trek through the maze in reverse. She heard people coming up on her before she could sense their presence next to her. When the floor began to rock beneath her, Rachael let out an involuntary squeal. More voices approached, laughing and screaming in regular intervals.

Rachael pressed herself against the wall to avoid touching the other people. Within seconds she was alone again. If she really strained, she could see the edges of walls, but even still there was nothing much to see anyway. She continued her way through the halls.

As Rachael hugged the wall, something clicked, and the wall behind her disappeared. She fell, spinning and tumbling. She landed on her butt and tumbled backward, falling head over feet. She dropped to the side and then fell out into empty air. She landed on her stomach, and the force knocked the wind out of her with a grunt. She rose on her hands and knees, gasping.

Panic caused her head to spin, and her mind threatened to close down. The darkness around her was impenetrable like the entire world had been painted in India ink. The ground beneath her felt damp, warm. When she gained her breath again, she crawled slowly, creeping along until she touched a wall. Following the wall, and using her sense of touch, Rachael searched anything that would get her out of there.

She heard breathing, heavy and panting, echoing in her ears, sounding like hurricane winds. When she froze, the sound stopped, and she realized then that it was her own breathing coming back at her in an echo. She tried to laugh at her own foolishness, but the fear was too deep, and she choked on a sob, instead.

"What is this place?" Her words sounded foreign in the drippy, dank underworld around her.

This is some kind of basement, has to be.

If there was a way in, there was a way out, and she would find it. She continued. The surface felt rough, feathery, like untreated wood. She took care not to get a sliver. There was no telling what kind of bacteria was brewing here in this dark, dirty dungeon. She suspected any cut in this place could turn into a death sentence.

After moving several feet in the dark, Rachael came to an edge—a door jamb. She followed it with her fingers until she found the doorway. Her hands fell into emptiness. As she took a step forward, hands still outstretched, she touched something soft, yet at the same time unyielding, like a sponge-covered rock. She probed with her fingers until she found a nose, a mouth...

It was the flesh of someone's face.

Rachael screamed.

Chapter Seven: Gina

She had thought Larry was cute when she first met him, and it was why she agreed to go to the fair with him. Sure, his complexion was mottled, and there were deep acne scars on his face, but he had pretty blue eyes. And though she agreed to accompany him to the fair, now that she was there with him, Larry distressed her. He seemed to be both arrogant and needy, self-assured, yet immature. She would probably not go out on another date with him.

"Stand over here." Larry indicated to his left.

Gina giggled and continued walking. She had no interest in changing her position.

"I mean it. Walk on the left please."

Gina shook her head, playfully. "Nah, I don't think so."

Larry gripped her by the shoulders and forcefully moved her to his left.

"Ow, you're hurting me." Gina pulled from his grip and stepped away from him, frowning.

"I'm sorry, but Jesus Christ, I'm trying to be a gentleman here."

"What are you talking about?"

"A gentleman always walks to the right of a lady." Larry smiled.

Gina glared at him. "I don't care about that. Keep your hands off me."

They walked in silence. Larry kept his head turned away from Gina. She wondered if he was crying. *He's sulking like a goddamned child.*

She refused to feed into his need for validation. Gina decided to give it another hour then cry headache or something, and ask to be taken home.

"What should we do now?" Larry stared at her, smiling again.

"Huh? Oh, I don't know. What were you thinking?"

He nodded at something in front of them. "I thought we could go on the Ferris Wheel."

"Ferris Wheel? I don't know. I have a thing about heights."

"I'll win a prize for you. What do you have your eye on?"

She looked around, searching for the hardest game she could find, something that would kill him. After a cursory circuit of all the nearest games, her eyes settled on the ladder game. She watched as one person after another attempted to climb the swinging ladder and fell to the mat below. She saw that the problem was both ends of the ladder were attached by a single rope, causing the ladder to swing uncontrollably. She couldn't wait to see him struggle with this one.

Gina pointed to the extra-large teddy bear. "I want that."

Larry laughed. "That's a lot of teddy bear to be carrying around all day."

A perfect reason to leave early.

"Don't worry about it, though." Larry chuckled. "I'll lug the big lug around."

Gina tried her hardest to smile.

As they headed for the ladder game, Gina hung back. For some reason, she didn't even want to be seen walking with him. Gina avoided him when he tried to hold her hand. She didn't want him doing that now.

The ladders were at a slight incline so that the top of the ladder was a mere three feet off the mat. The barker explained the rules quickly, and with a deep, authoritative voice.

"Start at the bottom and stay upright all the way to the top and ring the bell. If you can complete the climb five times, you win the mega-bear. Dollar fifty a try. One bear per customer per day. Ready to try your hand at it?"

Larry gave a single nod and pulled seven fifty from his pocket and handed it to the barker. He then stepped up to the first rope ladder not currently occupied and set his feet on either side of it.

Gina watched as he began to start up the ladder. It swung violently at times, but every time she thought he would spin off the rope, he steadied himself and continued up. When he finally reached the top, he pulled the string to ring the bell. People standing around the attraction clapped for him. He hopped off the ladder and returned to the start.

One down, and four to go.

When Larry made it halfway up the ladder a second time, it dawned on Gina that he might have learned the secret of this game. She had been trying to humiliate him, but instead, he was drawing a crowd. He was managing to do what most people had come to believe was nearly impossible. Even the game attendant seemed impressed. Gina felt a sense of dread building in her chest when he rang the bell for a second time.

Larry climbed the ladder a third time, ringing the bell, and with every toll, more people wandered over to watch him. He shook hands with people as they congratulated him.

A man standing next to Gina pointed at Larry. "Your boyfriend's awesome. Even if he falls off now, he's got my vote for the most impressive."

On the fourth ring of the bell, Gina thought about Larry's failure at the strongman's game, and how he lost control at the end. That could happen again.

She glanced up at the teddy bear.

That's not a toy; it's a roommate.

She didn't have it yet, but already she devised a plan for getting rid of it. She could donate it to charity, but she didn't know who would accept it, or want it, for that matter.

The bell rang a fifth and final time.

Larry dropped to the mat amidst a chorus of cheers. People met him at the exit with high fives and pats on the back. Larry grinned like a superstar. She saw a devilish glint in his eyes that not only gave her the creeps...it scared her. She wanted to flee, but her momentary paralysis lasted a moment too long. The attendant used a hook to lower the bear. Larry stood next to Gina, and when the attendant handed the bear to Larry; he, in turn, gave it to her.

Gina's chance to run vanished. She fought back the tears.

Larry wrapped the bear's arms around Gina's neck. She cringed when his hands brushed her chest. The bear's body dangled down her back, its feet nearly touching the ground.

"I don't know how long I'll be able to carry this thing."

Larry stood behind her and wrapped his arms around the bear, hugging the toy and Gina at the same time. "Don't worry, I'll help you."

Gina attempted to elbow him away from her, but he refused to move.

"Did you hear how those people were cheering for me?" His hot breath reverberated in her ear. "It was great, wasn't it? I've always had good balance. It was weird; as soon as I situated myself on the ladder, I knew I wasn't going to fall off. It was like magic or something."

As Larry continued expressing his joy over the fantastic skill he possessed, Gina stopped listening. She had tried to humiliate him and failed. She had never felt such rage over someone else's self-confidence before, but Larry seemed to push every one of Gina's bad vibe buttons. The prize was a symbol of Larry pride. She wanted to take a pair of scissors to that damn bear.

It's not coming home with me.

Gina didn't want it in her house, and she definitely wouldn't allow him to bring it in.

Gina glanced around. Did she not know any other people here? She needed to find another way home and didn't want to leave with him. Gina glanced at her phone. She could download that ride-sharing app, slip away— ("I have to use the bathroom.")—and catch a ride with a stranger. She wasn't thrilled with this idea either, but anything was better than going home with Larry.

He was still talking, and though she had no idea what he was saying, she nodded as if she agreed with it all. And she had no need to worry about being put on the spot. Self-absorbed as he was, he would not bother asking for her opinion. She need only to listen or pretend to listen.

When she could take no more, Gina shrugged out of her bear hug, pushing the stuffed toy and Larry away at the same time. She staggered forward, placing her hand to her temple, planting the seed of a headache.

Larry stopped taking. He looked at her. "Are you feeling okay?"

"I have a bit of a headache." She closed her eyes to avoid showing the lie in her eyes.

Larry placed an arm around her shoulder, and she flinched. She pulled away from him with a look that she hoped would let him know he had crossed a line. The expression must have worked, because Larry stepped back and raised his hands slightly, palms out, in the act of surrender. She relaxed, and they continued walking.

She thought of telling him she wanted to go home, but he would offer to take her home. She didn't want that. She would simply hold out until the opportunity arose to find an alternate ride.

"A soothing trip around on the Ferris Wheel will be the perfect remedy for a headache."

"I told you, I'm afraid of heights. I don't want to do it."

Larry took her by the hand and led her to the line of people waiting to board the ride.

Gina squared her jaw and clenched her fists. "This is the last thing we're doing. I'm going home after this."

She could feel Larry's eyes on her, but she couldn't look at him.

He shifted the bear in his arms. "Okay."

They didn't speak for the rest of their wait. Larry was a complete gentleman to her, playing the doting boyfriend.

As the couple before them boarded and moved away, Larry sidestepped the attendant and opened the gate for Gina. He climbed beside her and pulled the teddy bear onto the seat next to him. The attendant offered to hold the bear for them, but Larry insisted on including it. This put Larry snugly up against Gina. She only considered moving the bear between them after the ride moved away from the loading platform. In an attempt to step away, Gina turned and watched as the two teenaged boys climbed onto the carriage behind her. As the ride slowly allowed new riders, Gina felt herself being lifted moment by moment into the sky. When they reached the apex, the ride stopped. She looked down, between her feet, at the two teenage boys. They laughed and playfully punched each other's arms. The carriage holding the boys rocked excessively, and Gina felt herself getting sick. When her carriage moved again, she willed it not to sway.

We're up too high. Gina thought the words, too frightened to say them aloud. Her vocal cords, as well as her body, were paralyzed. She wanted to cringe away as Larry moved closer to her—tried to push him away—but she couldn't get her body to obey. The carriage moved again, and this time, it did rock. Tears filled her eyes. She moaned or thought she did, but Larry seemed not to notice her state of distress.

I need to get off. I hadn't known I was so terrified of heights, but I can't stay on this ride. I'll tell the technician when we reach the bottom that I need to get off. I'm sure I can function again once I'm back on the ground.

But Gina couldn't get the employee's attention. The ride began its cycle, and when they reached the bottom, she couldn't move. Within seconds, they were riding up and around once again. Suddenly it felt as if they were spinning out of control. She tried to scream, but her brain didn't want to function, though her hand managed to reach out and grip the padded seat between her and Larry. Her fingers flexed, and her fingernails dug into the fabric of the bench. Her hand brushed against Larry's leg, and he looked over at her.

He'll see I'm in distress and stop the ride for me.

Larry took Gina's hand in his. She couldn't resist, couldn't protest.

Stop the ride, please just stop the ride.

Larry pulled her hand into his lap. He uncurled her fingers and placed her palm against the stiffening erection under the fabric of his shorts, forcing her to rub his crotch. He leaned over and moaned into her ear.

"Oh, that feels good."

His breath was hot and moist. His tongue flicked out, and it felt like a worm crawling into her ear. Inwardly, she cringed, but if he noticed her repulsion, he gave no indication. He used his other hand to turn her head, and now that wet worm was questing for her mouth.

Her stomach lurched.

Don't. Please don't do this.

Still, the words wouldn't come.

Larry leaned over and covered her mouth with his own. Her lips quivered against his, but she made no move to kiss him back. He didn't care. He covered her face with kisses. He must have tasted her tears, but still, he did not stop. He whispered, "oh god," and moaned against the side of her face. He sucked at her earlobe. As the ride slowed, and they were once again at the summit of the ride, Larry reached down and unzipped his fly. She cringed when she felt something hard and warm flopping against her leg. She struggled against her paralysis, wanted to push him off her but unable to make her body obey. His full weight crushed against her and suddenly he was fumbling between her legs, pulling shorts and panties aside, exposing her vagina. With a sharp pain, like her insides being ripped open, he entered her. He pushed into her, grunting. Through tear-filled eyes, Gina looked up at the two teenage boys above her. The boys leaned back, nearly tipping their carriage to watch her.

How can this be happening? Why isn't anyone stopping him?

In a span that felt like hours, but in reality had been only seconds, Larry rolled off her. He tucked back in and zipped up.

Gina felt something warm and sticky running down her thigh. As her ability to move slowly returned to her, she managed to look down. Blood mixed with something white and glistening ran down her leg.

Larry leaned over and kissed her cheek. "That was so wonderful."

It took all of Gina's strength to slide away from him. She managed to turn her head slightly in his direction. Her body vibrated as she let out a tortured wail, and spittle flew from her lips.

Larry leaned away from her, a look of shock, making his eyes go wide.

Their carriage came stopped at the landing, and as the attendant opened their gate, Gina finally found the strength to move.

She ran.

She ran and screamed. Screamed and cried and ran. She ran past stunned and confused people, who looked at her with horrified expressions on their faces but didn't understand what she had just been through. She cried and screamed, and people covered their mouths and gasped as they watched her run by them. Some gave her angry stares, thinking she was crazy. Some were afraid of her. She ran, pushing people aside, bumping into them.

She ran, and Larry ran after her, still clutching that stupid bear. She ran out of steam, and he caught up to her. Her voice was hoarse and raw from screaming. He grabbed her arm and pulled her into a narrow gap between two buildings, a fence at the back of the alley blocked her in. Gina looked over Larry's shoulder, hoping that someone had seen the attack and would come to her aid. Several seconds passed, but no one came.

Larry dropped the teddy bear and approached her, panting. She backed up until she hit the wall of the building behind her. Gina tried to run past him, but he stopped her.

"Baby, what's wrong?"

"Let me go, Larry. Please."

"I love you, don't you understand that? I thought you loved me, too."

"I don't love you, Larry. I don't. You raped me, you bastard."

His brow furrowed. "No."

"Yes. You raped me. You raped me." She whispered it, looking down at her shaking hands. Tears dripped off her nose and landed in her palms.

Larry reached out to her, but she flinched away.

"Don't touch me."

He pulled away quickly.

"Gina, Sweetheart, what's happening? We were getting along so well. I don't understand."

Gina's fear turned to anger. Her lip pulled back in a snarl. "This was the first date. What makes you think we are going to begin a relationship after a single date? Halfway through this date, I was looking for an excuse to leave. I don't want a relationship with you, and there must be something wrong in your head if you think that after six hours it's okay to roll over on me and rape me on an amusement ride." She had more words to say, but her anger had run out, and she couldn't continue without breaking down in sobs. Instead, she just stared at him, seething.

Larry held her stare, saying nothing but with a look on his face between confusion and anger. She had the urge to turn away but steeled herself against averting her eyes.

Larry's stern, thin-lipped countenance cracked and he frowned. His head drooped, looking at the ground and sobbing.

"I'm sick. I need help. I thought you would heal me. I'm sorry. Can you ever forgive me?"

He looked up at her again, and Gina searched his eyes for sincerity. *Don't fall for his act.* She snapped back to her senses and shoved him away, hard. He stumbled backward, into the wall of the opposite building. She tried to run past him while he was off-balance, but he recovered too quickly and grabbed her by the arm. With a strength she could not match, Larry pulled her back, lifting her off the ground and slamming her into the side of the building. She crumpled to the stony ground.

He stood over her. "I'm sorry. I didn't mean to..."

He reached for her, but she slapped his hand away.

"I just wanted to help."

She stood. "I don't want or need your help."

She was about to say more, but something so bizarre happened that caused her to completely lose her train of thought. She stared at a spot behind Larry, mouth agape.

The wall behind Larry *moved.*

A section of the wall about the size and shape of a door came away. A dark opening formed. Gina watched in shocked silence as a towering figure — seven feet tall, at least — stepped out of the darkness. The shape wore a white-faced, rubber clown mask with a tangle of rainbow-colored hair. The clown's nose was a red rubber ball. The frozen smile showed silly happiness. She glanced down at the frumpy yellow costume the clown wore on its body, with elastic bands at the wrists and ankles. The clown's large hands were covered in white gloves, and it wore oversized yellow shoes on its feet. Gina had a moment when she wasn't sure if she wanted to laugh...or scream.

When Gina's gaze was once again directed at Larry, he fixed her with a questioning gaze.

Her ruined vocal cords only managed to croak. "Behind you."

Larry slowly turned around. He peered up at the clown and stumbled backward, tripping over Gina.

Pinned between the wall and Larry, Gina watched in stunned silence as the clown reached out with an eight-inch buck knife. The clown rammed the weapon into Larry's stomach, and the man released an explosive sound as if he had been sucker-punched. Larry fingered the hole made by the knife as it was pulled free. His head dropped and he gaped at his wound. When his head came back, the blade cut a clean gash across his throat.

Blood sprayed from his neck like water from a ruptured pipe. Larry spun away from Gina, and she screamed. She rocketed back and hit the fence that trapped her between the buildings. The clown lifted Larry and tossed the man into the hole from which the clown had appeared. Gina attempted to run toward the alleyway entrance, but the clown caught her effortlessly by one arm around her waist. Her scream turned into a grunt as her body pressed against the clown's torso, taking away her ability to breathe. The clown hurled her into the dark gap. She flew through the air, spinning, and landed on her ass. A lance of pain traveled from her tailbone, up her spine, to her skull.

Then she was tumbling down, sliding, moving in a spiral, as if on some kind of strange kid's amusement ride. When she reached the bottom, she lay sprawled across something lumpy.

It was Larry's corpse.

She scrambled off him and found the edge of the slide. She gripped on its sides and tried to climb back up. She looked above her at the rectangle of light that was the exit. In another moment, the sun disappeared, and she was alone with the clown and Larry's corpse.

A scream formed on her lips but turned to a sob. She sat on the edge of the slide and waited for the clown to come for her.

Chapter Eight: Shaina

She sat up with her heart pounding in her chest and a scream on her lips. Shaina glanced around quickly, the unfamiliar surroundings confusing her. As her racing heart and rapid breathing slowed, she remembered being at the fair, in the manager's office to be precise.

She also recalled the dream that had awakened her so abruptly. In the dream, something chased her through the darkness, but with every waking moment, the vision slipped away. Good riddance; it had been a bad dream, anyway. She stood and tested the strength of her legs. Searching her phone, Shaina found there were no missed calls, and she groaned inwardly.

Damn you, Tommy. Where are you?

In one corner of the office, Shaina spotted a water cooler and a stack of six-ounce Dixie cups on the shelf nearby. She grabbed a cup and dispensed some of the water, downed it, and poured herself another.

Her thirst sated, Shaina scurried out of the office.

As she entered the central control room, she stopped as her eyes landed on the two strangers standing next to the monitors.

Dashiell turned to look at her and smiled. "Welcome back, sleepyhead." He noticed her eyes were on the new people. "Shaina, this is Wanda and Dylan."

The short woman approached and held out a stubby arm. The small, pudgy fingers felt odd in her grip, like shaking the hand of a baby.

"Glad to meet you," the woman said in her high-pitched voice.

"Glad to meet you, too." Shaina felt like she was in a daze.

She glanced up as the man approached. He held out his hand, and Shaina shook it as well.

"Dylan," He said.

He held her grip a moment longer than Shaina would have deemed necessary.

"Nice to meet you." Shaina pulled her hand free.

"Dash tells us you were with Miss Helen. You brought her here."

"Yes, that's right."

"Where is that treacherous bitch?"

Shaina's eyes tracked the voice to its source, and she stared at the small woman named Wanda.

"I don't know." Shaina's voice was still heavy with sleep.

"She didn't hurt you, I hope," Wanda said.

Shaina took a moment to answer. "No, not really. I mean, she held me at gunpoint, but the gun turned out to be empty. She kept insisting that the fair was a dangerous place."

Wanda waved a tiny, dismissive hand. "This place is no more dangerous than a Chuck-E-Cheese's. I don't know what she's talking about."

"That may be," Shaina said. "But my kids are out in that park somewhere, and until I know they are safe I'm not taking any chances."

"I just hope she doesn't start another fire." Dylan glanced around when all eyes landed on him. "What?"

Shaina felt a tightness in her chest at the mention of the fire. Her kids were out there somewhere. "I can't stand around anymore. I have to go out and actively look for my family."

"Understandable," Dashiell said. "I'll be your escort."

"I'll go, too." Dylan grinned. "As security."

Dashiell raised an eyebrow at him.

"I'm good in a fight."

"I'll stay here and continue to monitor the cameras," Wanda said.

Dashiell opened the door and allowed Shaina to exit first.

Shaina walked down the steps and followed the path leading to the park. She walked along the midway with Dashiell on one side of her and Dylan on the other. As they moved deeper into the park, the crowds of people grew more abundant and louder. Soon they were being jostled and pushed and moved away from each other. When Shaina thought she had lost Dashiell completely, someone gripped her by the arm. She almost pulled away until she realized it was Dashiell. She moved closer to him. Dylan drew between the two and wrapped an arm around each of them. Shaina turned, and their faces were mere inches apart.

"Cozy." Dylan laughed and kissed Shaina's nose.

Dashiell leaned across Dylan's chest to speak directly to Shaina. "I think he likes you." Then hooked his thumb to indicate Dylan. Shaina giggled.

"Aw, don't be sad." Dylan kissed Dashiell on the nose as well. "I like you, too."

Shaina laughed. "Are all carnival people as nuts, as you?"

"Yes," Dylan said, smiling.

Dashiell took Shaina by the hand, pulling her away from Dylan.

Dylan shrugged. "Just trying to cheer you up."

Shaina gripped Dashiell's hand tighter when he tried to pull away, and he looked, first at their intertwined hands, then at her.

Shaina leaned in. "I don't want to lose you."

As she and Dashiell walked hand in hand, weaving in and out of the throng of fairgoers, Dylan did his best to keep up.

Shaina stopped abruptly and released Dashiell's hand. "Have I shown you a picture of my family yet?"

"As a matter of fact, no. I have no idea who we're looking for."

Shaina pulled her phone from her pocket, turned it on, and immediately looked for any missed calls. There were none, just as she had expected. "One sec, I need to try this first." She dialed Tommy's number, but again it went straight to voice mail. She ended the call without leaving a message and flipped through her pictures until she came across a still of Tommy and her kids. She enlarged the image and handed the screen to Dylan. Dashiell glanced over Dylan's shoulder to look at the picture as well.

"Cute kids." Dylan handed the phone back to her.

"Thank you. I certainly think so." She tucked her phone into her front right pocket for easy access in case Tommy finally came to his senses and called her. She kept her hand at the pocket for a few seconds, as if touching a talisman. She willed it to vibrate against her hip. It didn't.

The crowd around them slackened, and it made it easier for Shaina to see individual faces. Shaina watched people passing by for her brother's distinctive gait—he had a slight limp from a motorcycle accident a year ago. She scanned the faces of the people who were not moving, but none matched her brother's features. She scanned the faces of children as well, but none were familiar to her.

She stopped looking when she heard Dylan speak to her right.

"I'm in the mood for a slushy, who else wants in?"

"Sounds good. A red one." Dashiell shoved his hands into the pockets of his slacks and pulled out a wad of bills.

"You're paying?" Dylan frowned. "You own the place. Shouldn't you get your food for free?"

Dashiell lifted his chin. "I own the land, not the vendors. I don't presume to take anything for free." Dashiell handed Dylan the money.

Dylan shrugged. He turned to Shaina. "How about you? Thirsty?"

"Yes, but I can pay for my own."

"No, you can't." Dashiell stopped her when she reached for her money.

"No worries." Dylan waved the wad of money. "What flavor do you want?"

Shaina hesitated. "Blue raspberry, I guess."

Dylan walked away before she could protest.

When Dylan was out of earshot, Dashiell leaned his head toward Shaina, his hands still jammed deep in his pockets. "He likes you."

"Pardon?" She wasn't sure she understood what he said.

Dashiell pulled a hand from his pocket and yanked his thumb at Dylan. "He likes you. He's flirting."

Shaina turned and caught Dashiell's eyes, managing to hold his gaze for several seconds before he turned away.

I'd prefer to know how you feel about me. But Shaina let the thought die before it moved across her lips.

The silence between them stretched until Dylan returned, balancing the three large cups. Shaina thanked him as she took her drink. He handed the red slushy to Dashiell and slurped at the giant straw of the remaining blue drink. After a considerable drag on the straw, Dylan let out a loud cry of distress and grabbed his head. Both Shaina and Dashiell spun to face him.

"Brain freeze."

Dashiell laughed.

"Hold your tongue against your palate and keep it there until your warm saliva begins to reassert itself."

She couldn't tell if Dylan was doing as she said, but after a few seconds, he opened his eyes, and his hand fell away from his head.

Dylan smiled. "It worked. Thanks, doc."

"I'm a nurse, but you're welcome." She raised her own drink to her mouth but stopped. "Drink more slowly this time."

Dylan lowered his head. "Yes, Mother."

Dashiell laughed. "You're a grown man. You're old enough to know you shouldn't drink cold stuff too fast."

Dylan offered a goofy grin that got a laugh from both Dashiell and Shaina, but he said nothing.

They walked along quietly for several steps. Shaina had taken to half-heartedly searching the crowd for her family. The task seemed herculean, and she doubted very much that she would be successful. They had a better chance of running into her brother and kids by accident.

As Dylan walked, he chewed on the end of his straw, not really ingesting the sugary drink inside the cup. He stopped. "You know what I think? We will have a better view of the crowd if we get on the Ferris Wheel. We could probably see the entire park from up there."

"Most of it, maybe," Dashiell said.

"Sounds like a good idea to me." Shaina looked up at the apex of the ride. It was high.

"Sounds like Dylan just wants an excuse to go on a ride."

Shaina repeated her previous statement, more forcefully this time. "I think it's a good idea. Let's do it."

Dashiell bought their tickets.

As they stood in line, the attendant released a sharp whistle. When Dashiell glanced up, the attendant waved him over. He motioned for all three to come forward.

The attendant held back the next group in line. "Climb aboard, Boss."

"Hey." The man in line pressed against the hand that was holding him back.

"This is the park's owner. Back off."

Dashiell shook his head. "I don't have to skip the line."

"Bull shit. Hop on."

Dashiell relented, and they climbed aboard.

Shaina tried to take the outside seat, with Dashiell on her right, but the men were too fast, and she was stuck sitting between them. She took the central spot, and the attendant closed their gate. The gondola moved forward and stopped. Shaina stared ahead as she perceived, peripherally, that the men were both looking at her. The carriage moved up again. Shaina realized the middle seat was the optimal placement for scanning the fairgrounds below them. If she had been sitting on the left side, she would have trouble seeing what was below them on the right. In the middle seat, however, she could see clearly on either side.

She missed her kids terribly.

"My son, Jeremy, takes excellent care of his sister." She didn't know why she was telling these virtual strangers about her kids, but she just felt the need suddenly to talk about them. "He hates to see her in distress. When she was afraid of the dark, it was Jeremy who went through her room showing her there were no monsters. He opened her closet door and shined a light in to show her there was nothing in there to be afraid of. He and she would get down on their knees and shine a light under her bed to show that nothing was hiding there, either. Every time she mentioned a place, Jeremy showed her there was nothing that could hurt her. He'd walk her to the park for the swings, and would always hold her hand when crossing the street, even though the other kids picked on him for it. I'm sure they poke fun, but he doesn't care. He's a real trooper."

Dylan placed a hand on her hand. "I'm sure he is protecting her right now."

She hadn't been aware of the tear streaking down her cheek until it reached her chin and she wiped it away.

She cleared her throat. "Oh, I know they are safe. And I'm not saying that I don't trust my brother to take care of them. I know he is. I'll just be happier when they are back in my arms again."

Dylan released her hand. "They will be."

As the ride finished its rounds, and everyone was in place, they picked up speed. After about the fourth or fifth rotation, she felt sure she had scanned every face in the crowd she could see from her vantage point. She saw no one who looked like her brother or kids.

They could be inside a building, or behind the flap of an awning. Also, I can't see the entire park. The Ferris Wheel was a good idea; it just didn't pan out, that's all. I just have to keep looking.

The Ferris Wheel made a few more rotations, but she had been unable to locate her brother or the kids.

"We could stay on for another go-around if you like." Dashiell glanced at the attendant for confirmation and received a nod.

"No. Thank you, but I would rather hoof it at this point. I felt helpless up there. I mean, what would we have done if we did spot my family? Even if we got the ride to stop right then and there, by the time we got to where we'd seen them, they would be gone again. I want to be face to face with my brother when I finally find him."

"You're right," Dylan said. "It was a stupid idea."

Shaina placed a hand on his arm. "No, it was a good idea. It was a nice, soothing distraction from my problems. I really enjoyed it."

Dylan smiled.

"Maybe you have a brain in your head after all," Dashiell said. "And you're not just standing around like the dumb, handsome animal that you are."

"Thank you?" Dylan said.

The three walked around the park again, aimlessly at first, but then Shaina began ducking into tents that she thought her brother would like. She searched the Tee-Shirt Hut but failing to find him there, entered a tent devoted to fantasy paraphernalia. Glancing around, she did not see him in there, either.

As she exited the little structure, she scanned the crowds around her. She tried to imagine what she would want to do if she were her brother. She suspected that there was plenty of stuff he would want to do if he was alone, adult shows and such, but those places were not appropriate for kids. She debated for a moment if he would entertain these notions anyway, but decided to give him the benefit of the doubt.

Shaina scurried through the crowd, and the men struggled to keep up with her as she searched one place after another. She only slowed down when she was panting, and there was a cramp in her side.

"I don't get it." She took a couple of deep breaths to calm her racing heart. "We should have run into them by accident. Where are they?"

"They will turn up," Dashiell said. "It's just a matter of time."

Shaina nodded, feeling calmer now.

"I contacted Wanda by radio. They still haven't found Miss Helen, either."

Dylan nudged Dashiell in the side. "That's not helping, Buddy."

"Oh." Dashiell shrank back a little. "Sorry."

Shaina let out a little laugh. "It's fine. I've known her long enough to decide she's not the monster you make her out to be."

The trio continued their search.

Chapter Nine: Amber

As the oppressive crowd undulated around them, Amber Hicks held a bone-crushing grip on her boyfriend's hand. Christopher Scarver's yellow muscle shirt exposed big arms, and his dark skin glistened with sweat as he and Amber pushed through the throng of people. Amber chanted under her breath. "Hang on tight, hang on tight."

Why had she let him talk her into coming to the fair in the first place? She hated crowds. She hated being around people in general. Maybe hate was too harsh a word, but she definitely feared to be around people. She could barely stand to go to the store for fear of someone in line, turning around talking to her. To avoid being in such a situation, she was happy to send Christopher in her stead. He complained about having to buy her feminine needs products, but as long as he was willing to do it, he could protest all he wished.

"Where are you taking me?" she asked when the crowd thinned out enough that they could walk side by side. She didn't release his hand, however.

"I have an extraordinary place in mind."

That didn't tell her anything at all.

Amber wanted to be home. She was quite content staying inside her studio apartment, creating her disturbing sculptures. Her latest work was of a man being strangled by a tourniquet until his eyes bulged. The man would be life-sized when completed, sitting naked and spread-eagled, with a micro-penis dangling between his legs. When she showed a maquette of the figure to her agent, he loved it. Her agent, Jeff, gushed that all the galleries he had demonstrated the figurine to were clamoring to be the first to display the finished work.

She should be home working, not running through a fairground trying to avoid being touched by the strangers around her.

"We're almost there." He whispered into her ear and then kissed her on the cheek.

His excitement vibrated into her like a tuning fork.

He pulled her in a new direction, and they were once again fighting through more crowds. As the people around them brushed up against her, she felt her throat closing. She couldn't breathe. She squeezed his hand, trying to communicate her distress. He squeezed back, which let her know he acknowledged her plea, but he didn't stop dragging her forward. She pressed her lips tightly together to suppress a scream building there and closed her eyes. When he finished pulling her, she opened them again.

The first thing she noticed was all the people moving through a metal stanchion that alternated directions to fit more people in a smaller space. The next was that she and Christopher were in line as well.

She looked up at the building near them and read the sign. She smiled, and then she laughed.

A spook house.

He knew her so well. She might have been agoraphobic, but she was also a freak for all things horror.

She studied the mural of people in different states of distress. She felt giddy over the alien and the hockey-masked killer. There was blood dripping from axes and a man in a boiling caldron.

She hugged him. "I hope it's not lame."

Christopher kissed her on the lips. "I have high hopes it's going to be epic."

They moved forward as people began to file through the entrance.

"How does this work? I mean do we walk through it? Ride? Will we have to be around other people?"

"I don't know, hon." He stood behind her with his arms wrapped around her waist. "We'll know soon enough."

"I hope it's a rider and we are the only ones in the car. I like how those rickety carts clack and bang around. Adds to the uneasiness."

"I hope that this is well planned and will inspire you."

She leaned back so he could kiss her.

They moved forward again.

Amber looked down at Christopher's hand, reassuring herself he was truly there with her. She watched as the next couple entered the doors. It took several minutes before the next group was allowed to enter.

She and Christopher moved forward.

When the hand touched her shoulder, she first thought it was Christopher. She gasped when she realized it was not her boyfriend holding her shoulder. She flinched away from the hand.

The woman standing there put her hands up. "I'm not going to hurt you."

Christopher stepped between Amber and the woman.

"What are you doing?" Christopher scowled at the woman.

"I didn't mean to startle you." The woman glanced around furtively. "Just hear me out. You can't go in there." The woman pointed to the door where two more people entered the attraction. "I need you to understand that this place is not a good place. I sense something terrible is going to happen if you go through those doors. Do not go in there. Go home." She glanced around again. Something to her right upset the woman, and she scurried away.

Christopher and Amber glanced at each other. He shrugged.

Their confusion compounded when a police officer approached them. Several other officers ran by them.

"Excuse me," the officer said. "But did the woman who was just here speak to you?"

"Yes," Christopher said. "She told us to go home."

The officer nodded. "Did you know her?"

"No, not at all. That woman scared my girlfriend."

The officer nodded again. Without saying a word to Amber or Christopher, he leaned into a mic attached to his jacket. "Yeah, the suspect was just here at the spook house. She approached two patrons."

The mic crackled and a gruff voice issued from the speaker. "Spook house, yeah? Suitable place for her."

"Nice, Chuck. Ben and Stan are trying to track her down now. Send someone over to interview the couple, will you? I'm going to help my guys try to stop her." The officer turned back to Amber and Christopher. "Some officers are on their way here. I'm going to ask you to step out of line and speak to them when they get here. Will you do that?"

"We really don't have anything to say."

"That's fine. Speak to the officers, please." The cop rushed off.

Amber took a step.

"Where are you going?" Christopher asked.

"He told us to wait for the cops to come."

Christopher shook his head. "He asked us if we would. If they want to hear what we have to say they will wait for us to come out the other side. I say we keep going. Besides, it's our turn."

Amber glanced at the entrance then looked around. There were no cops in sight. "Whatever."

They entered the spook house.

The room was dark, but dim lights allowed them to see some kind of gate in front of them. Seconds passed, and there was movement from the left. A red, beat-up old cart stopped in front of them. They waited for a few seconds, expecting an assistant to come along and tell them what to do. When no one came, Christopher climbed into the car and motioned for Amber to join him. Reluctantly, she did. As soon as they sat on the springy bench seat, a bar came down and locked in place in front of them. Amber squealed when the cart jolted and began moving them deeper into the darkness of the attraction. She giggled.

The car rolled along on a track, turning a corner and busting through a pair of double doors. The doors slammed shut behind them, sealing them in complete darkness. The car rumbled on.

Something brushed against their heads from above, and Amber screamed. Strobe lights revealed a ghostly apparition made of cloth hovering over them. Amber uttered a nervous laugh.

Amber tried to look behind them, but the surrounding darkness did not allow for even shadows to be discernable.

She leaned against Christopher. "I don't like this." She touched his arm, just wanting to make sure he was there. Then, strangely, she wanted him to speak, so she knew it was him sitting there next to her. "Chris."

"This is great. Really spooky."

Amber's muscles loosened at the sound of her boyfriend's voice. "I don't see anything very inspiring."

"Give it time. We are only a few feet in. It'll get better."

Amber reached out a shaking hand, found his hand, and wrapped her fingers around his fingers. "This feels strange."

"My hand?"

She giggled. "No, this place. It feels like there's something...extra going on. I don't know. It's hard to explain."

The cart jolted, and a loud crash was followed by a trap door opening, and a witch popped up, cackling and screaming. Amber had been startled, but the effect had been less than frightening. They moved on.

"This is kind of lame." Before Christopher could respond, she continued. "And no, it's not going to get better."

He groaned, defeated. "I tried. I really had high hopes for this place."

Another trap door opened and another lame attempt to scare her. This time it was the wolfman.

"I don't blame you, but the scariest thing I've seen so far was that woman from the line who warned us not to come in here. We should have listened."

Something touched her neck, and she screamed.

Christopher laughed.

"Was that you?" She punched him on the arm. "That doesn't count."

As the ride rounded a corner, a form looking like the Grim Reaper leaped forward swinging a scythe. The automaton stopped inches from Amber's face and gave a deep-throated, bellowing laugh as it turned back into place.

Amber screamed, then laughed. "Okay, that was good."

"That's the spirit. If you're open to the experience, you'll enjoy it more. I promise."

A low moaning cry began to swell from somewhere in front of them. Amber braced herself for something to jump out at them. She moved closer to Christopher and slid her hand into his again. He leaned in and kissed her.

The moan became a bellowing yell. Lights flashed, and a form took shape ahead. Amber let out a little squeak of alarm. She slapped her free hand across her mouth, stifling a scream. The specter seemed to be moving of its own accord, and not through animatronics.

"Chris..." Amber shuttered in his grasp.

What's happening? This doesn't feel like part of the ride.

The figure ran by on a platform running parallel to the track, screaming. As the car passed by, the scream became a laugh. The shape faded behind them, and all sound ceased. The lights went out again, pitching them in inky darkness once again.

Christopher breathed in deeply and exhaled. "I didn't know they had real people running around. That was intense."

The seat beneath them rumbled and bumped, the cart pushed through another pair of swinging doors, and the tracks clicked on as they trundled farther into the attraction.

"Do you think there are emergency exits for people who can't take it?"

Christopher pulled away from her. "You're not thinking of chickening out on me, are you?"

"No, not at all. I was just thinking out loud."

"Didn't you see the sign at the beginning? Pregnant women, fat people, and heart patients are discouraged from riding."

"It didn't really say that did it? Fat people? That's discriminatory."

"They'd probably rather have you sue them for discrimination than for wrongful death."

She couldn't argue with that.

Their boxcar slowed down, and another door opened. They slowly entered the doorway, and the car came to a rumbling halt.

They sat in complete silence, complete darkness.

"Uh, what...what happened?" Chris stood. "Did the ride die on us?"

When Amber felt his body moving away from her, she clung to him, forcing him back down in his seat.

"Don't leave me."

"I wasn't leaving. I'm hoping to get a better view of our surroundings."

Amber heard the rumble of another car going by behind them. Voices chittered. Something roared, followed by screams, and then laughter.

Then there was nothing again.

"Hello, is anyone there?" Chris stood again. "Hey, we're stuck here. Is anyone out there? What's going on?"

To their left, a dim light flickered on, lighting up what looked like a door with no handle. Amber and Christopher turned and stared at each other, then turned toward the door again. As they watched, the door opened by sliding right. A small room was illuminated by a light in its ceiling.

"Is this part of the ride?" Amber didn't expect Christopher answer.

Her boyfriend turned around and peered back to where the car had come. He stepped out of the wagon and walked back along the tracks to the gate. She quickly followed him, snagging his shirt to keep from losing him in the darkness.

Christopher pushed on the gate, kicked it. He used an open hand to bang on it. "Hello, we're in here? Is anyone there?" He stepped back and waited.

There was no answer.

Amber pointed to the small room. "Should we go in there?"

Christopher shrugged. "It's either that or we climb this gate and start walking back along the track."

Amber shook her head violently, though she doubted he could see that. "No, that's not going to happen. We'll get lost. I think the ride is telling us to take that little room."

Amber walked over to the dimly lit doorway and looked into the room. Christopher came and stood beside her.

"What's in there?" His voice echoed into the room.

"Only one way to find out." She stepped into the room.

After a moment of hesitation, he joined her. As they turned around inside the room, the door slid shut. A grinding moan filled their ears, and the floor jolted.

Amber grabbed his arm. "We're moving."

He placed a comforting hand on her arm. "Feels like a rudimentary elevator. Not very stable at all."

"Feels like we're going down."

"Yeah, I think so."

When the elevator—or whatever it was—stopped, the door slid open again. Amber gave a dry little cough as the dusty air of the room beyond the doorway was sucked into her lungs.

Christopher raised a hand and waved the dust away from his face, then rubbed at his watering eyes.

When they had grown accustomed to the stuffy air, they stepped over the threshold into this new room. The door closed, shutting out all light and leaving Amber and Chris in complete darkness.

Amber spun around and tried to open the door, but the smooth surface of the door left no handholds or any other way of opening it from this angle.

"What the hell?" Christopher's voice echoed in the darkness.

"Chris, I'm scared." Amber reached out and latched onto him.

He pulled her into an embrace. "We'll be okay."

A light came on, and Amber flinched. She relaxed when she saw that the light was coming from the flashlight feature on Chris's phone. He scanned the empty room; there was nothing to see.

"Do you have cell service? Call someone and let's get out of here."

She studied Christopher's expression as his phone's glowing video screen cast a pale light over his face. His eyes seemed to be lit from inside, and his brown skin looked like it was made out of modeling clay. The effect that made her shiver. She placed a hand over her mouth, afraid she might scream.

In the cell phone's glow, she saw his frown.

He shook his head. "No service."

She checked her own phone and learned that she, too, had no cell service.

Christopher placed a hand on her phone and forced her to turn it off. "It's the only light we have until our batteries die. We need to conserve."

She turned her phone off and shoved it back into her pocket.

Christopher scanned the empty room with his light. He searched the walls for a doorway, but there didn't seem to be any way out. He knocked on one wall.

"What are you doing? Do you expect someone to answer back?"

"No, not really. I want to see if there is a change in the sound of the knock."

"What does that signify?"

"I guess that means the space behind it is hollow."

"Where did you learn that?"

He laughed. "The movies."

"Any luck?"

He knocked again. "No." He dropped his hand. "I'm not sure if it even works."

She followed him around the room as he searched the walls with his little light. There were no cracks to indicate a hidden doorway. Even the door to the elevator seemed to have disappeared.

"How can that be?" Amber felt the wall where she thought the door should be. "We just came through it. Why can't we find it now?"

The cellphone light swiveled as Christopher moved away from that wall and searched another area of the room.

She followed him. As they shuffled along, Christopher staggered.

"What was that? Something tripped me." He stepped back and shined the light at his feet.

"Is that a—?" Her hand flew up to stifle a gasp.

"Looks like an arm." He tapped it with his foot.

"Oh, God. Is it real?"

"Real? No, I...no. Can't be." He scratched the stubble on his cheek. "I mean it's part of the attraction, right?" He reached down.

"Chris, no. Don't touch it."

He glanced at her. We need to know if it's real or not, right? I have to touch it to know for sure."

Amber shivered, and a groan escaped her throat.

After a moment of hesitation, Christopher reached down again, picked the object up by the wrist, and held it away from his body as far as he could. "Feels hard, and it's heavier than I thought it would be." He handed the phone to Amber and took the limb in both hands. He turned it, and the hand flopped at the wrist.

Christopher dropped the arm and stepped back. Amber screamed and nearly dropped the phone. Christopher pulled her closer and wrapped his arms around her. She searched his face, but the look of fright in his eyes scared her more than the darkness.

"What is it, Chris?"

"Nothing." His voice was small, timid. "It's nothing. Just creeped me out, is all."

She didn't believe him. "It's real, isn't it?"

Taking a deep breath, he stepped away from her. "No, not at all. Just a really creepy replica."

"I don't get it. Why would the people running this place..."?

Christopher staggered over to the wall where the elevator door should have been. He banged on the wall.

His actions scared Amber, and she started to cry.

"Help. Help us. We're down here. Someone, please help us."

She wiped her face and joined him beating on the wall. The sound they made was a solid thumping that she knew wasn't carrying very far.

She stopped. "This isn't working."

He tapped the wall a couple more times and stopped as well.

Christopher swept his cellphone's flashlight around the room. He focused on another wall. "Look at this."

His light illuminated one small part of the wall. Amber stepped closer to see what he was showing her. She saw a rectangular hole in the wall the size of a small window. She reached out and touched its edges.

"There's a hole here."

Christopher shined his light into the gap, and Amber peered through to another room.

"I think I can crawl through to the other side." Amber gripped the edges of the hole and braced a foot against the base of the wall. "Boost me up."

Christopher pulled her back, and Amber stumbled away. She fell onto the hard dirt floor.

"What did you do that for?"

Christopher helped her to stand.

"Before we go crawling through strange holes, we should examine it a little more." Christopher shined the light around until he found the severed arm. "Our friend here might have had a similar idea on the other side of the wall. The rest of him might still be over there."

"What are we going to do then? That hole seems to be the only way through here. I don't want to be stuck here forever."

"Just settle down."

Settle down? Amber panted. *I'm not a hysterical female.* She took a few calming breaths, and when she spoke, her voice was low and even. "I'm fine."

Christopher reached down and picked up the severed limb again.

Amber's calm demeanor broke. "What are you doing?"

Chris shined the light of his cellphone into the gap. He aimed it at something inside the hole without breaking the threshold. "Look."

Amber stood next to him and looked at where the light was pointed.

A slit ran along the top of the hole lengthwise, halfway between the two rooms. Amber tried to think of what this crevice represented.

Christopher forced her to back away. He raised the severed arm and placed it in the hole. He moved the arm toward the other side. As the hand reached the halfway mark, a blade slammed down like a guillotine then shot back up to disappear into the slit.

Amber screamed.

Christopher stumbled back, dropping the limb. He shined the light on it, and they both stared in shocked disbelief.

The hand was missing.

"What's happening?" She spun into Christopher's arms and cried against his chest. He stroked her hair.

Christopher waited for her to calm herself. He lowered her to the floor, and they sat together with their backs against the wall.

"This isn't a funhouse anymore." He squeezed her by the shoulder and pulled her to him. "It's a murder house."

"What's that?" Amber sniffled.

"There was a hotel in Chicago where people slipped behind the walls and were trapped by a serial killer. They would look for a way out only to fall into traps." He pointed to the hole in the wall. "Like that one. People would fall into holes with spikes sticking out of them, or get gassed."

"Gassed?" Amber whined.

"We need to stop moving around, Am. God knows what other traps there are around here."

Amber's head snapped up, eyes wide. "God, I'm so scared. We could have been killed by any number of other traps." She shuddered. "Chris, what are we going to do? I don't want to die."

He pulled her tighter to him. "We're going to wait. Help is sure to come, sooner or later. I won't let anything happen to you."

They sat there for several minutes, not speaking or moving. Amber listened to their synchronized breathing, the only sound in the room. Amber's pounding heart slowly ebbed to a dull thud that she felt in her ears. She nuzzled against Christopher, enjoying his scent. Her head lifted slightly, chin raised, as his lips came down to meet her and they kissed. Amber turned to face him, and her questing tongue darted in and out of his mouth. She moaned.

She heard a sound, like something being dragged across the stone floor and pushed away from Christopher. "What was that?"

Christopher jumped to his feet. She stood and stayed behind him.

She heard the sound again, and she was sure now that Christopher heard it, too. They turned and looked at each other.

Something was coming.

Christopher whispered into her ear. "It's coming from that other room."

She nodded with her head pressed against his neck. The two of them slowly made their way over to the hole in the wall.

After a few more seconds passed, they heard human voices echoing through the hole.

"Someone is coming."

Amber tensed. She couldn't tell from the tone of his voice if he thought this was a good thing, like someone coming to rescue them.

Or something much worse.

Chapter Ten: Rachael

"Rachael?"

Alan's voice broke through her terror, and Rachael stopped screaming.

"Alan? Is that you?" she asked. "I—where are we? I came in looking for you and fell through the wall."

A female voice responded — the Bimbo.

"We dropped through the floor and landed in this basement. We've been wandering around ever since."

Rachael backed away from Alan as the female shape with him moved closer, but still, the Bimbo reached out and touched Rachael's arm.

"Do you remember the way out?"

Rachael looked down at her hand. She stepped away from the woman's touch. "No, I don't know how I got in here, to be honest. The wall opened up, and I dropped several feet. I tried, but I couldn't find the ledge from where I fell. I tried but couldn't find a doorway anywhere. Until I found you, that is."

Alan stepped closer to Rachael. "That's how it was for us, too."

"What do we do now?" April asked.

Alan was close, very close, and she could smell his cologne. She closed her eyes and inhaled his scent. She wanted him, still.

She backed away from him and returned to the wall. "We keep looking for an exit. There has to be an exit somewhere."

As Rachael moved along the wall, she heard shoes scraping along the floor behind her. She wasn't sure when or how she became the leader of this group, but she didn't care. She planned to save herself, and if they wished to follow her, they could do that, but she wasn't expecting or desiring their companionship.

Rachael listened to the Bimbo squealing and yelping at every little imagined threat, and she knew Alan was there to wrap his strong arms around her, protecting her. At one point, she heard them kissing, and she wanted to throw up.

The room narrowed, and she understood that they had entered a hallway. As they walked through the passage, Alan leaned into her hear and whispered.

"Do you think this leads to an exit?"

His breath in her ear tingled down her body. She almost moaned.

Her response was breathy. "I hope so." She shivered a little and broke his spell over her so she could speak normally. "Maybe."

"It's just that April's so scared, and I want to get her out of here."

Oooo, April is scared. That's high on my priority list to solve...not. She hissed through clenched teeth. *How about you and I get out of here, and let her wander through these dark halls forever.*

The group reached the end of the hallway and Rachael searched for a doorknob or handle. She found none, but she did feel an upraised edge along the right side and used her fingernails to get underneath it. Rachael thanked her sturdy genes that her nails were strong enough to drag the slab of wood toward her. She took the stress off her nails when she managed to get enough of a gap to put her fingers in the hole.

"Help me, please." Rachael's voice strained from the effort.

Alan rushed forward and added his strength, and they were able to open a big enough gap through which to fit. April went first, and Rachael followed. Alan squeezed through last, and without his strength holding the slab open, the wooden plank snapped back into place.

"I don't think that was a door," April said.

But at least they were through. And as a bonus, the new room had a light built into the ceiling and, dim as the bulbs were, it was still better than the impenetrable darkness. Being able to see did not improve their situation. There were no visible doorways, and thick wooden beams with slabs of cement between them made up the walls. It would take a jackhammer to break through these barriers. Also, cobwebs and dusty, rust-colored splatter marks that might have been paint, or something more sinister covered the surfaces. Rachael shivered at the thought.

"What do we do now?" April asked.

Rachael scowled. The Bimbo hadn't done anything to improve their situation, and as far as Rachael was concerned, she had only hindered their progress.

"I guess we keep moving," Alan said. "See if we can find another secret door. The lights are a good sign, right?" He glanced at Rachael (as if she had all the answers), but continued his thought without a response. "Lights mean we're getting closer to the exit."

The Bimbo bought his fuzzy logic, but Rachael wasn't so sure. They had fallen through the looking glass. This wasn't part of the funhouse. They were someplace else, and she didn't think this place was necessarily survivable. She had a feeling their only hope was when—or if—a search party came looking for them. And what were the odds of that happening?

She thought pretty low.

She didn't share her negative thoughts with the others because she doubted the Bimbo could handle hearing it, and Rachael had no interest in giving that useless bitch any more reason to go running into Alan's waiting arms.

They walked through the room slowly, searching the walls for any sign of an exit. There was darkness stretching out in front of them that the lights were not strong enough to light up. As the minutes passed, the notion that they were getting closer to the exit dwindled.

Surely, even the Bimbo could see that.

Rachael turned around and watched as the couple walked several paces behind her, holding hands and talking in low voices. The Bimbo bopped him playfully on the arm and laughed at something he said.

Rachael faced forward and pretended she wasn't a third wheel in this expedition.

After several paces, Rachael reached the point when she could finally see the end of the long passage. She stopped, and when the couple reached her, they stopped, too. The three of them stared ahead.

In the far wall, there was a door. It was a real door, with a door handle, and not some strange secret doorway.

Rachael turned to Alan. "Is it the exit?"

Alan didn't look at Rachael but merely shrugged.

April said: "It has to be, right?"

Rachael ignored her, and Alan said nothing.

April took a tentative step toward the door, but Alan touched her arm, held her back.

"Let me go first." Alan stepped past the two women and walked toward the door.

Rachael's first thought was that it would be locked, but as the knob turned and the door opened, her second thought came in a wave of panic.

It's booby-trapped.

Alan stepped through the doorway, but nothing happened. He motioned for the others to follow. April followed Alan through, and Rachael entered the new room only after nothing happened to her predecessors.

The light revealed the new room to be similar in shape and length as their previous room, though narrower. Adding to the narrowness were tables on both sides of the room with a walkway between them.

Rachael cautiously approached one of these workbenches. There were no tools, but she did note that there were shackles bolted to the tabletop. There were locks on the chains as well, and it wasn't hard to imagine why.

Brown blotches covered the wooden tabletop.

"This is interesting," Alan said.

Rachael turned to look at him.

Alan's table had chains as well, and he lifted them with a rattle that made Rachael think of the old eerie apparition of Scrooge's dead partner, Jacob Marley. She shivered.

"What kind of attraction is this?" April asked. "I get the sense that this is where they create the horror displays for the rest of the show."

"So, what?" Alan asked. "You think we slipped behind the scenes? We're where the magic happens?"

This isn't a stage, and it isn't fake. Though Rachael couldn't give voice to the thought, it still caused the skin on her arms to prickle.

"We need to get out of here." Rachael brushed past them and headed to the other end of the room. She didn't wait for them to follow. She searched the walls as she passed by other tables. There were eight tables in all, four on each side of the room. The back wall was bare timber. She found a seam in the wood that she suspected was another hidden door. How to open it was a whole other issue. She used her fingers to examine every inch of the door.

When April and Alan caught up to her, they realized what she was doing and tried to help.

"Is there a button or something that releases it?" April asked.

"If there is, I don't see it." Rachael didn't let the others see her eyes roll. "Why don't you make that your goal."

As April moved away, Alan moved closer to Rachael, and his proximity to her made her heart race.

But Alan didn't feel what Rachael felt.

"I know what you're doing, and you should lay off her."

Rachael's face heated. She turned toward him and lifted her hands to express she was innocent. She returned to the task of opening the door.

"Just play nice, okay?"

She nodded relenting. "Okay." *But just until we get out of here.*

Rachael's agitation increased at the door that refused to open, and now that she had to play nice with the Bimbo. *No, you promised. Her name is April.*

Rachael took a step back and studied the door from a distance. She looked around the room but saw no tools or equipment she could use to pry the door open. An ax, or even a hammer, would have alleviated some of her frustration.

Rachael considered kicking the door.

"Hello, what's this?"

Alan leaned over to see what April found.

Rachael hesitated, but she, too, looked.

April pointed to a hole in the wall under one of the tables. It was small, but someone with a tiny hand could fit in there. As April reached for the hole, Alan stopped her.

"I don't know if you should do that."

"Why not?"

"What if there is a rat or something in there?" Alan said.

April's body gave an involuntary shake. "Ew, don't say that I'm squeamish enough and someone has to check it out."

"I'll do it," Rachael said.

Alan and April glanced at her.

"No, I got this." April crumpled her hand into a cone shape and slowly reached into the hole.

"Maybe I should…" Alan's voice trailed off.

"Your hand won't fit. Besides, I feel something."

April scrunched up her face as if concentrating on a difficult math problem. She groaned and squealed, falling backward into Alan. He caught her and together they fell to the floor.

"What happened?" Alan asked, holding April on his lap. "Are you okay?"

Before she could respond, the door slowly began to swing inward.

"There was a lever in there," April said.

Rachael scurried through the doorway. April jumped up from where she and Alan had fallen and followed Rachael.

"Will you guys wait for me?" Alan rushed to catch up. "What if there's something bad in here?"

As he finished passing through the threshold, the door closed again. With the sealing of the doorway, what little light was afforded them in the previous room was gone. In total darkness again, Alan tried to open the passageway but could find no handle, and the slab that served as a door wouldn't budge.

Rachael reached out and touched his arm. "Exactly why we had to hurry."

Alan shrugged Rachael's hand off him. "You almost left me behind."

Rachael giggled.

Alan sighed. "Whatever. What now?"

Rachael placed her hands against the wall and started feeling around.

"Hold on." April touched Rachael's back. "The cellphones don't have a signal, but we can still use them as flashlights." Amber reached into her pocket and pulled out her phone. She ignited the flashlight feature.

In the opposite side of the room, April spotted a dark rectangular hole in the wall. She tapped Alan's shoulder.

"Look."

Alan put out his hands and indicated the girls should stay behind him as he approached the wall.

Rachael stepped closer and spotted something moving in the darkness beyond the hole. She gasped and stepped back.

Alan peered into the hole. "Hello, is someone over there?"

"Hello?" the male voice came from the darkness.

Rachael rushed over to the hole. Standing about a foot away, she peered into the dark space, but she could see nothing.

"My name's Rachael."

"I'm Christopher, and my girlfriend, Amber, is here too. We came down in an elevator."

"There's an elevator on your side?" Alan studied the gap. He placed his fingertips on the ledge, stood on his toes. He leaped forward, driving his upper body through the hole.

The people beyond the wall cried out in protest. Rachael understood they were trying to warn him of something and she rushed forward and grabbed one of his pant legs, tried to pull him out of the hole. She heard a swish of something moving very quickly through the air, and a hollow thump. Then the people in the other partition were screaming. Rachael's heart raced, and her hands shook. April's light focused on Alan's body as it slumped from the hole, bringing with it a river of blood that sprayed against the wall.

Alan's head was gone.

April screamed and dropped the phone.

Rachael's body went cold, convulsing. She reached down to help Alan but recoiled. Her hands shook uncontrollably. There was a scream on her lips that she couldn't let loose. She looked up and watched as April ran around the room, screaming and pulling at her hair.

She couldn't worry about April. Rachael was suffering, also.

Rachael returned to the hole. The screaming over on the other side had begun to die down. Through the hole, she heard crying: the woman. Somewhere behind her the Bimbo (*April, call her April*) had stopped screaming and babbled like a baby. The Bim—(no, April) seemed to have lost her mind. She was talking gibberish and switching between laughing hysterically and sobbing uncontrollably.

Ignoring the headless body on the floor, Rachael called through the hole. "What's happening? Where is this place? Why are we here?"

The man, Christopher, replied. "We're trapped in here, too. It's an escape room. There are traps— deadly traps. We knew there was a trap in that hole. It's why we're still over here. The elevator is not an option. It brought us down here, but now we can't get back into it. We were hoping there was a way out in that room you're in."

"We've been traveling through several rooms, but there doesn't appear to be a way out where we came from, either."

"Oh, God, what do to do?"

Rachael heard the woman on the other side, crying again.

"Wasn't there an armless body over there?" Christopher's sharp voice caused Rachael to flinch.

Rachael took a step back. "No, there isn't." She spotted something she hadn't noticed before. She bent down but ratcheted back up quickly. "My God, there's a severed hand."

"The hand was attached to an arm over here. That's how we learned about the trap. I used this arm to test the space inside the hole. A sensor or something must have caused a guillotine to come down. But I don't get it...there should have been a body over there."

Rachael didn't answer.

April had quieted down, though Rachael doubted the woman would ever be right again. She couldn't let herself worry about April right now. If April didn't have the good sense to show self-preservation, that was her problem. *I'm not getting killed trying to reassure you that you'll be okay.*

Rachael turned her attention back to the couple on the other side of the hole. "The three of us came through some strange doorway in the funhouse. Is that where you got stuck as well?"

"No," Christopher said. "We were in a go-cart going through the House of Horrors. The ride took a sudden turn and then stopped. When the door to the elevator opened, we just thought it was part of the attraction and got in. When we were brought down here and stepped out of the elevator, the door shut behind us. We can't get it open again."

Rachael nodded. "Looks like all ways into this madhouse are a one-way ticket. But god, there has to be a way out."

"Did any of you guys bring cell phones?" Christopher asked.

"Yes, but they don't work down here."

"Neither do ours." Christopher sounded defeated. "There's no light on this side. My battery died from me using the flashlight feature. Amber's battery is still okay, though."

"We've been finding secret doors. Did you find anything that might be something like that?"

Christopher puffed out a held breath. "It's too dark over here to see anything."

When Rachael hadn't heard the mumbling idiot for a while, she turned and saw that April was staring at Alan's body, tears glistening in the woman's eyes.

Rachael walked around the body and wrapped an arm over April's shoulder. The woman flinched but didn't pull away. Rachael walked with April to the other side of the room and forced the woman to look away from Alan. April stayed facing the wall, but her body continued to convulse uncontrollably. She was probably going into shock.

"Stay with me, April. I can't help you right now." Rachael rubbed her back.

"Talk to her," Christopher said. "Get her to respond to you. I think that will help."

Rachael came around to face April. She waved a hand in front of the woman's eyes. When April didn't respond to that, she snapped her fingers near her ear. April merely stared blankly into space.

"Can you hear me, April? I need you to look at me." She shook the woman's shoulders slightly. "Look at me."

Rachael heard a strange rustling sound behind her; it was a kind of swishing sound. April's glassy stare turned into wide-eyed panic, and she released an ear-piercing scream.

Rachael wheeled around. The entire wall behind her had slid to the right, creating a gaping maw of open space. Standing in the opening was a gigantic person wearing a clown costume. The puffy yellow suit—complete with gathered wrist and ankle bands—was dingy and covered in several layers of grime. The dark eyes peering from the eyeholes of the rubber mask regarded the two women briefly then strode into the room. As the clown passed, a noxious odor of boiled cabbage, sour milk, and the bitter stink of stomach acid hit Rachael's nose, she wretched but managed not to throw up. Rachael slapped a hand over her mouth and nose. April wasn't as strong-willed and doubled over, vomiting up bile, and whatever other contents were still in her stomach.

"What's happening?" Christopher said.

Rachael couldn't speak. She instinctively pulled April to her and shielded the woman's eyes from the intruder.

Rachael watched as the giant inspected Alan's headless body. Its head lifted and looked toward the gap.

"What the fuck is that?" Christopher said.

Again, Rachael didn't respond because she didn't have an answer to give. She watched as the thing looked down at the severed hand. The clown reached down and picked the appendage off the floor and crammed it into a pocket of the yellow clown suit. The giant then sauntered over to the opposite corner from where Rachael and April cowered, balled up one gloved hand, and slammed its fist against the wall. A secret door popped open next to the small hole, and the clown disappeared inside.

Amber screamed.

April flinched and quaked in Rachael's arms.

The clown reappeared gripping Alan's head by the hair in one hand and the severed limb in the other. It tossed the arm on Alan's chest then gripped Alan by one foot, dragging the body back the way it had come.

As the clown took Alan away, Rachael held April's face against her chest, preventing the addled woman from seeing what was happening.

The new doorway between the rooms remained open, as did the wall-sized door through which the clown had passed. After a few seconds, Christopher took a tentative step into the room with Rachael and April. Amber followed. Spotting the terrified woman huddled in Rachael's arms, Amber scuttled over and took April by the hand. When April turned, Amber took a tissue from her pocket and cleaned April's face. Rachael approached the handsome black man as he studied the smear of crimson on the floor.

"You're Rachael, right?" Christopher asked. He pointed to the two women huddled in the corner. "And it's April?"

Rachael nodded.

Christopher pointed to the bloodstain. "Was he your boyfriend?"

Rachael's impulse was to say yes, but she stopped herself. "No, he was with her." She tipped her head toward April. "But Alan and I were friends."

Christopher stepped over the puddles of blood and joined Amber. Rachael tapped him on the shoulder.

"Should we go that way?" She pointed toward the opening.

Amber's eyes flew wide open, and she swiveled to face Rachael. "Bitch, are you crazy? You want to follow that thing?"

Rachael's eyes narrowed. "No, I don't want to follow him, but if there is a way out through there, I'll take my chances. You all can do what you want."

Amber sneered. "You'd leave your friend, frail as she is, with strangers?"

Rachael stepped toward the opening. "She's not my friend. She's the Bimbo that stole my boyfriend." She stepped into the room beyond the opening, which looked like a giant warehouse.

"Wait, Rachael." Christopher put up a hand. "We should stick together. Amber, I think she's right. There isn't a way out in here. We can't sit here and wait for that clown thing to return. If there's a way out, we should try to find it. Besides, this woman needs help that we can't give her."

After a moment of hesitation, Amber led April out of the room. She leaned into Christopher's ear and spoke in a whisper, but she intended Rachael to hear the conversation. "That woman is trouble. Should we be following her? She's no leader. She'll get us all killed."

Rachael spun around. "Keep it up, and I'll leave you behind. I'm in no mood for bullshit. As I said, I don't care if you follow me."

"Okay, wait." Christopher stepped between the two women. "I do think it's best if we stay together. We aren't doing ourselves any favors being at each other's throats. We need to stay together and get along."

After a moment of silence, Rachael shrugged. "Whatever. Just stay out of my way."

"We should be careful. There could be more traps."

This gave Rachael pause. She hadn't thought of that.

"You know what?" Rachael said. "Your girlfriend is right. I'm not a good leader. I think you should lead the way." She stepped aside and allowed Christopher, Amber, and April to go ahead of her. "I'll take up the rear and keep an eye on our flank."

Christopher met Rachael's eyes. "I'm okay with that plan. I think you're frightened, and that's fine, but I'm not taking leadership of the group. I'm simply going ahead to look for pitfalls, and to keep everyone safe. We can be civil about this."

Rachael said nothing and followed behind the group.

Chapter Eleven: Gina

Using her phone's light feature to get a bearing on her surroundings, Gina illuminated Larry's corpse laying at her feet. With a yelp, she fell away from it and dropped her cell. The light went out.

Oh, God. Please don't say it landed near him. Her skin prickled as she imagined Larry's cold, dead hand reaching out to touch her, and she peed a little. When her groping hand found her phone, she snatched it up, then staggered away from the place where she believed Larry's corpse to be. She pressed herself against a cold stone wall, breathing heavy and trying hard not to throw up. When she had relaxed enough to feel at least somewhat normal again, she started to follow the wall away from the slide and the corpse. She used the light again only when she was sure she was far from Larry.

Using the light now and not touching the wall — she found its texture to be too dusty and covered in cobwebs — Gina headed for the end of the room where she could begin following the adjacent wall.

She stopped when she reached the corner, wondering if she would end up going entirely around the room without ever finding an exit. In the back of her mind, she also feared running onto the murderous clown.

After traveling several feet along the second wall, Gina managed to find a small metal door and tried to open it. The door seemed locked. She kicked at it but only managed to make a warbling gong sound.

She thought of moving on, find another door, but she was exhausted — physically and emotionally. It was hard to believe that only an hour ago, she had been trying to think of a way to sneak off from her date and go home. Since then, she had been raped, watched her rapist die, and now was trapped in an underground funhouse with no discernable way of escape. She couldn't humor the idea that she could be stuck in this room forever. She sat down with her back against the door to think about her options. Her mind wandered to the moment on the Ferris Wheel when she knew that Larry's true intentions had been to rape her. The memory of those two boys staring down at her caused her anger to bubble up again. Would they grow up to think that what Larry had done was normal?

Gina's hands balled into fists, and she slammed them into the door behind her. She stopped when she remembered Larry was dead. She wondered if he had raped other girls besides her.

That monster clown did the world a favor if you want my opinion.

She didn't know what the clown had in mind for her, and she doubted it had killed Larry for her, but still, she felt a touch of gratitude that Larry was dead.

With the initial dose of adrenaline wearing off, Gina dozed. Her head bobbed, and she shook herself to wake up. A few more minutes passed, and her eyes fluttered again. She stood and paced, trying to keep her mind alert. She sat back down, and within minutes she was asleep.

She dreamed that she was still at the fair with Larry. He is the perfect gentleman, and she holds his hand as they walk. She laughs when he tells a joke and kisses him on the cheek.

Now her mother is at the fair with her. Her mother is screaming obscenities at her, calling her a whore, a slut.

"You deserve everything you get when you leave the house like that," her mother says.

Gina looks down at her clothes. She is wearing a pink spaghetti strap top and red shorts. The only skin showing is her shoulders. "What's wrong with the way I look?"

"Your breasts," her mother says. "Your breasts are sticking out. Look at the way your nipples jut out as if they could cut glass. You are asking to be raped."

Then something miraculous happens. Larry sticks up for her.

"You don't know what you're talking about, old lady. She looks great. She isn't a whore at all."

Her mother is circling them now, studying them. "You are both doomed." She spits out the words with the venom of a rattler. "He's going to punish you for the trouble you've caused."

"Who?" Gina asks. "What trouble."

"The clown." Her mother's eyes grow wide. Her voice is full of warnings and glee. "The clown is going to get you because you've been nothing but trouble for me since the day you were born."

When Gina turns, Larry is gone, and in his place is a dirt-encrusted clown who begins to clap his filthy, red-gloved hands together, and it's the sound of metal hitting metal.

Bam. Bam. Bam.

Gina awoke with that sound following her out of the dream.

She jumped up and spun around when she realized the banging was coming from the other side of the metal door. She considered running, but the door had already begun to open, and her chance to flee evaporated.

Light seeped through the crack. There was light on the other side of the door.

She balled her hands into fists and prepared to ram the clown but was surprised when the small pale face of an older man appeared in the doorway. Her protective stance relaxed.

"Oh, hello." The man pulled the door the rest of the way open, revealing an older woman standing next to him.

"Hi," Gina said in a small voice.

"And who might you be?" the old man asked.

"Gina."

"Are you lost, too, dear?" the old woman asked.

Gina nodded.

The man marched through the door but stopped when Gina stepped back from him.

He tilted his head quizzically. "No need to be afraid. We're certainly not going to hurt you."

"Have you..." She cleared her throat and tried again. "Have you seen the clown?"

"Clown?" the old woman said. "No, no clown."

"We were in the mirror maze. We stepped into a dark space between two mirrors, thinking it was the exit and ended up down here. We've been searching for a way out. Did you see a clown?" The man stopped talking, but before Gina could respond, the man started talking again. "Where are my manners.

I'm Clifford Javes, and this is my battleax wife, Cary Lynn."

The woman batted at his arm. "You shut your mouth, Cliffy."

"I'm happy to meet you both. My name is Gina."

The woman stepped forward. "My dear, by any chance, have you come across a bathroom since getting stuck here?"

"I told you, Cary, just find a dark hole and squat."

The woman's eyes grew wide, and her mouth opened in an O. "Clifford, shut your mouth."

Gina turned away from the squabbling couple. "I'm afraid I haven't." She couldn't help but notice her bladder was beginning to protest.

"I don't recommend going back that way," Clifford said and stepped out of the doorway, letting the door close behind him.

Gina squealed and rushed for the door but missed, and the door sealed shut. "Oh, no. The door doesn't have a handle on this side." She pressed her face against the cold steel.

"Nothing back that way. We already tried to get out every other way back yonder."

She would like to have seen that for herself.

Gina was still mourning her open door when she heard the old couple's jibber-jabber heading in the direction of Larry's corpse.

"Oh, I came from that way. There's nothing there. I think we should…"

"This way is as good as any," Clifford said. "We'll see for ourselves that there isn't a way out."

Go that way then, old fool. Hope you trip over Larry's —

Gina jogged to catch up and took the lead with the light from her phone, illuminating their way. Maybe she could get them to circle without ever seeing the corpse.

"I think I might have to warn you that something happened this way. Something that might be hard to hear — or believe to be true — but I assure you, it is."

The couple continued walking, and she didn't feel she had their full attention. "I think you should stop and listen to this. I wasn't alone when I came to the fair. The person I came here with was…" *Killed.*

Still, the old couple walked on, and Gina struggled to keep the light steady. When the slide came into view, she stood in their way and forced them to stop.

"What is it, dear?" Though Cary Lynn's voice sounded pleasant, the irritation was there as well.

"I need to tell you about — " Gina shined the light on the ground at the base of the slide.

Larry's body wasn't where she had last seen it. She scanned everywhere Larry's body should have been. She looked to the right and left of the slide.

But Larry was gone.

"Did you lose something, my dear?" Cary Lynn asked.

Yes, the corpse of my rapist.

Gina shivered. She had been sure Larry was dead, but she hadn't checked his body. Could he have survived the attack? Was he stumbling around in here, ready to attack her again?

Gina groaned.

"What's the matter, little lady?" Clifford said.

Gina swallowed hard. Her throat felt tight, hoarse. "We're not alone in here."

"You were saying you came here with a friend —"

Gina turned on the older woman with the light, causing Cary Lynn to shield her eyes. Gina lowered the cell's beam to the floor.

"No, not a friend."

Larry was dead; she was sure of that. Someone moved the body, that's what happened.

We haven't seen the last of the clown. Gina took a deep breath. "What I'm saying is that we aren't safe here. There's someone here with us. Someone who isn't friendly at all."

Clifford waved away her concerns with a gnarled hand.

"Now, now. Don't go getting hysterical. I suppose you already tried to climb this slide?" Clifford said.

"I'm telling you we are in danger."

Clifford ignored Gina and placed his hands on the slope of the slide.

"Don't get any ideas," Cary Lynn grabbed her husband's arm. "You'll break a bone if you try to climb it yourself, Cliffy."

"Actually," he said. "I was going to send you up, my dear."

"Shut your mouth."

Gina listened in the darkness, wondering if the clown could be nearby. "I...I think we should keep moving."

"Okay, yes." Clifford waved a dismissive hand. "Feel free to lead the way, young lady."

Gina stepped forward reluctantly. Without turning around, Gina sensed the couple following a few steps behind her.

She led the couple along the stone wall to the far corner. If there were a way out, it would probably be where the last door had been, only on the opposite wall. She realized that she had no idea what was in the center of this large room. And the lighting was so bad that she couldn't see more than a few inches in front of her face. It was impossible to know what could be hiding in the darkest spaces. Larry's stumbling, bloodless corpse, came into her mind. Larry could be following them, and they would never know it.

"Sorry, Missy. You're going a little too fast for our old legs to keep up."

Gina stopped and let them catch up. "I'm sorry."

"No worries, dear." Cary Lynn touched Gina lightly on her back.

When Gina stopped letting the darkness mess with her mind, she calmed down. After a few more paces, they came to another door.

Clifford tried the door, and it opened. He walked through, and Cary Lynn followed him. Gina entered passageway last.

The new room was smaller, with wooden walls, and lit with bulbs in the ceiling. Gina turned and tried the door they had just passed through, and just as she suspected, it was locked.

We're being led like cattle. But where? And why?

The thought was unsettling, but at least she could see the entire room. If something were coming for them, she would see it coming. As much as she hated the idea, she continued. The couple shuffled along beside her.

It took the crew only a few seconds to get to the other side. Another door appeared, and Gina feared it wouldn't open, trapping them, but when she turned the knob, it opened. She mumbled a prayer of thanks and passed through the opening. The elderly couple followed.

Gina and her counterparts stepped into a hallway.

Gina took a couple of tentative steps forward. She looked back, but the couple was not following. Clifford seemed transfixed.

Gina headed for a door near the center of the hall on the right. When she turned back, she saw the couple were not following.

She shrugged, turned back to the door, and reached for the brass knob. She thought it strange that it would have such a dazzling knob.

She reached out and placed her hand on the knob, began to turn.

"Stop." The deep, demanding voice caused her to flinch away from the door. She turned in the direction from which the voice had come. She stared at the black man standing at a door opposite from the one she and the Javes's had used. His hand was out like a cop directing traffic. Three women stood behind him. Two helped a third to stay upright.

"I'm sorry," the black man said. "But I don't think you understand. Some doors are trapped."

"Trapped?" Gina repeated the word as if she didn't understand its meaning.

The man approached and gently directed her a few steps away from the door. He pointed toward the ceiling, and Gina glanced up.

Gina saw four holes in the ceiling directly above where she had been standing when she had been reaching for the knob. Still, she wasn't quite sure what she was seeing.

"Stand back." The man flattened himself against the wall and reached his left hand out to grip the knob. He touched it gingerly. When nothing happened, he turned the knob and pushed the door open with his fingers. He jumped away from the door as if expecting a bomb to go off.

Gina watched in horror as four thick steel bars shot down from the holes in the ceiling and embedded into the floor. The metal poles then quickly rocketed back up and disappeared again. The man stepped through the doorway first, peering up at the holes as he moved. Nothing happened. He waved the others to follow.

The two women with the invalid woman followed him through. They guided the woman to a sitting position on the floor and returned to help Gina and the elderly couple.

Gina still shivered from the thought of having been nearly skewered. She shook her head.

Mr. and Mrs. Javes passed through the doorway next.

Still, Gina did not pass under those deadly holes.

"It's okay," the black man said. "The trap has to be reset. Everything seems to be spring-loaded. I don't know how much longer this door is going to stay open. You have to come through now."

Tears flooded Gina's eyes, and her hands trembled. She screamed, spittle spraying from her lips, and rushed forward. The black man caught her in strong arms and pulled her into the room. She fell on top of him and stayed with him on the floor for long seconds, sobbing, until he finally helped her to stand.

The door slammed shut.

The man looked at the door then turned to Gina. "Hi, I'm Christopher."

Gina wiped the tears and slobber from her face and nodded at him. When she was able, she told him her name.

A blonde woman stood next to Christopher. "I'm Amber. He's my boyfriend." She pointed to the other standing woman. "Her name is Rachael. And that's April." She pointed to the woman on the floor.

"We're Mr. and Mrs. Javes," Clifford said.

Cary Lynn scolded her husband. "Tell them our first names."

"Uh, Clifford and Cary Lynn Javes." Clifford stepped forward and shook Christopher's hand.

"Nice to meet you, folks," Christopher said.

Gina stared at the girl crouched on the floor. "What's wrong with her?"

"She's..." Amber caught Gina's eyes and stared into them. "Seen things."

Gina felt a rush of heat enter her head. "Did she see the clown?"

Christopher gripped Gina by the shoulder and spun her. "You know about the clown?"

"I... uh...I—yes, I've seen him."

"Do you know who he is? What does he want?"

"I don't know any of that. I know it stabbed the person I was here with and killed him." She thought about the missing body. "At least, I think he died."

Christopher blinked. "You're saying he killed somebody?"

Gina looked around at the stunned faces surrounding her. "Yes. We were in an alley at the fair. He seemed to have come from out of nowhere. He stabbed Larry and then threw me and Larry's body into this strange place. I thought the clown would come back and finish me off, but it never did." Then she thought about Larry's missing body. "I guess he did eventually come back for Larry. The body was missing when I returned to where I had left it."

Christopher and the blonde woman shared a look.

"What do you know of the clown?" Gina asked.

The woman, Rachael, was the one who responded. "He didn't try and kill us...well, not directly. We were with a guy named Alan, April and me. He was...killed by one of those traps. Then the clown came along, ignoring all of us, and carried the body away. I should say bodies. Apparently, there had been another victim before us."

"We have since come across other traps," Christopher said. "Opening doors around here can get you killed."

"We've seen no such traps," Clifford said.

"Still, it's best not to open doors without a little caution."

Clifford clapped his hands together and rubbed them as if trying to keep warm. "I'd like to know more about this clown people keep talking about."

Gina turned to face Clifford. "He isn't wearing clown make-up. It's a full rubber mask pulled down over his head."

Amber stepped forward. "He's wearing a dingy yellow bodysuit."

Gina nodded and continued. "He's tall, very tall."

Cary Lynn placed a hand to her mouth. "What's happening to us? Are we going to die?"

Clifford placed an arm around her shoulder and pulled his wife into him. She put her head on his chest.

"If we stick together, and all keep our heads..." Christopher's eyes flitted to April. "Then, we should be able to make it out of here okay."

Gina had caught Christopher's slight indication to April, and it made her want to voice her concerns.

"Is she going to be okay? I mean, will she snap out of whatever funk she's in?"

"Hey," Rachael said. "She just watched her boyfriend get beheaded. Leave her alone."

Cary Lynn gasped, and delicate fingers fluttered to her lips. "Beheaded?"

Gina put her hands up, palms out, in supplication. "I understand. And I'm not complaining. I am just worried that if we come across that monster again, will she protect herself?"

"I'll see to it she's safe," Amber said.

The blonde woman, amber, gave the brunette standing next to her an odd, unfriendly look, and Gina wondered what animosity had been brewing between them. The brunette, Rachael, seemed equally antagonistic.

"We both will," Rachael said.

Gina ignored them and turned to Christopher. "What are we going to do?"

Christopher pointed. "We're going to go through this door. But we have to do it carefully. A previous door opened into a pit. We couldn't go that way because April couldn't jump over. If we hadn't been paying attention, one or more of us would have fallen in."

"Could you see how deep the pit was?" Clifford asked.

Christopher nodded. "It was only a few feet deep, but spikes were sticking up from it."

"Oh, my Lord," Cary Lynn said.

"Luckily, we found another door, and this one seemed trap-free. From there, we passed through another room to get to this hall."

April screamed and bolted to her feet. Every head turned in her direction and then turned to see where she was looking.

At the opposite end of the room, through a thick-paned window, the clown stared at the group. It pounded a fist on the glass and then raised both fists in the air, shaking them in an unearthly rage. The thing bellowed a wrathful cry that was only slightly muffled by the window.

Screams erupted from the group, and pandemonium gripped them as they clambered through the doorway that Christopher had pointed out. No longer worried about traps, Gina's only thoughts were to escape the clown. Even April moved without assistance from the others. Christopher, the last through the door, slammed it behind him. As a single mass, the group ran to the opposite side of the room.

As they clustered together, panting and exhausted, they watched for the clown to approach, but nothing happened.

Gina's heart hammered in her chest, causing her breastbone to ache until her heartbeat slowly returned to normal. She glanced at the other frightened faces around her and supposed they could see the same fear on her face as well.

"We're never getting out of here." She didn't mean to say it, but now that it was out, she couldn't take it back. Cary Lynn began to cry. Clifford did his best to console her, but she only cried harder.

"Stop," Christopher said. "We're going to be okay. We need to keep calm. Don't freak out on me now."

"There's another door," April spoke so softly she nearly went unheard.

But Gina heard her and turned her gaze in the direction April was looking, seeing the door as well.

"There's a door." Gina's voice cut through the crying and shouting.

Cary Lynn stopped crying and glanced in the direction of the other door. "A way out?"

The door stood off to the right. It was nothing more than a panel in the wall. Gina was surprised they could see it at all. It blended into the surroundings so well as to be nearly invisible.

Most shockingly of all was the one who had spotted it.

April must be getting better. She's standing and walking on her own, and now she's even talking.

No one made a move right away. All heads turned toward Christopher. He, in turn, looked back at each one of them. After another moment of hesitation, Christopher walked away from the group and headed for the door.

Gina followed him.

"What does it matter?" Rachael said. "There's no way out of here anyway. We're all going to die."

Several members of the group shushed her simultaneously.

As Christopher studied the door, Gina stood nearby, watching for the clown. He used his hands to feel along the edge of the door. There was no doorknob. His hands stopped along the top side. After a second, Gina heard a click, and the door popped open.

Gina and Christopher shared a glance.

He hooked his fingers around the edge of the door and pulled it the rest of the way open. Gina realized she was backing away and stopped.

Christopher stood slightly to the side and peered into the doorway. Nothing came out of the gloom to impale him, and nothing grabbed him. Gina stood next to him and peered into the room.

A short hallway led to another door.

"God damn it." Christopher sighed.

Everyone gathered around to stare into the hallway.

Clifford cussed. "Not another damn door."

"Who's going to go in there and try that one?" Rachael asked.

Christopher grunted. "I guess I will."

"No, Chris." Amber grabbed his arm. "Why you?"

"It's fine," he said to her. "I'll be fine."

"No, wait," Clifford said. "Let my wife do it." He nudged Cary Lynn lightly.

"Clifford," she said with a nervous laugh. "Shut your mouth."

Clifford stepped forward. "I'll do it."

This took the smile off his wife's face. "Clifford, no."

Clifford stood in front of her and rubbed her arms. "I'll be fine, my love. Don't worry. I love you."

She opened her mouth to respond again, but he leaned down and planted a dry kiss on her lips, effectively silencing her. He walked away from her before she had a chance to recover.

"Be careful," Christopher said as Clifford walked by.

The older man nodded.

Clifford walked the few paces through the hallway with slow, deliberate steps. When he reached the second door without setting off any traps, he took a second to study the door, which had no knob.

He placed a hand on the wooden surface and pushed.

The door opened easily.

Gina immediately noticed the brightness of the room beyond Clifford's door. *No more barely lit rooms or complete darkness.*

Then she noticed the look on Clifford's face.

"What the hell?"

Everyone rushed forward to see what Clifford had found.

Chapter Twelve: Shaina

As she passed by the Himalaya, Shaina searched the ride for Tommy or her kids. The speeding cars rocketed along the circular track and many faces passed by in a blur, but Tommy and her kids were not among the screaming and laughing riders.

Dashiell stopped to touch her arm. "What's wrong? You're getting discouraged, aren't you? I can see it on your face."

She shrugged. "I'm just getting frustrated, I guess. Where are they?"

"Have you tried calling again?"

Shaina nodded. "As suspected, still no answer. I have no messages on my voicemail, either."

Dylan stood in front of Shaina and Dashiell. Shaina stared at him. His wide eyes and broad smile suggested he had an idea.

"What is it?" Shaina asked.

"One word." Dylan made explosions with his hands. "Face recognition." He dropped his hands and shrugged. "Okay, two words."

"Face recognition?" Dashiell asked.

"The police must have face recognition software. Let's borrow it and go at this another way."

"The cops aren't going to let us use their expensive equipment to search for my kids."

"We have Wanda use it to search the crowds for Miss Helen, and if she happens to find your brother, well sorry police people."

Dashiell laughed.

Dylan glared at him. "I'm serious."

"We're wasting time," Shaina said. "We need to keep looking."

"I don't think aimlessly wandering around is getting the job done, is all I'm saying."

"If you're tired, go back to the office," Dashiell said.

Dylan laughed. "That's not it."

"I don't have time for this." Shaina brushed past Dylan. Her feet hurt as well, and she didn't think she got enough rest during her nap, but she wouldn't give up the search for her kids.

"Wait up," Dylan said.

She sensed that the two men were following her again and smiled.

The three of them weaved through crowds of people, stopping when Dylan decided to buy a churro. He offered to share it with her, but she declined. Dashiell ate her portion.

As they walked through a narrow section of the midway, Shaina stopped and caused the others to bump into her. She pointed up.

"What about that?"

The name of the ride was The Insane Drop Tower, which consisted of a long row of seats, three tiers high, that shot up several hundred feet along a large steel tower, and then dropped its screaming riders back down to the platform below.

"What about it?" Dashiell asked.

"Let's repeat our attempt to get a higher point of view." She stepped into line for the ride.

"Forget that." Dashiell took her hand and pulled her to the front of the line. He spoke briefly to the attendant. The attendant nodded, and the three of them climbed aboard. The attendant roped off the rest of the potential riders even though there were still some empty seats. There was a rumble of complaints passing through the crowd, and a sea of confused faces.

Shaina took a seat in the back row because they were on the highest level, and the men followed her. The ride started abruptly and shot up in the air. It stayed there at the apex.

Shaina shielded her eyes from the glaring sun as she peered out over the crowd to the west. The sun had begun to sink toward the horizon, and it dawned on her that she didn't know what time it was. She wasn't wearing a watch, and her phone was tucked away in her pocket. She made a mental note to get an accurate count of the time as she searched the faces below her for one that looked familiar.

Dashiell cursed. "I'll be damned."

"Did you see something?" Shaina asked. Her excitement shined in her eyes.

"Not your family, but I did see our mutual friend."

Dashiell motioned the attendant to lower the ride, and the trio disembarked. Dashiell thanked the attendant quickly and shot off toward the eastern end of the fairgrounds.

Shaina panted as she ran to keep up. "What's going on?"

"Miss Helen was right up here."

She caught up to him and ran beside him. "The police are looking for her. We're looking for my kids."

"I know." He stopped running, looked around. "But what if she knows where your kids are?"

Shaina scanned the surroundings, searching the people wandering around, as well as those standing alone. She did not see Miss Helen.

"What's happening?" Dylan said when he caught up to them.

"We're looking for Miss Helen," Shaina said.

"She was standing right here." Dashiell pointed to the exact spot. "She was here. She couldn't have gotten very far." He began looking around and behind buildings. He searched large groups for anyone hiding amongst them. With every unsuccessful examination, he grunted in exasperation.

"Are you sure it was her?" Shaina asked.

Dashiell stopped and turned and glared at her. It lasted only a second and then his eyes softened. "Trust me. I would never mistake her for anyone. I have her image seared into my memory."

"Why is that?"

That glare returned and stayed this time, but Shaina knew this time it wasn't meant for her. "You don't forget the person who threatens your livelihood. When she tried to burn this place down, she made an enemy of me."

Shaina understood, she supposed. Dashiell, as far as she knew, didn't have kids. If he cared about his fair half as much as she cared for her kids, she couldn't blame him for being so emotional.

Still, it was just property, and not living breathing people. It was probably even insured. She had a feeling he was overreacting. But who was she to judge? She wasn't the owner of such a grand menagerie as this fair.

When Shaina's phone rang, she almost didn't know what to do. She pulled her cell from her pocket and stared at it.

Dashiell and Dylan gathered around her.

"Who is it?" Dylan finally asked.

She stared at the name that came up on the screen. "It's Tommy."

"Answer it, for god's sake," Dashiell said.

She accepted the call. "Hello."

"Hi, Sis." Tommy's voice sounded sleep-heavy. "Sorry. My battery died, and then I took a nap and the kids…"

"Tommy, where are you? Where are my kids?"

"We're home."

"You're okay? You're all safe?"

"Yes, why? What made you think we weren't? Where are you? The kids have been asking for you."

"I'm at the fair. I've been here all day looking for you."

Tommy laughed, and if he had been within her reach, she would have strangled him.

"Were you able to enjoy it while you were there?" Tommy asked.

Shaina's face heated. "I'm not here for fun. I came here looking for you." She took a couple of deep breaths and let each one out slowly, trying to calm herself down. "How were the kids? Did they enjoy themselves?"

"They did. Well, Susie did. Jeremy, not so much. He's not big about crowds, I guess."

"And you're sure they're okay? Where are they now?"

"They're fine, Sis. I promise. They've taken baths and gotten into their PJs. They're in watching TV right now. Do you want to talk to them?"

"No, don't bother them. I'll see them when I get home."

"Okay. See you soon?"

"Yeah, and Tommy?"

"Yeah, Sis?"

"Thank's. You take good care of my kids."

"You know it, Sis. Bye."

She clicked end on the call. She stared dumbly at the two men. "My kids are home safe and in their pajamas." She let out a slight, humorless laugh.

"You going to let him have it when you get home?" Dylan asked.

She laughed again, only more sinister this time. "Oh, he's getting an earful when I get home."

When Shaina began walking, the men followed her.

Dashiell strode next to her. "This is good news. Now that your kids are okay, we can concentrate on finding Miss Helen."

Shaina stopped walking and turned to him. He paused, as well.

"I'm going home. Helen is your problem. She's a matter for the police to handle."

Dashiell's look of shock caused Shaina's brow to furrow.

"I thought you would stick around for a little while and help us track her down," Dashiell said.

"I want to go home to my kids."

"And I can appreciate that. But with all due respect, we helped you look for your kids. At least stick around for a little while longer until she is back in custody. I mean, it's in your best interest, too."

"How do you figure?"

"If she gets away, what's to stop her from going back to your house."

She groaned inwardly. "Okay, you've got an hour. If she isn't in custody by then, she's your problem. I have to be home by eight to put my kids to bed."

Dashiell's shoulders relaxed, and he smiled. "Thank you."

"Where do we start?" She had hoped her manhunting days were behind her.

"I think we need to spread out. I saw her standing right about here. If we search in a spiral, we might be able to cover more ground. I'll go this way." He pointed to his left. "Dylan, you go that way." He looked to his right.

"I guess I'll go this way then?" Shaina pointed north.

"What do we do if we find her?"

"Take her to a policeman. Cops are patrolling everywhere."

Shaina shrugged. She still thought this was something better left to the authorities, but Dashiell had sufficiently guilted her into staying. Shaina waded through the crowds of people, looking at faces and trying to cover more ground by spiraling outward. If Miss Helen had been able to go unseen for this long, she doubted three amateur sleuths would be able to pin her down. The woman was crafty.

Shaina made it through another thick cluster of people and stopped to survey the new surroundings.

As she searched the faces of those within her sight, her mind wandered back to something Tommy had said.

Jeremy doesn't like large crowds.

That didn't make sense to her. Tommy loved taking his sister and had been looking forward to going to the fair right along. She wondered what her brother had done to piss off her son? More than likely, it wasn't the fair that had put Jeremy in a mood, but her brother's teaching that had done it.

When she had had enough of the search, she returned to the meeting spot near the ticket booth and waited for news from the others.

Dylan appeared first. She watched him approach, shaking his head.

"Nothing," he said.

"She's not just a psychic; she's a ghost. She appears and disappears at will."

Dylan laughed. "She claims she can see ghosts." He hesitated as if wanting to say something more, but unsure how to proceed. Then he continued with his thought. "Do you believe in such things?"

Shaina considered it. "I've never given it much thought. I suppose it's not impossible. If people can believe in God and the Devil, I suppose they can believe in ghosts as well."

"I'm not asking you what other people believe. I want to know what you believe."

"I guess I think I want to believe. How is that?"

"It's good enough, I suppose."

"Why do you ask?"

Dylan looked around. He stepped in closer to her.

"Do you know what my talent is? What I do here?"

She thought a moment and recalled a discussion she had had with Dashiell about Dylan. "You're a geek. A shock artist. You purposely put yourself though painful situations for entertainment."

"Do you understand how I can do that?"

She shrugged. "I guess you have a super high tolerance for pain."

"That's exactly right. But the reason I can do that is not altogether…natural. The truth is much more complicated." As he paused in his speech, he flexed his fingers. "How do I say this? I've wanted to share my secret with someone ever since I came here. I expected it to be easier than this." He took a deep breath. "Oh, boy. I…I'm…"

"There is no sign of her anywhere." Dashiell approached from behind Dylan.

Dylan spun around.

"Any luck?" Dashiell frowned. "What's going on? You look like a kid caught with his hand in the cookie jar. What are you two conspiring about?"

"Dylan was about to tell me—" Shaina wasn't allowed to finish.

"I was about to tell her that I couldn't find her, either."

Dashiell furrowed his brow. "I don't know if that's the truth."

Dylan barked a nervous laugh. "Of course, it is. What else would we be talking about?"

A little confused, she responded to Dashiell but kept her eyes on Dylan. "Yeah, we were discussing having no luck here, as well." When Dashiell stepped away to look around the ticket booth, Shaina stepped closer to Dylan and whispered into his ear. "I expect us to finish this discussion at a later date. I'm intrigued."

Dylan nodded.

Dashiell returned, looking defeated. "No luck."

"What's the plan now, boss?" Dylan asked.

Dashiell didn't respond.

"I think it's time to—" Shaina stared to her left. Stunned, her hand came up to point at what had caught her attention so completely that words failed her. The men turned to see where she was looking.

Miss Helen stood in line at the funhouse. She handed the ticket taker her pass and turned to look directly at Shaina and the others. She slipped into the darkness of the building and disappeared.

They rushed over to the entrance, and Dashiell explained their situation to the attendant with explicit instructions to not let anyone else in until further notice. The attendant nodded his understanding.

"Dylan, stay at the exit and wait for her to come out the other side."

The man didn't hesitate and ran to the exit door.

"Come with me?"

Shaina nodded, and Dashiell led the way through the funhouse entrance.

The interior was dark and cold. It took Shaina a moment for her eyes to grow accustomed to the darkness to see shadows and vague shapes. They used their hands to feel along the wall.

A doorway took them into a lighted room with many colors on the wall. They rushed while there was light, but the room grew smaller and smaller. After moving through the golden door at the end, they entered the mirrored hall. Shaina tried not to laugh as Dashiell bumped into a mirrored surface. Then she did the same thing.

"This is your attraction, but have you ever been in here?" Shaina asked.

"Never." Dashiell laughed.

She liked his laugh; it was so carefree.

"In fact," he said. "I inherited this place from my uncle. The place was in disrepair, and it took years to get it visitor-ready, though I didn't see it in that condition. I didn't lay eyes on the place until a couple of months ago. The biggest problem was that we couldn't keep help."

"Large turnover?" Shaina asked.

"Yes, but the strange thing is, they left without saying a word. No one even collected a final paycheck. I have about twenty checks inside my desk. As soon as I track down their relatives, I'll start mailing them out."

"You're right. That is strange."

They moved along in silence for a time, and the room changed back to complete darkness. The pair stumbled along until the floor began to wobble underfoot. Shaina yelped. Dashiell laughed. This time she was not so impressed with his laugh.

"It's not funny."

"A little funny."

As a strobe light flickered, Shaina watched Dashiell trying to keep his feet on the unsteady floor, which made it seem as though he was breakdancing. She started to laugh, but lost her footing and fell into

Dashiell's arms. He caught her with ease, but a hand brushed her left breast.

"Hey, watch your hands, buddy."

"First day on your new feet? You fell into me, remember?" He didn't release her, and she didn't pull away. Their lips inched closer together.

The floor rolled again, and the strobe effect ended, leaving them in complete darkness. Both fell toward the wall, still holding each other.

Only the wall wasn't a wall. Shaina felt herself falling into space. She slipped out of Dashiell's hands, and she reached out, searching for him. Shaina hit something that felt like a ramp, then tumbled again, rolling down a freaky slide. She landed on her back against something soft. She heard an "oof" and understood what she hit.

When she could see again, Shaina glanced at Dashiell laying beneath her. They both panted as if just having run a marathon.

"Should I give you two some privacy?"

Miss Helen stood with her shoulder leaned against the wall.

Dashiell jumped up and helped Shaina to stand. Shaina brushed herself off.

"Where is this? It's not part of the funhouse." Dashiell's head swiveled as he looked around.

"This is what I was trying to tell you. This--down here--is the black fair."

Shaina shrugged. "What does that mean?"

Dashiell tried to climb the ramp.

"Forget it," Miss Helen said. "I already tried that. There's no going back that way. She hooked her thumb behind her. "There's a door over here, leading to another room. And another slide. Another dead end. I saw another door, though, so we can try that one."

She turned and walked away.

Shaina followed.

"You need to explain yourself," Dashiell said. "What do you know about this underground area? And why did you try to burn the fair down?"

"I tried to burn the fair to force people out. I wasn't sure what lurked in the fair, just that something unnatural was going on. I intended to evacuate so I could investigate the grounds without the interference of the workers. I intended to save lives. You stopped me before I could cause enough panic to get everyone out."

"Call *me* psychic." Dashiell hooked a thumb at his chest. "I knew something was endangering my fair and when I went in search of danger, I found you."

"Then that boy went missing, and everyone began pointing the finger at me."

"Billy," Shaina said. "Does your psychic ability tell you what happened to him?"

"Yes," Miss Helen said, but didn't elaborate. "Black fog was hiding this place down here from me. Now I can see with all the strength of all my gift that there are ghosts in these halls, and I can see them with perfect clarity. The black veil has lifted." Miss Helen pointed. "We go that way."

They entered a large room and moved left along the wall until they reached another door. When Miss Helen tried the knob, the door opened. They walked through to the hallway beyond.

"You know the way out of here?" Dashiell asked.

"I do not. And I think the ghosts are leading us somewhere else." Miss Helen walked halfway down the hall and opened a door.

"Who is leading you, Miss Helen?" Shaina asked.

The woman looked deeply into Shaina's eyes. "The dead lead."

Dashiell scoffed and walked away. He reached

"Stop," Miss Helen said.

"What now?" Dashiell turned to face her.

Miss Helen scanned the room, looking everywhere but at Dashiell.

Shaina touched her arm. "What is it?"

Miss Helen glanced over at Shaina and then returned to searching the room with her eyes. "We're very close to the source of all the trouble."

"Really?" Dashiell sneered. "How do you know?"

Miss Helen locked eyes with Dashiell. "Because you are surrounded by the dead right now. There are at least thirty dead people around you, protecting you. They don't want you going through that door."

"Why not?"

Miss Helen put out her hands. "I don't know, to be honest."

"What do you suggest then? Are they telling you that?"

"I don't know," said Miss Helen. "They don't talk to me."

Dashiell laughed. "You're one crazy lady."

"What do you see?" Shaina asked.

Dashiell turned his gaze on Shaina. "Don't fall for her tricks."

Shaina ignored him. "Who do you see?"

"I see several people. Men, women, children. They are circling you, Dashiell. They are looking at you with distrustful eyes."

"I'm not going to get sucked into your delusion," he said.

"Do you recognize any of them?" Shaina asked.

"Yes," Miss Helen said. "I think I do. I see a man who I once saw working on a building at the fair just before it opened. Yes, he is wearing bib overalls, has a thick gray beard, and stunning blue eyes."

"Jessie?" Dashiell said.

"Yes. He nodded. He is Jessie."

Shaina looked to Dashiell for an explanation.

Dashiell looked around himself as if sensing something. "Jessie disappeared. One of the workers I mentioned. He left without picking up a final paycheck."

"He never left," Miss Helen said, and there was a hint of sadness in her voice.

"He thinks I killed him?" Dashiell frowned. He turned to Miss Helen with imploring eyes.

"No, he doesn't think that."

"How do you know?" A touch of the old skepticism returned to Dashiell's voice. "I thought that they don't talk to you?"

"I know because he's answering your questions. When you asked if he thought you killed him, he shook his head. No. So, you see, the dead don't talk, but they do speak."

"Now you're talking in riddles." Dashiell reached out a hand as if trying to touch the ghosts.

Shaina giggled at his behavior. "I thought you didn't believe in this stuff?"

Dashiell didn't respond to Shaina but stopped.

"Hush, a boy is coming out of the crowd now. He's..."

"Does he think I killed him, too?" Dashiell said. "Where is he?"

"No, this boy isn't interested in you."

Shaina's throat constricted when Miss Helen's eyes tracked the child ghost. Miss Helen's gaze suggested the spirit was standing in front of Shaina.

"Are you saying he's looking at me?"

Miss Helen nodded. "He knows you, this boy who disappeared the night I tried to burn down the fair. He seems to know you, Shaina."

"Billy Meyers? You're saying he's dead?" Shaina's voice was a whisper. It was all she could manage.

"I'm sorry," Miss Helen said. "But yes."

Shaina shook her head, not wanting to believe it. "He had been playing with Jeremy the day he disappeared. He and Jeremy had been riding bikes." Shaina's hand flew to her mouth, and tears stung her eyes.

"What happened to him?" Dashiell's voice was harsh, accusatory.

The psychic woman did not get agitated. "I had nothing to do with his passing, and I do not know what happened to him. I only know he's still here, on these grounds somewhere." She tried to soften her next words by speaking quietly. "His...body, anyway."

Shaina's hand dropped away from her mouth. "Can he show us where to find...him? Can any of them?"

Miss Helen nodded her head. "He's going to show us how to find him." She indicated the direction to go. "This way."

Miss Helen's eyes grew wide. "Oh, my."

"What?" Shaina said.

"They are all going in that direction."

"What?" Dashiell spun around. "What is over there?"

"Only one way to find out." Miss Helen began walking.

Shaina's pulse thudded painfully in her neck as if a fist was tightening around her throat, choking her. She didn't want to see what Ghost Billy Meyers meant to show her. She rubbed at her neck, but the sensation did not improve.

After taking a few deep breaths, she followed Dashiell and Miss Helen deeper into the dimly lit room. The three of them stopped in front of a door.

"What are we going to see beyond this door?" Shaina asked.

"I honestly don't know," said Miss Helen.

The two women looked at Dashiell to lead the way.

Chapter Thirteen: Tommy

When the kids headed to the playroom, Tommy took the opportunity to change the channel on the television from the Cartoon Network to HBO. He scanned through the several HBO stations hoping to find something worth watching. Tommy had a bad habit of channel surfing without settling on any one thing. He was doing that now, having no luck finding something on the pay channels to watch Tommy decided to turn it back to the Cartoon Network, and a Family Guy episode he had seen before but thought it was funny enough to see again. Laughing at something Stewie said, Tommy turned to see Jeremy entering the living room. Tommy turned the volume down on the television.

"Hi, Bud. What's going on?"

"I wanted to ask you something."

"Great, Bud. Does your mom let you watch Family Guy?"

Jeremy gave the TV a cursory glance. "Yeah, sure. Sometimes."

"Okay. Good. What do you have to ask me? Oh, but first, would you mind getting your old uncle a glass of iced tea?"

Jeremy said nothing but walked into the kitchen. Tommy heard a cupboard door open and the tinkle of glasses knocking into one another, and then a few seconds later, ice jingled from the automatic dispenser built into the door. Tommy heard the fridge door open and the sound of liquid cascading over the ice.

"Hey, do you mind grabbing me a box of the Chips Ahoy, too?"

Jeremy returned to the living room with the refreshments and placed them on the coffee table in front of Tommy.

Tommy ate a cookie and washed it down with a swig of tea that reduced the amount of liquid in the glass by half.

The boy stood in front of Tommy, waiting.

"Okay. You wanted to ask me something."

Jeremy climbed up next to his uncle on the sofa. "Did mom say when she would be home?"

Tommy thought back to the conversation he had had with his sister. "No, just that she had some unfinished business to take care of, and then she would be home."

Jeremy stared at Tommy.

"Was there something else you needed?" Tommy's attention split between the boy and the muted TV show.

The boy hesitated, with a thought forming on his lips, but did not speak right away. When the boy's eyes teared up, Tommy turned the TV off and gave the boy his full attention.

"What's the matter? Tell your old Uncle Tommy everything." He wondered when he would be old enough to be known simply as Tom, or Thomas, and not by the childhood moniker of Tommy. Never, he supposed, when it came to family. He would be forever known as Uncle Tommy, even when these kids were old enough to have their kids, and Tommy was 90 years old himself. He supposed he was okay with that.

Jeremy squared his shoulders and cleared his throat. He blinked away the tears. The boy's bravery made Tommy's throat tighten.

"I was hoping mom would be home by now. I don't think she should have gone to the fair. None of us should have gone there."

"Why do you say that, Bud?"

"I...I know...something..." The boy's voice cracked, and he stopped. He blinked hard and tried again. "I know something about the fair."

"What is it? What do you know?" Tommy said when a few seconds passed without Jeremy speaking again.

Now Jeremy's façade broke, and Jeremy exploded in tears and wild sobs. "I saw when it took Billy away." Jeremy threw himself into Tommy's arms.

Tommy hugged the boy, tightly. He struggled not to cry, himself. After he let the boy cry himself out, Tommy held him out at arm's length and looked into Jeremy's red-rimmed eyes. "I need you to calm down and tell me what you're trying to say. You can do that."

Jeremy nodded.

"Okay, go."

Jeremy took in a deep breath that hitched a little when he released it, but he seemed more relaxed. He spoke softly at first, but as he gained confidence, his words came out quickly and with more volume.

"I was with Billy that day he disappeared. We were riding bikes. When I said I had to go home, he told me he was going to sneak into the fairgrounds that night. He said he had a secret way into the fair. I didn't want to do it, but he kept calling me a baby. He said he was going to tell everyone at school what a baby I was. I said, 'I'm not a baby.' But I was afraid he would say something at school, so I told him I would go, too. Billy told me to meet him at midnight at the oak tree down the street. He said to bring my bike, so I snuck out of my window and got on my bike. I met him at the tree, and I followed him out of town. He took me down a road that led to the back of the fair. We hid our bikes in the field, and he showed me a hole. We got in and were looking around, but I got scared and wanted to go back. I started heading to the fence. When I turned around, Billy was yelling at me to stay. He was saying I was a baby again. I said I didn't care what he said, but a big clown appeared behind Billy. I started to tell Billy that he was standing in front of a clown when the clown grabbed Billy, covering his mouth. Billy kicked and tried to scream, but the clown carried him away."

Jeremy started crying again. Tommy rubbed the boy's arm and waited for him to continue.

"I hopped on my bike and rode home. I climbed back into my room and waited for the clown to follow me. I was afraid to tell anyone what I saw because I didn't want to get in trouble. I waited for the cops to come and take me away for being bad. Then people started talking about Billy being missing, and I got even more scared. I don't want to get into trouble. I'm sorry, Uncle Tommy. I'm sorry I let Billy get taken away." Jeremy let loose with even more tears.

Tommy gripped Jeremy by the back of the head and pulled him into a fierce hug. Something terrible had happened to the boy Billy, he knew, but he had no idea how close his nephew had been to falling to the same fate. He hugged Jeremy and cried.

"You didn't do anything wrong." Tommy struggled to get his tears under control. "You aren't in any trouble for this. But thank you for telling me what you know."

Tommy peered over Jeremy's shoulder as Susie entered from the hallway, hugging her stuffed animal from the fair to her chest.

"I'm lonely," she said. "Jamie, are you coming back to play?"

Tommy waved her over. "Come sit with Uncle Tommy. I want to see you for a little while."

The little girl dropped her hands and dragged the stuffed toy behind her as she approached. She climbed up onto the sofa and sat on the opposite side of Tommy from where Jeremy sat. Tommy wrapped an arm around her and pulled her into a hug.

"Is Jamie in trouble?" Susie asked in a voice that said: "Is Jamie in trouble *again?*"

Tommy laughed. "No, he's not in trouble." He ruffled the boy's hair.

Jeremy quickly tried to comb it out with his fingers.

"Now I want you both to go in the playroom and wait there till Uncle Tommy figures some stuff out. Will you do that for me?"

They nodded in unison. Tommy kissed both of them on the top of the head and rushed them off. Once gone from the room, he reached for his phone and dialed Shaina, but she didn't answer.

"Damn it." He didn't know who else to call.

Well, that wasn't entirely true. He did know who to call; he just didn't want to.

He dialed the three numerals.

"911," the operator said. "What's the nature of your emergency."

Tommy fumbled for words. "It, uh, it's not so much as an emergency as information."

"This line is for emergencies, sir. If you're looking for information, you should call 411. Please do not tie up this line…"

"I don't need information. I have it." He sputtered. "I have info on the disappearance of Billy Meyers."

Tommy was not surprised when the police showed up at the door in roughly twelve minutes.

Tommy allowed them to enter. A male officer entered first as a female police officer stood in the doorway and surveyed the situation.

"You say you have information on the William Meyers case?" The policeman flipped open a note pad.

"I do," Tommy said, and the nervousness in his voice caused him to squeak. He cleared his throat. "I do. Well, I mean, my nephew does."

"Is your nephew here?"

"Jeremy, can you come out here, please?"

Jeremy strolled down the hallway. At the sight of the police officers, the boy burst into tears. "I'm sorry. Don't take me away from my mom. Please…"

Tommy rushed over and took Jeremy's head in his hands. He placed his face close enough to touch noses. "You're not in trouble, Jer. I promise. I love you, and I won't let anyone take you away. Do you hear me?"

Jeremy sniffled, nodded.

The female officer gave Jeremy a tissue, and he blew his nose.

Susie appeared from the hall. She cried and ran to Jeremy. She wrapped her arms around her brother so tight he gasped for breath. "Don't go, Jamie. Don't take my brother." She cried harder.

"No, he's not in trouble." After a struggle, Tommy pulled Susie away from her brother.

The female officer tapped Tommy on the shoulder. "What's her name?"

"Susie," he said.

As the female officer squatted down next to the girl, tight polyester and leather apparel squeaked and groaned. She took the girl gently by one arm. "Susie. That's a pretty name. My name is Rebecca. You can call me Officer Becky. How does that sound?"

Susie nodded as Officer Becky helped wipe her runny nose.

The policewoman continued. "I want you to know your bother is not in trouble. He's in no danger. It's the opposite. He's a hero."

"He is?" Susie said.

"I am?" Jeremy said.

"Yes, you have information on a case we haven't been able to crack. You coming forward is a courageous thing."

Susie wiped her nose on the sleeve of her pajama top.

"How about you show me your playroom," Officer Becky said.

Susie sniffled. "Okay."

The officer followed Susie down the hall.

The male police officer stepped toward Jeremy. "Okay, young man. Will you tell me what you know?"

The boy nodded. He told the policeman everything he could remember, leaving out no details. When he couldn't remember parts he had already told Tommy, his uncle coaxed, and Jeremy continued. When he finished telling all he knew, the policeman stopped writing.

"You've been a big help, young sir," the cop said. The police officer turned away and spoke into a CB mic clipped to his shoulder. There was a squelch, and then someone on the other end replied in a tinny voice. Tommy couldn't make out what was said. He turned to Jeremy.

"Do you think I would betray your trust?" Tommy said.

"No," Jeremy said. "I guess not."

Tommy fell backward as if pushed. "You guess not? You guess not?"

Jeremy laughed. "No. I know you got my back."

"Damn right, I do." Tommy hooked his thump at the police officer. "They're going to help get your mom home."

A squelch on the cop's belt radio caused Tommy to look toward the officer. The female officer came back from the hallway.

"We got it," a male voice on the CB said. "We found the bike, right where the kid said it would be."

"Good work, Joe," the cop in the room said into his mic.

"What now?" Tommy said.

"Now we search for a needle in a haystack, and hope we find this mysterious clown." The cop turned and placed a hand on the front door's knob, hesitated. He turned back to Tommy. "We'll send an officer to keep an eye on you and to keep you posted. We also might have a few follow up questions."

"We'll be here," Tommy said.

The cop walked out, followed by his female partner. Before she had closed the door, Jeremy asked, "Did I help?"

"Kid," Officer Becky said. "If we crack this case because of you, I'll see to it that you get a key to the city."

Chapter Fourteen: Dylan

"Clowns?" Dylan said to Wanda through the two-way radio. "Did we even hire any clowns?"

The radio shrieked, followed by Wanda's high, squeaky voice. "I'm just telling you what I know. Be on the lookout for a clown. The police have shifted their focus from Miss Helen to any clowns we have on the premises."

Dylan grumbled under his breath before pressing the talk button. "Okay. If you hear from Shaina and Dashiell before I do, let me know."

"You know I will," Wanda said. The walkie returned to a steady stream of static.

He didn't understand how his two comrades had gotten away from him. He had been standing by the exit for nearly half an hour, waiting for the others to emerge. Miss Helen had once again managed to disappear and had taken two of her pursuers as well this time. Dylan waited an extra few minutes before going back to the entrance and asking the attendant if anyone had emerged from that way. He assured Dylan no one had.

The facts didn't add up. Dylan searched the exterior of the building for any other doors where someone might have slipped out and found two emergency exits. Dylan had concluded that they had come out one of these exits.

He couldn't waste any more time on them. They would show up either with or without Miss Helen, and then he could let them know about the new focus. He clipped the walkie talkie to his belt and headed out in search of the elusive clown.

Unsure where to begin his search for this mysterious clown (at least Miss Helen he knew existed), Dylan decided he would begin in the place he knew best and headed to the camp for the performers of the freak show.

He entered the mess tent and waved to Brenda, the bearded lady. She was a large woman—over three hundred pounds of pure love-- also but was so much more than just a Performer. She also cooked for the entire camp. Brenda sashayed over and sat him down, placing a plate of food in front of him.

"Eat." She sat down on the opposite bench, her girth causing his side of the table to lift slightly. "You're too skinny."

He ate the mash potatoes and meatloaf without argument. He hadn't realized how hungry he had been until he started eating. When he finished, he pushed the plate away. He drank the glass of milk Brenda had placed in front of him as well.

"I'm on a mission," he said.

She leaned in. "Sounds important."

"The cops are looking for a clown. Have you seen any around here?"

"A clown?" She huffed. "No clowns here. This isn't a circus."

"They think a clown possibly abducted the boy that went missing a few days before we opened."

She folded her arms over her massive bosom and leaned on the table, which groaned under her weight.

"They say they have a witness who saw the boy get abducted by a clown on the fair's grounds."

Brenda leaned back and stroked her beard. She used her hands on the table to leverage herself into a standing position. "Sorry I can't help you."

Dylan also stood. When he reached for his dirty dishes, Brenda elbowed him aside.

"Get your hands off those dishes."

Dylan raised his hands and backed away. He laughed then reached out to hug her. She pulled him into her arms and gave him a closed-lip kiss on the mouth, a personal contact he found strangely alluring.

After releasing him and backing away, Brenda scooped up the dirty dishes. "You can try asking some of the others, but it all sounds like hokum to me."

Dylan strode through the camp, nodding hello to various performers and asking if any of them knew of a clown. Some responded by shaking their heads; some asked what he needed with a clown, and some just scowled and walked away. He wasn't surprised by this reaction; freak show camps were a close-knit community, and many found unwanted questions to be an intrusion into their world.

The wolf boy, Jake, caught Dylan's eye, and he headed toward the teen. Jake was covered head to toe in hair due to hypertrichosis and was one of Dylan's favorite people. He smiled and waved as he approached, and Jake waved back.

"How was the show today?" Dylan asked.

Jake shrugged. "Not bad, I guess. Some days are better than others, as you well know. What are you up to?"

Dylan whistled. "I am chasing ghosts, my friend. Do you remember the Psychic, Miss Helen? Well, we've been trying to pin her down. Can you believe she came back to the scene of her crime here at the fair?"

Jake looked down at his feet. When he looked up again, he met Dylan's eyes. "I know she tried to burn her hut, but she didn't hurt anyone. I hope she's not in trouble." The boy shook his head with fierce determination. "And I know she didn't kidnap anyone."

Dylan brought his hands together and rubbed them. "The cops have lost interest in her at the moment. I don't know what she is facing for arson, but they are no longer looking at her for the missing kid. They think a clown did the deed."

"A clown?" Jake asked.

Dylan nodded. "And it happened right here at the fair. Have you seen any clowns lately?"

"Here?" Jake waved him away. "No, no one here did that."

"Still, I need to look for all the clowns here at the fair, if for no other reason than to help rule them out. We don't want cops coming in here and hauling away everyone in a costume if we can help it, right?"

Jake shrugged. "I guess not. You can talk to Ezra, the tall man. He's been known to dress as a clown sometimes. There is also the stilt-walker Jonas. He wears clown make-up. But neither of them has it in them to kidnap someone."

"You are just an optimist, aren't you? But have you seen them today?"

Jake nodded. "Ezra is in his tent, and Jonas is probably in costume walking around the fair."

"Thanks, guy," Dylan said and walked away.

Dylan tapped on the canvas door to Ezra's tent, adding sound effects. "Knock, knock, knock."

Ezra opened the flap. "Dylan." The tall man dipped back into the tent with no further invitation. Dylan entered anyway.

"How goes it, Ezra?"

The tent ceiling was high, but Ezra had to slump anyway. Dylan had asked him how tall he was when he had first met the man, and Ezra had answered proudly, "7 feet 11 inches, just one foot under the tallest man who ever lived, Robert Wadlow."

Ezra took a seat that put him at eye level with Dylan standing.

"Goes well, my friend. What do you need?"

"I'm looking for a clown."

"When do you need him by?"

Dylan frowned. Once he realized what Ezra was implying, he clarified. "I mean, I need to know if there is a clown on the grounds. Have you been in clown make-up lately?"

Ezra moved his head in a quizzical lilt. "Not recently, why do you ask?"

"Well," Dylan thought carefully about what to say next. "There is a possibility a clown may have been last to see the missing boy, Billy Meyers. You wouldn't happen to have been dressed as a clown that day. Maybe the boy was snooping around the fairgrounds, and you scared him off?"

Even as Dylan watched, the tall man's face turned red. All the saliva in Dylan's mouth dried up, and he suddenly found it hard to swallow. Instinctively, his head swiveled to look for the door, judging his chances of reaching it before the giant's long arms stretched out and wrapped those strong hands around Dylan's throat.

But as fast as the anger had come upon Ezra, it subsided just as quickly. Dylan's flight instinct ebbed.

"Don't you think if I had seen the boy, I would have told the police when they questioned me?" As Ezra resituated his weight, the wooden chair beneath him groaned. "Besides, I thought that Psychic chick was on the hook for that."

"She's been set aside for the time being. A witness claims a clown had been near the boy Billy when last seen."

"There's a witness now?" Ezra moved in his seat again, and the sound of groaning wood echoed through the tent. "It wasn't me. I only dress up when I perform. I'm not one of those fruitcakes that run around dressed as a clown all the time."

If Dylan was honest with himself, he had only known the tall man for a few months. He knew Ezra to be straight-forward and no-nonsense, but was the man capable of throttling some little kid and killing him, then packing him away in a suitcase? Dylan couldn't say.

"I'm just passing along what I know. I'm sure the witness is referring to some other clown."

"Uh, yup."

"Sorry to bother you, big guy." Dylan backed toward the door.

"No bother," Ezra said. "Come back any time."

Dylan ducked through the tent's flap and headed off in search of his next...suspect? He smiled, feeling like a gumshoe detective from the 40s or 50s.

He didn't expect to have trouble finding a 12-foot person, but he hadn't seen Jonas in the past few days and wasn't sure where to begin his search.

As Dylan passed the orange mesh fencing that blocked off the part of the fairgrounds where Miss Helen had set the fire, he stopped. There was no one beyond that section of the grounds, and he doubted the stilt walker Jonas would be in there, but Dylan ducked under the nylon mesh anyway and strode over to the hut where Miss Helen had planned to do her fortune-telling. The small shack was scorched, but there was little damage to the structure. Helen's belongings were still inside the hut.

Why had she done this? She hadn't even packed up her stuff. She merely set the place ablaze and walked away.

Dylan used his shoe to kick some debris on the ground, not sure for what he was looking. He spotted something that didn't seem to be touched by fire and squatted down to get a better look.

He picked up the crystal ball and held it out at arm's length. He stared into its elusive depths and dared it to show him what he needed to know to solve his mystery. When nothing happened, he laughed at his silliness.

He hadn't known Miss Helen all that well, but he did recall her claim that a black mist covered the fair. He distinctly remembered her saying that even her crystal couldn't penetrate its evil.

She said the particular word: evil.

Looking into the globe now caused a shiver to run through his body.

Evil.

Dylan couldn't help but think about his secret. He had thought he might tell Shaina, but the moment passed, and he hadn't told her. Now he wondered if Miss Helen's gift might hold some validity. Did she see through the veil of deception Dylan had constructed around his secret? Had she been speaking of him when she referred to an evil presence at the fair? Dylan, himself, believed something hidden deep within him was sinister. This secret he harbored but dared not speak of directly resulted in his ability to heal, but whether this aspect of his secret might have been a good thing, the rest of the — ability, for lack of a better word — was terrible, and dare he say evil.

When he thought he heard movement outside the hut, Dylan dropped the ball he was holding. It hit with a heavy thud and rolled away. He stepped out of the shelter and glanced around but was alone.

Dylan noticed the dilapidated building near Hellen's hut, which was also behind the cordoned area and walked that way. Peering into the window, he saw that the building was a vast, unused warehouse. Dylan walked around to a small utility door next to the large bay door. He tried the knob, locked. He glanced around, and when he was sure he was alone, Dylan squeezed the doorknob until the metal began to crunch in his grip.

The radio on Dylan's belt crackled, and he pulled his hand away from the door.

Wanda's voice issued from the speaker. "How are you doing out there, Dyl?"

Dylan cleared his throat before answering. "Still searching for the elusive clown."

"Good luck," she said.

Dylan lifted the radio to his mouth and pressed talk. "Wanda, any word from Dashiell yet?"

A squelch came to the radio's speaker, and she replied. "Nothing yet. I'm not surprised, though. He doesn't have a radio and would have to come back here to check-in. If he hadn't found Miss Helen yet, he's not going to waste time coming back here."

"Maybe he and that lady he's with went off to find a dark corner somewhere to make out."

Dylan ignored the comment. "He's probably not even aware we have switched focus from Helen."

"No," she said through the radio's speaker. "He probably doesn't."

"I'll sure let you know if I see him."

She responded. "Don't you mean *when* you find him?"

He laughed and pressed the button. "Yes, you're right. Out."

Dylan exited the quarantined area and headed back to the din of the crowds. The sun dipped below the Ferris Wheel, limning the riders in a halo-like glow. The ride moved around, and the baskets filled with people cast the fair in a stuttering light and shadow pattern that seemed at once hypnotizing and stimulating. He set off to search for another clown to interrogate.

Dylan weaved in and out of crowds, keeping alert for the tall stilt-walker. He wasn't sure if there were any other clowns on the grounds, but Dylan thought he might also talk to Roger, the balloon animal maker, who might wear clown make-up as well. Dylan pivoted and headed to Roger's station. But he still hadn't given up the plight of finding Jonas. The elusive performer was still on his list of suspects to rule out, of course.

As Dylan came upon the balloon man's station, he could see the artist was not there. He then had to decide to wait around for the man, or move on. He decided to wait.

The balloon maker, a heavy-set man with bulldog jowls, returned moments later, his face painted white with big, red, rosy circles on his cheeks and a smile drawn in red dye from the corners of his mouth. He looked more like a happy mime than a clown, that was if mimes were different from clowns. Dylan didn't know.

"Hello," Dylan said as the man took up his place behind the balloon rack.

"Good afternoon, my fine fellow," the balloon man said with a flourish and a lithe dance that belied his heft. "Do you want a balloon wiener doggie, or maybe a giraffe?"

"I'll pass on both of them. No, I'm here because the police are looking for a clown. I want to get the jump on them and warn any potential clowns and to rule them out as a suspect."

The man frowned, causing the painted red smile to appear like a squiggly line. "I'm not a clown."

Dylan put his hands up in supplication. "I'm just passing along the information. Don't kill the messenger."

After another second, the man's smile returned to its original shape. "Hey, no harm, no foul. What are they gathering up clowns for? What did a clown ever do to draw the attention of the police?" Under his breath, he added, "Other than those terror clowns that pop up from time to time, that is." The balloon man bellowed laughter that morphed into a coughing fit.

Dylan couldn't help notice how closely this man resembled the killer, John Wayne Gacy.

"They think a clown may know something about the disappearance of that boy Billy Meyers. Wouldn't happen to be you, would it? Did you see the boy?"

The man's smile stayed plastered on his face, but the eyes told a different story. "What are you trying to say?"

"Honest, I'm not trying to say anything. It's a simple yes or no question."

The smile still in place, the man said, "It's a no."

"Okay, so noted."

"I thought that witch woman offed the kid."

"First of all, no one is saying he's dead yet. I guess new information came to light, and now the cops are looking for a clown that might have been a witness to what happened to the kid."

"Wasn't me."

Dylan nodded. "Noted. Sorry to have bothered you."

"No bother at all."

"Before I go, I wonder if you have seen the guy on stilts. Believe his name to be Jonas. I still need to talk to him."

Roger's face brightened. "Ah, yeah. That's Squeakles. He comes by here now and again. Brings all the little kiddies trailing behind him. Great for business."

"Has he been by today?"

Roger shook his head. "No, not yet."

"Okay, thanks."

"Good luck finding your clown."

Dylan turned his head and waved as he walked away. "Thanks."

He wasn't one to judge other people—and certainly didn't want to be judged by others—but Dylan couldn't stop thinking Roger did not belong working around kids. The guy made Dylan's skin crawl.

He thought to have the cops look into the balloon guy and moved forward with his investigation.

Dylan had wandered around aimlessly for several minutes. He considered checking in with Wanda but figured that if there had been any changes to their situation, she would contact him. Dashiell and Shaina were still MIA.

He looked to the east and the setting sun. There were parts of the fair in enough darkness that lights had begun to turn on. The sound of people enjoying the rides, winning—and losing—at the games of chance, and talking amongst themselves as they enjoyed various treats, helped to drown out Dylan's thoughts of doubt and inadequacy. He tried to think of what else he could do to bring this investigation to a close.

After giving up looking for the man on stilts, the man on stilts found him.

"Ex-squeeze me." The voice was so high pitched and distorted, Dylan wasn't even sure he had heard it correctly.

When Dylan turned around, he stared up at the twelve-foot-high clown-faced stilt-man. When the man spoke again, he understood why the voice sounded the way it did. The man had some voice altering gadget between his teeth.

"I get by you?" the squeaky voice asked. "P-p-l-l-ease?"

"You're Squeakles?" Dylan asked.

The clown honked a hand-held horn twice.

"Can I ask you a few questions?"

The horn honked twice again.

I'll take that as a yes.

"Can I convince you to take that thing out of your mouth and talk to me like a normal human?"

A squeaky laugh emanated from the mouth, and one honk from the hand-held horn.

"Well, I tried." Dylan glanced down at the tiny little shoes attached to the bottom of the stilts. Long, baggy pants hid the actual height of the man.

The stilt man hopped back and forth, from one foot to the other, like a child waiting to open a present on Christmas eve.

Dylan sighed. "Let's get started then, I guess. Were you around on Wednesday night? It's the night before the fair opened. The boy Billy was last seen here, allegedly, and a clown was spotted at the scene by a witness. Would you know anything about that?"

"No, not me, officer." The stilt man's squeaky-toy voice sounded, at once, solemn and yet wholly ridiculous.

A vein throbbed in Dylan's head. *Okay, that's it. I'm leaving this up to the professionals. I'm dealing with a bunch of nutcases.*

Dylan decided to go at this another way.

"We're looking for a little boy who's gone missing. Don't you want to help get to the bottom of this?"

The tactic worked.

The stilt man removed the apparatus from his mouth. His real voice was deep and rumbling. "Look, man. I'm sorry about this kid's deal, but I wasn't there. How much clearer can I make it?"

"Does anyone you know fit that description? I'm running out of clowns to question. I already spoke to Ezra and Roger. They say they didn't see Billy, either."

"How reliable is your witness?"

"I don't know. But the police are looking for a clown. Just a head's up, they might drag you to the station. Thank you for talking to me, man to man. I appreciate your time." Dylan reached up to shake his hand, but the clown only honked the horn.

The man popped the speech altering device back into his mouth. His squeaky voice came back. "Go away. You scare the kids."

Chapter Fifteen: Shaina

The enormity of the room shocked her, but that wasn't the only surprise waiting for Shaina and the others. There also appeared to be an entire underground fair, complete with rides—flashing colored lights dancing across shiny metal surfaces, and a calliope playing a tune that was at once cheerful and eerie. She saw people milling around, and that confused her. Were they out of the trap?

Her eyes lifted toward the room's ceiling, if you could call it that. She saw what looked like a giant circular tent top. A large pole ran down the center of the room, presumably to the floor, though she couldn't see where it stopped. From higher on the pole, cords radiated outward and connected to the canvas in the farthest reaches of the room. At second glance, she thought it looked less like a tent and more like an enormous umbrella.

In several places, the canvas was in tatters, and strips of the heavy fabric hung down like torn curtains.

Nearby, Shaina spotted a pillar that shot up and passed through the canvas to whatever served as a real ceiling up there.

In the places where the tears were heaviest, she saw light pouring through the gaps. Sunlight?

Shaina turned to Dashiell. His face mirrored her shock.

"What is this place," she asked.

He shook his head slowly. "I have no fucking clue."

"Is there a roof up there? Does this go out into the real world? Nothing here looks familiar to you?"

Dashiell stared up and up. "No, there is nothing like this at the fair. This place is completely below the surface. A fair beneath the fair."

"This is not what it appears to be," Miss Helen said. "It's an abomination." The last word was a portentous whisper.

Shaina ignored her. "Are you telling me this is your fair and you have no idea what's under it?"

"Honestly, I know nothing about this—" He waved his hand around, indicating the menagerie in front of them. "None of it is on any of the plans I've seen. I've been through every inch of my fair, and have never seen anything that led me to believe this place existed." His eyes never deviated from the rides and people in the distance. "Who are those people?"

Miss Helen stepped past them and walked toward the crowd. When the others didn't immediately follow, she spoke over her shoulder. "We aren't going to get the answers standing around. Let's go."

Shaina and Dashiell followed her, reluctantly at first.

As they grew closer to the crowd, she noted the look of shock and fear on their faces. Only one of them came forward to meet them. The elderly man waved to Shaina and the others with her.

"Hi there, folks. Are you all new to the underground *funhouse*?" The last word dripped with sarcasm.

So far, nothing about this place seemed fun for Shaina. "Who are you people?"

"My name is Clifford Javes." An old woman walked over and stood next to him. "This is my beautiful wife, Cary Lynn."

One by one, the people gathered at the fringes of the park stepped forward and introduced themselves. When the other group finished, Shaina shared her name with them. Miss Helen was next to offer an introduction.

Dashiell was last. "I'm Dashiell Pearson."

Shaina looked at him, wondering why he chose to ignore the detail that he was the owner of the fair but realized this calm, unstable group could quickly turn into an angry mob if they thought he was responsible for what had happened to them. Miss Helen said nothing, protecting Dashiell's identity as well, no doubt out of self-preservation. Since she had arrived with him, they would think she was in on it as well.

"Have you seen the clown?" Cary Lynn asked.

Shaina wondered if the clown was a mascot. "No, I haven't. We only just got here. You are the first people we've seen since falling through the trap door."

Christopher moved through the group. He approached Shaina. "You aren't aware of what's happening here, do you?"

"What do you mean?" Dashiell asked.

Miss Helen caught Christopher's gaze. "He's referring to the fact that this isn't a funhouse at all. It's a house of horrors."

Christopher nodded his agreement to what the psychic said. "The clown isn't a beacon of joy. He's a killer. There are…things beyond this point that need to be seen to believe. But I warn you; it's not something you'll *want* to see."

Miss Helen walked away from the group toward the cluster of rides and attractions.

"Lady, you're not going to want to see what's over there," Christopher said.

"Did any of you bring food?" asked the woman who introduced herself as Rachael.

Shaina shook her head absently, but she was already following Miss Helen. Dashiell walked behind her. She turned to the cluster of grave faces, which left her wondering what she was about to see.

As they moved toward the merry-go-round, Shaina studied the people as they went around. Upon closer inspection, Shaina decided these weren't people but manikins, with pale faces and stiff limbs. After thinking about it, she couldn't recall seeing the attraction stop. It was less of a ride and more like a bizarre display. When she looked around, it was the same everywhere. They were in a museum, not a park. The Merry-go-round seemed to be the only genuinely functioning attraction because the other rides were just displays.

Dashiell stopped walking in front of her, and she bumped into him, but Miss Helen continued. She climbed over the small fencing surrounding the merry-go-round and slipped onto the platform, even as it continued to go around. Her curiosity hindering her reason, Shaina followed Miss Helen. Dashiell grabbed her arm, but Shaina shook loose of his grip and continued forward. As she reached the fencing, Shaina tried to comprehend what she saw yet, not seeing. There was something strange about this attraction, but she couldn't quite understand what was confusing her.

"Shaina, no. Come back," Dashiell said. "Don't you see?"

Shaina watched as Miss Helen examined one of the manikins. The psychic reached out tentatively but pulled back. After a moment, she reached out again.

Shaina stepped over the knee-high gate, stopped at the edge of the platform as it continued around. The ride moved just like others of its kind. The horses went up and down. There were poles where parents could stand and hold on as they watched over their kids. Loveseats, strategically placed, allowed lovers to dream of the day they had kids of their own.

As the ride continued around, Shaina saw a familiar face sitting alone on one of the love seats. As the manikin came around again, she focused on the face. Why did that child-sized manikin look so familiar?

Dashiell shouted to her again. "Shaina, please come away from there."

But it was too late. Shaina now understood. She stumbled onto the spinning platform, which almost threw her, but she gripped the leg of a horse and pulled herself entirely onto the ride. She stumbled through the bobbing horses to the loveseat. Miss Helen followed Shaina, guiding her to the destination. Shaina peered down at the manikin that wasn't a manikin at all.

Billy Meyers's dead, accusing eyes stared at Shaina. There was screaming from somewhere nearby, but she didn't know from where it came. Shaina spun, nearly falling from the platform. Though her vision was suddenly blurry, she could see it wasn't Miss Helen screaming.

As the tears streamed down her cheeks, it hit her that the screaming was coming from her lips. Miss Helen pulled her down to the floor and held her as she continued screaming, stroking her hair, trying to calm her down.

Shaina couldn't stop thinking about the boy. He had been a living, breathing boy only a few days ago, playing with her son.

Dashiell was there now, too. Both of them held her.

She wasn't sure when she had calmed down, but when the screaming and the tears stopped, she allowed them to help her to her feet. The three of them climbed carefully down off the ride. They returned to the others who were still standing at the edge of the attraction. She didn't need to look up to know all eyes were on her.

The older woman, Cary Lynn, helped Shaina with an arm around her waist. She led Shaina to a bench, where the woman introduced as April sat.

April turned to Shaina. "The place is full of them, you know. There are dead people everywhere." The woman's puffy eyes were glazed, and there was a maniacal grin on her red and blotchy face. April laughed. "My boyfriend is in there, too, I think. Without a head." She laughed again.

Shaina moved further down the bench, away from April.

"What's happening?" Shaina spoke directly to Dashiell.

He could only shake his head.

Cary Lynn spoke quietly to her husband, but in the hushed silence, everyone could hear her. "I still have to go pee."

"I'll take you, Cary," Rachael said.

The older woman looked around. "Where would we go? There are no bathrooms anywhere around here."

Rachael looked around. "I'll take you behind that old hunk of junk over there." She pointed to a rusted-out piece of equipment. "Looks safe enough and private enough."

"I hope you aren't saying I should cop a squat out here in the open." Cary Lynn placed a hand to her throat.

"Go ahead, you old bitty. You lost all dignity years ago," said Clifford.

"Shut your mouth." Cary Lynn took Rachael's hand, and the two walked away.

"It's easy," said Rachael. "Pretend you're squatting over a dirty toilet."

"Well this just gets better and better, doesn't it?" Cary Lynn puffed out an exasperated breath. The two disappeared behind a clump of scrap metal that looked like it had once been the shell of an amusement ride.

April had calmed down and sat quietly, staring at her hands.

"Has anyone looked for a way out of here?" Dashiell asked.

Christopher shot Dashiell a sharp look. His eyes softened. "We have been looking for a way out since getting trapped here. We haven't explored this place yet, but mostly because of what we found when we got here. It's taking all our strength to stay sane."

"Can you tell me more about the clown?" Dashiell asked.

Christopher pulled Dashiell aside, but Shaina followed them. Christopher eyed her, and she could tell he was sizing her up, wondering if her sanity could handle what he had to say. Shaina met his gaze.

"I'm okay."

"She is," Dashiell said.

Christopher nodded, reluctantly, and relayed the story of what happened to April's boyfriend, Alan. He then explained when the clown first appeared to them. Dashiell listened without interruption. When Christopher stopped talking, Dashiell continued to stay quiet, though Shaina's mind filled with all kinds of questions.

"Where did the clown come from? Why is he here? Is there more than just the one dweller?"

Dashiell continued to stay quiet, and Christopher only shrugged.

After several minutes, Rachael and Cary Lynn returned.

"Do you feel better?" Clifford asked his wife.

"Oh, you don't know the half of it." She turned to Rachael. "Thank you."

Rachael said, "If anyone else has to go, I have wet wipes in my purse."

"I do," said Gina.

Dashiell stood apart from the others and surveyed their surroundings. His eyes settled on the carrousel, which was still turning. Shaina joined him.

"What's on your mind?" she asked him. She sensed he wanted to talk about something to do with the running of the fair and didn't want to divulge his little secret to the others.

He looked toward the rest of the group. Shaina was sure the others were too far to hear what he had to say. Dashiell turned to her.

"I'm looking at the way this place is set up, and I can't help but notice the only working attraction is the carrousel. The rest of these…rides…are just for show. In fact, the parts seem to have been taken from broken-down rides that used to be up top." He hesitated. "I'd been getting reports that dilapidated rides had been disappearing. I thought it was thrill-seekers looking for souvenirs, but now I can see they were brought down here."

"Do you think there are more dwellers down here? I mean, can one oversized clown do all this alone?"

Dashiell shrugged. "I have no clue. This has been going on for years. Years and years. Long before I came into the picture. My guess is some homicidal, homeless hobo found this place and set up camp down here. Who knows how long he's been here."

"If there's a way in here, there has to be a way out. Do you think we should look for an exit?"

"Maybe we should ask our resident psychic. She should know a way out."

Shaina noted the wisp of sarcasm in his words. "You don't think she is…"

"No. I don't think that. I guess my prejudices against her are hard to go. But no, I don't think she trapped us down here."

Shaina suddenly wasn't so sure. They were there because of her. Maybe she knew they would follow her. When she thought back on it, she recalled Miss Helen looking right at her before disappearing into the funhouse. *I dare you to follow me,* her eyes said.

She wouldn't share her suspicions with Dashiell just yet. She would want to be sure before she started spreading rumors. After all, she had been on Miss Helen's side all through this. Even when the woman was holding a gun on her, she never truly felt a threat from the woman.

Dashiell and Shaina joined the others.

Amber, eyes fixed on Miss Helen, stood up from the bench where she had been consoling April. She strode up to the psychic and stood face to face with her. Miss Helen did not back away.

"I remember you," she said.

Miss Helen stood her ground, waiting for the other woman to continue.

"You told us not to go into the House of Horrors." She hooked her thumb at Christopher. "You warned us something would happen if we went in there. We didn't listen, and now we are trapped here."

"I can only tell you of the danger. It's up to you to heed it."

Miss Helen didn't flinch when Amber slapped her hands together in front of the psychic's face.

"How did you know there was danger?"

Miss Helen blinked. "I'm psychic. I sensed it."

Christopher stood next to Amber. "If you knew there was a danger, why did you come down here yourself?"

"I am out to clear my name. I came here because my ability was leading me here. My fate is the same as yours. I am blameless. Getting angry will get you nowhere. We can't start turning on each other or—"

Cary Lynn joined the conversation. "If you're psychic, why can't you tell us how to get out of here?"

"My ability doesn't work that way. I didn't know anything until I entered this place. I fell through the rabbit hole, just like everybody else."

"You stupid bitch." Rachael rushed forward. "Work your voodoo and get us out of here. People are dying."

Shaina nudged Dashiell and motioned with her head to interfere.

Dashiell stepped forward. "All right, guys. No need to get hysterical. She's not to blame for us being here."

Shaina mentally slapped her forehead. A man told a bunch of women not to get hysterical. She sensed her impending involvement in the confrontation. Before she could make a move or say anything, Dashiell made things a hell of a lot worse.

"She's no more to blame for any of this than I am."

Dashiell turned to look at Shaina, and his eyes said it all. *I fucked up.*

"Why would we blame you?" Clifford asked. "What do you have to do with all this?"

Dashiell sighed. "It's bound to get out, so I might as well tell you and get it over with." He paused, noting that all eyes were on him. "I own the fair."

"What?" Christopher balled his hands into fists. "What?"

"Remember that I'm trapped down here, too. I had no idea this place existed. I don't know where this place is or how to get out again."

When Christopher stepped forward quickly, Shaina rushed to stand in front of Dashiell. He stepped back again and turned away.

"Is this some kind of game?" Amber asked. "Do you trap people down here and then watch them go insane, like Jigsaw or something? Because I'll tell you what…" She laughed. "I'm fast approaching just that."

"We'll all be okay if we just…" Shaina couldn't finish her speech.

Everyone began shouting and talking over each other. No one was making any sense. Dashiell backed away from them.

"Stop." It was April, and the word was so loud and aggressive that all shouting ceased. "Just stop."

Everyone turned to look at her.

Cary Lynn screamed.

The clown stood behind April. It grabbed her by the hair and lifted her off the bench. Her expression changed from anger to confusion, and then to horror and pain. She kicked and screamed, holding onto the hand that had lifted her.

Too horrified at first to move, everyone stared. The clown pulled her over the back of the bench, dragged her away and disappeared behind a useless clump of broken amusement ride parts. Christopher sprinted after her. Dashiell followed, but the clown moved fast, and soon, Aprils screams were too faint to hear.

Cary Lynn cried against her husband's chest. Rachael and Amber stared stoically at the spot where April had disappeared. Miss Helen stared at Shaina. Shaina had trouble meeting the woman's gaze.

"I'm not a part of this." Miss Helen's voice was heavy with emotion.

"I know. I..." Shaina's voice trailed off. Had the woman known her thoughts? She couldn't defend that.

"Oh, God." Amber paced. "Christoph..." She cried, and her voice trailed off. Rachael placed a hand on her shoulder, but Amber shrugged it away.

"He'll come back," Rachael said. "They'll bring April back."

Amber whirled on her. "You didn't even care about that girl. You showed her no sympathy at all. You picked at her mercilessly. You teased her for being afraid—for losing her boyfriend—for god's sake." Amber seethed.

Silent tears streamed down Rachael's face. "He was my boyfriend first. He left me for her. He..."

"And now he's dead." Amber chocked back a sob.

Rachael's silent tears turned to sobs. "I still loved him. I still loved him, and he left me. He left me for that..."

"Go ahead and say it. Make some derogatory comment about that poor girl."

Rachael took a deep breath and physically relaxed. "Look, yesterday I was as madly in love with Alan as April. I didn't know until late last night he was seeing her. He broke up with me. I still loved him, never stopped. I don't know how to process any of this." Tears sprung to Rachael's eyes, and she rubbed them away with a fist.

Rachael turned to Shaina. Her imploring eyes caused Shaina to go up and hug Rachael.

Amber grunted her displeasure but said nothing more.

Rachael stepped away from Shaina when Christopher and Dashiell returned. All eyes turned to them, but their glum faces and Christopher's mournful shake of the head told them what they needed to know without saying a word.

Chapter Sixteen: Tommy

It had been an hour since they told him his sister had gone missing, and Tommy had been pacing a groove in the carpet ever since. He peered out the window, hoping to see her car pulling into the driveway, but saw only the police cruiser parked at the curb in front of the house. Tommy wasn't sure if this comforted him or worried him. He was glad for their protection, but why did they need protecting? For that matter, why would Shaina be in danger? What did she have to do with any of it? He looked toward the sofa where the two kids sat huddled together, watching the *Aristocats* for the third time. He heard the popcorn popper stop and headed to the kitchen, returned to the living room with the bowl of popcorn and sat down between them. They attacked the bowl of snacks greedily.

He couldn't tell them that their mother wasn't on her way home. At least, he didn't think she was. He hoped she was okay, delayed by some unseen but benign thing. She had just forgotten to call.

Only, that wasn't Shaina. He was more apt to forget to check in than she was. She was a stickler for punctuality and transparency. The only reason that he could think of for Shaina not contacting him—her children—was because she was in danger.

Tommy smiled when Susie looked at him, and she laid her head on his arm. He let her cuddle up next to him. She was a sweet girl, and her naiveté was a blessing. Her brother had no such protections. He fidgeted and roiled next to Tommy with the knowledge that something terrible was happening.

Tommy wanted to comfort the boy but didn't know how.

Shaina had to be safe. She had to return to them. Tommy wasn't ready to take care of these kids on his own. Sure, he was the fun uncle, and it was a part he played well, but in the end, it was his sister who kept the kids safe and grounded, and him, as well. When he thought about it, Shaina had three kids.

Tommy grabbed a handful of popcorn and threw it into the air. Susie giggled, and even Jeremy laughed. He needed to do something, had to get his mind away from thinking that Shaina was not coming back. He didn't know why his brain always went to the worst scenario it could dream up. Shaina was coming back to her kids. And she would yell at him for making a mess with the popcorn (because he wasn't going to clean it up).

He caught himself about to look toward the door and stopped to look at Susie instead. *If I look anxious and nervously waiting for her to come through the door, they will be worried, too. I have to think of them.* Instead, he crammed a handful of popcorn into his mouth like the Cookie Monster would eat it. As he made an even bigger mess, Susie laughed some more.

He loved hearing her little laugh.

"I love you, Uncle Tommy," she said and hugged his arm.

"I love you, too, Little Princess."

"When is Mommy coming home?"

Damn, all his plotting and pageantry hadn't fooled her one bit.

"Soon, honey," he said. "Your mom will be home sooner than you know. You might have to go to sleep first, but she'll be here when you wake up."

"You promise?"

"I do. I promise." Tommy swallowed hard. *Please, Sis. Don't make me out to be a liar.*

The kids quieted down and continued watching the movie. Susie yawned, which was a good sign, but the contagion of it made Tommy yawn, too. Within a few minutes, Susie's eyes began to flutter, and her head to nod.

"You're sleepy. You should head on off to bed."

"I'm not sleepy." Susie's eyes were closed, and she yawned again.

Tommy smiled. He would let her stay up a little longer. It wasn't like he couldn't carry her off to bed if she fell asleep on the sofa.

Tommy turned to Jeremy. "How about you?"

"I'm good." Jeremy turned the TV and then back to his uncle. "But when she falls asleep, can we watch something else?"

"Sure, what do you want to watch?"

"Scarface," Jeremy said.

"Uh, no. It'll give you nightmares. How about something fun? Like Mrs. Doubtfire?"

Jeremy shrugged. "How about Jurassic Park?"

Tommy thought a moment. "Still might give you nightmares, but if you don't tell your mom, I'll agree to it."

Jeremy leaned forward to get a look at his sister on the other side of Tommy. "She's asleep. Let's do it."

Tommy glanced down. Susie was leaning against his arm and looked to be asleep. "Give me a sec to put her to bed, and then I'll start the movie, okay."

Jeremy nodded.

Tommy skillfully wiggled out from under Susie and stood. He lifted her into his arms. She fidgeted but did not wake. He made it halfway across the room when there came a knock at the door. Tommy stopped and looked toward the door. He contemplated continuing to Susie's bedroom before answering the door but decided against it. There could be news about his sister, and he was anxious to know what was going on.

With Susie still sleeping against his shoulder, Tommy walked to the door and looked out. A plainclothes officer was standing out there looking at something in his hands. This man had a detective's badge around his neck. Tommy opened the door.

"Mr. Salvador?" the detective said. "I'm Detective Berber."

"No, I'm Tommy Warner, Shaina Salvador's brother."

"Oh, sorry, Mr. Warner. May I come in?"

"Yes, of course." Tommy moved aside, and the detective entered. Tommy closed the door.

"I'm here to follow up on the latest development on the Billy Meyers case."

"You didn't find my sister?"

"No, I'm afraid not. Do you want to finish what you were doing, and we can talk?" The detective gestured to Susie.

"Uh, yeah. Just a minute."

Tommy disappeared down the hall and put Susie to bed, covered her, and kissed her forehead. She moaned and turned, but did not wake. He returned to the living room where the detective was still where Tommy had left him. Jeremy peered over the back of the sofa at the officer.

"Would you like to have a seat?" Tommy led the cop to the sofa, and they sat down. "Jeremy, do you want to…"

"I'd like for the boy to stay if you don't mind. You see, Mr. Warner, we have a few photographs we'd like the boy to view. We're trying to pin down this clown he said was there when the boy disappeared. We want to get a better idea of what we're looking for." The man held out the item in his hand. It looked like a photo album. "We'd like young Jeremy to look at a few pictures, and see if he can recognize the clown he saw that night." The cop turned to the boy. "Will you do that?"

Jeremy glanced at his uncle. Tommy nodded. Jeremy turned back to the detective with his lips pressed tightly together. He gave a single nod of the head.

"Great." The cop opened the book and held it out for Jeremy to see.

The boy scanned the pictures of the clowns inside the book.

"Clown mug shots," Tommy said with a wry smile. "Now I've seen everything, I think."

The cop ignored him and concentrated on Jeremy. The boy screwed up his face as he stared at the pictures. He shook his head, and the policeman flipped the pages. There were more clowns on the subsequent pages as well, and again the boy shook his head in the negative. On the next page, he barely scanned the pictures before shaking his head.

"Son, are you sure you're taking the right amount of time to look at these photos? I feel like you're going a little fast."

Jeremy waved his head over the book. "These aren't the right kind of clowns."

"What do you mean by that, Buddy?" Tommy asked.

Jeremy looked at Tommy. He looked scared. Tommy placed a hand on his shoulder and looked him in the eyes.

"You're doing fine. Tell us what you're trying to say."

Jeremy looked at the pictures in the book again. "These clowns are all wearing make-up."

The detective and Tommy shared a look. They were both thinking the same thing: *what other kinds of clowns are there?*

"The clown had a normal face?" The detective didn't understand.

Jeremy shook his head again. "No, he had…" The boy used his hands to mimic putting something on his head. "He was wearing a clown mask."

The cop slammed the book closed. "Jesus Christ."

Jeremy flinched away.

Without apologizing, the cop stood. "This is useless. It could be anybody."

Tommy stood. He was about to tell the cop to relax, but the detective beat him to the punch.

Detective Berber sighed heavily. "I didn't mean to barge in here and waste your time. Your help has been invaluable, young man. Thank you."

Tommy followed the cop to the door and saw him out. He spoke quietly to the detective. "That boy hasn't seen his mother in over 24 hours. When you come back, I hope it won't be to look at more useless pictures in a book. We want you to bring his mother back to us. That's not too much to ask for, is it?"

The detective nodded. "You're right. We're working tirelessly to resolve this situation. I didn't mean to lose my temper. When I return, I hope it's to bring your sister home."

The two shook hands, and the cop stepped out the door. Tommy closed and locked the door before returning to Jeremy on the sofa.

Tommy dropped onto the sofa next to Jeremy. "What was that all about?" Tommy laughed. "And did you see that book? I mean, I've heard of clown college, but clown mug shots? How many bad clowns are there out there?"

"All of them," Jeremy said.

"All of them?" Tommy repeated.

"All clowns are bad."

Tommy flopped his head against the back cushions of the sofa. "There are no good clowns in the world. Who would have guessed that?"

"Okay, maybe not all. But most."

Tommy turned and looked at Jeremy. The boy looked into his uncle's eyes. They both spoke at the same time.

"Nah, they're all bad."

Tommy and Jeremy laughed. They laughed so loud Tommy checked to see if they woke Susie. When the girl didn't appear, they started laughing again.

When they had gotten that out of their system, Tommy picked up the remote. "Should we watch Jurassic Park now?"

Jeremy didn't respond. Tommy thought about the cop again and nodded.

"You're right. We earned it. Let's watch Scarface."

"Yeah," Jeremy said.

Before Tommy started the movie, he turned to his nephew. "Keep in mind that if it gives you nightmares, I warned you. And one more thing; it's important. Do not tell your mother I let you watch this."

Jeremy put a lock over his lips and threw away the key.

Tommy started the movie.

Chapter Seventeen: Shaina

After the clown took April, the group huddled together in a small, terrified group; but as time passed without incident, the assembly began to split up and sit in small clusters, yet still stayed within sight of each other. Rachael and Gina sat on the floor, quietly talking. The Javes' sat on a bench seat that looked to have once belonged on a roller coaster. Amber and Christopher sat a few feet away from Dashiell, Shaina, and Helen. The couple sat with their backs against the metal shell of what had once been part of a kid's train ride. The train's conductor was a corpse wired to a bar in the center of the car.

Dashiell sat on a fake log used for the water ride called Timber! He angled his body to face Shaina. Shaina sat next to him and turned to face him. Helen sat a few feet away from the pair, turned to look out at the vast expanse of the room.

Dashiell's eyes pointed down, but his gaze seemed fixed on some long past moment in time.

"What?" Shaina asked him.

"Oh, nothing." He slapped the log. "I remember when I first took a ride on this one. It was sort of like a roller coaster in the water. First, you rode up this track to the top of the rail, and then you were pushed along by water until you got to the drop. Then it was like riding a waterfall to the pool below. Then you floated along, pushed by the waves to the end where you got off and went around to do it again."

"Sounds fun." Miss Helen sounded less than thrilled by the memory.

"When did the fair close for the first time?" Shaina asked.

"I think it was about 1985. About ten years after my cousin, Owen Jr. died. My uncle was devastated. He became an introvert. When I think about it, this underground bunker might have been there then. I would assume Uncle Owen had plans to expand the fair to something more down here. He probably abandoned those plans after his son died. I think the carrousel was the first thing he built down here before he gave up on it. That's why the carrousel is whole and functioning, and everything else he pinched from the abandoned fair up above."

"Where does the clown fit into all this?" Shaina asked.

Dashiell shrugged. "Maybe an escaped lunatic who found his way down here and made a home for himself."

"What do you make of those traps? The guillotine in the wall, and the spikes that nearly impaled everyone?"

"The only thing I can figure is they were derived from other parts of the fair and rigged to kill intruders, maybe?" He shrugged again. "I'm only speculating. I don't know what to think of all that."

Shaina turned to Miss Helen. "Does your extra sight help to illuminate what's happening here?"

Miss Helen stared at Shaina for a moment, as if debating whether or not to answer. Then she cleared her throat. "I'm not getting a reading about any part of this. It's sort of like making a phone call, but the party you're calling is giving you a busy signal. I'll be of no help to you right now. If anything changes, I'll let you know."

The group fell into silence for a time.

The silence ended when Shaina turned to Dashiell again. "Do you have any memory of your cousin Owen?"

Dashiell shook his head. "I was just a baby when he died."

"How did he die?"

Dashiell lifted his chin. "Ah, that's the magic question."

"What does that mean?"

"My father said Owen died of a disease, and my uncle always claimed it was a car accident that killed his son. When I asked my father why Uncle Owen thought he died in a car accident, my father said it was because of his grief."

"What disease did he have?"

Dashiell shook his head. "My dad never said."

The silence returned until Dashiell spoke again.

"I'll tell you something else. I have the eerie feeling of being here before. I feel a sense of déjà vu when I look around. But can't—for the life of me—remember when I might have been here before. I certainly don't know how to get in and out of this place. And it's only here that I have that feeling of familiarity. The place as a whole means nothing to me."

"I'm trying to picture what you were like as a kid." She laughed.

"I was a normal kid, as kids go, I guess."

"Did you have any nicknames growing up?"

"Yeah, the most popular one was Dash. I had one friend who called me Dashi. Still another…" Dashiell chuckled under his breath. "David used to call me Dot dot dot dash dash dash dot dot dot."

Shaina smiled. "Why?"

Dashiell turned to her as if shocked. "Why it's Morse code for SOS."

Shaina slapped her forehead. "Of course. How could I forget my boy scout training?" She giggled. "So, your nickname was Save Our Souls?"

Dashiell full-out laughed at her.

"What now?"

"That's not what SOS means."

"What does it mean then, smarty-pants?"

He shrugged. "It doesn't mean anything. It was intended to get your attention. The point is to keep hitting dotdotdotdashdashdashdotdotdotdashdashdash over and over again until you get someone's attention."

"Is that true?"

He put up his hand: scout's honor. "David told me so, and he wouldn't lie."

Miss Helen stood and walked away without giving any explanation.

Dashiell watched her go. "Did I offend her?"

Shaina shrugged. "Nah, you probably bored her."

Dashiell nudged her with his shoulder. "Do you say that because I bore you?"

Shaina answered quickly. "No, not at all. I—"

Dashiell quieted her with a quick kiss on the lips. When he pulled away, he turned his head, but Shaina could see the redness creeping down the back of his neck.

He's embarrassed.

She placed her hand on his. "It's about time." The words were a whisper.

Dashiell turned to face her. She leaned in and kissed him back, and as she pulled back, they stared into each other's eyes.

"I've been throwing hints at you all day, you know."

His lip curled up in a slight smile. "I don't know. I'm horrible at picking up cues like that."

"I see that now." She interlocked her fingers in his so their palms touched. "This is how people hold hands." She looked into his eyes again. "Is there anything else I can teach you about boys and girls?"

Dashiell leaned in. "No, I think I can figure it out from here." They kissed again. "Thanks for the tips, though."

She giggled and leaned against him.

Shaina glanced over at Miss Helen, and the psychic woman was looking back at her, nodding.

Shaina lifted her head from Dashiell's shoulder. "Do you think she knew and gave us a little privacy?"

Dashiell looked toward the woman. Miss Helen looked away quickly.

"Who knows what she knows?" he said. "She probably knows we are talking about her right now."

"How can she not? We keep looking at her."

"Sometimes I think she's a quack, a fake. Then there are times when I think she's spot-on, the real deal. Is she, or isn't she?"

Shaina nodded. "I've had similar thoughts. She's a—"

A scream cut her sentence short. Shaina and Dashiell jumped up. Christopher and Amber also stood. Shaina scanned the vicinity. All were still present.

Miss Helen said what everyone was thinking. "April."

The girl screamed again, closer this time.

Christopher and Amber ran in the direction of the scream. Shaina and Dashiell followed close behind. Shaina cringed every time she passed by a display with one of the corpses modeled to look like a living spectator at a fair.

Keep telling yourself they are manikins.

But the ruse didn't work because she knew what they were. She could smell the decay. She could also see how they were made to stand. Bindings tied some bodies to posts like scarecrows in a field, and some had the poles driven directly into them like skewers. She ran close to Dashiell and shielded her eyes as best she could to keep from having to look at the abominations any longer. She focused on April. She prayed they weren't too late.

When they reached the source of the screaming, the sound stopped. She struggled to keep standing when she saw the fate that awaited the girl and managed a faint whisper. "Oh, God."

April was on a stage surrounded by a large cage, of which there appeared to be no way in or out. She wore a pink tutu and an orange halter top. Shaina distinctly recalled this was not what April had been wearing when the clown took her; it must have redressed her. Straps held the girl's arms outstretched, and her legs spread on a giant wheel similar to ones used by gamblers, or magicians.

And April was not alone.

The clown stood in front of her, placing tape over her mouth and stifling her screams.

"What do we do?" Amber asked, her voice choked with emotion.

Christopher pulled Amber closer to him. He tried to shield her eyes, but she refused to look away. Shaina thought she was brave for that. Shaina wanted to look away, but she couldn't, either. She needed to know — to see — what was about to happen.

The clown spun the wheel. Momentum took over, and the wheel turned in a continuous motion. Each time April's head came to its lowest point, her hair hung down and brushed the floor of the stage.

Shaina noticed the clown wore a brown leather vest over the brightly colored, yet dingy costume. The garment, too, had not been on the clown when it took April.

The clown turned to its audience and opened the vest to show the insides of the garment. Shaina could see the six throwing knives tucked into slots, three on each side of the vest.

The clown reached in with a flourish and removed one of the knives. The clown then lifted the dagger over his head, holding it straight up by the blade. The clown stayed in this position for several seconds and then let the knife fly.

The crowd screamed in unison.

April fought against her restraints, eyes wide with terror. The knife hit under her left arm as the wheel continued to turn.

The girl uttered a muffled scream against the tape sealed to her mouth.

It isn't an act; it's a cat toying with a mouse. "He's going to kill her. We have to get her out." Then another thought hit Shaina: *we are all the mouse.*

Christopher jumped onto the stage. He circled the cage, searching for a way inside. "Hang in there, April. We'll get you out. We'll help you. Just hang in there, girl."

Christopher tried to climb the bars, but it was no use. The bars were vertical, with no horizontal bars to stand on. He managed to climb halfway up before sliding back down. Even if he managed to get to the top, Shaina saw no way in from up there. She did spot large braided wire cables attached to iron rings at the top of the cage. The cables extended upward, higher than she could see.

Inside the cage, the clown threw another knife at the spinning girl, and the blade embedded in the wood between April's thighs with a thud. The girl seemed too far gone to comprehend what was happening to her. She babbled against the tape, crying and laughing all at once.

"She's losing it," Shaina said.

"No, she's already gone," Dashiell said.

Rachael looked at him with tear- and rage-filled eyes. "No, she's going to be okay. We'll find a way to get her out." Rachael climbed up onto the stage and went as close to April as she could get. "You'll be okay. Do you hear me? You're going to be okay."

If April heard her, she gave no sign.

As the clown threw the third knife, the weapon hit above April's right arm. Rachael squeaked and fell back. Shaina watched the clown ready the fourth knife. Rachael rolled off the stage and took refuge low to the floor, where the clown would not be able to reach her with the knife if he threw it at her.

The clown's focus did not waver from April, however.

The fourth blade spun through the air. Shaina watched as it tumbled, moving as if in slow motion. Christopher stopped trying to climb the bars, and he watched the knife as well. There was a collective gasp as the blade stuck into the wood between April's legs. The knife stuck precisely in the center of the circle.

But still, the blade did not touch her skin.

April's wide, bloodshot eyes stared at nothing. *She's no longer here with us.*

Dashiell's right. The shock has blinded her and destroyed her mind.

Rachael returned to the edge of the stage, though she didn't climb back up, and talked soothingly to April. Amber was there, too.

"I'm gonna kill you, Motherfucker." Spittle flew from Christopher's lips. "I'm gonna fucking kill —"

The fifth knife embedded in April's right eye.

Gina screamed and turned away.

The clown's final knife flew out and struck in the girl in the throat.

The crowd stared in, stunned silence. The clown walked over to April's still spinning, limp body, and removed the blades. Reaching behind the wheel, the clown must have flipped a switch, because the wheel stopped spinning. Blood dripped from her wounds and soaked into her hair as she hung nearly upside down.

The clown charged toward Christopher, and the man jumped back, but after reaching half the distance, the clown disappeared.

Christopher explained why. "There is a trap door. He ducked down a secret doorway in the floor of the stage."

A few seconds later, the whirring sound of machinery started, and the cage began to rise. Christopher waited until enough space had appeared, then crawled beneath the cage and rushed to April, unbuckling the straps that still held her to the wheel. The limp body dropped into his arms, and he carefully lowered her to the floor.

When the cage reached its apex, the machinery stopped. Amber rushed over to cradle April's head as Shaina tested her for a pulse. Finding none, Shaina dropped her hand away, not needing to report her findings.

Christopher stomped over to the trap door and began kicking at it. The thick, oak wooden door wouldn't budge.

Miss Helen stood off the stage, looking up. "I would suggest you all get off there before he decides to drop that cage again. You'll all be trapped."

Christopher and Dashiell lifted April off the floor and carried her off the stage. The others followed. They gathered in a nook created by the side of the stage and another adjacent building. Christopher laid April prone on the floor and folded her arms across her chest.

The survivors sat on the floor and stared at her still form.

Chapter Eighteen: Rachael

April's dead body invoked no emotion for Rachael. She was happy that someone had covered it up, but that was all. She had tried to think of the group but had failed. Every fiber of her body told her that only she would be responsible for her survival. She suspected any one of these people trapped here with her would throw her to the wolf (or clown) if it meant saving their own asses. She didn't trust them to keep her safe; that's what it boiled down to, she supposed.

Rachael had lived an entire lifetime in the last six hours. Had it only been that long since she came to be in this hellish place? Rachael had seen the love of her life die, and then the woman who stole her love also die. In another world, this would have been bittersweet justice, but right now, all she felt was numb. When she stared at the dead woman, Rachael saw her impending death mirrored there.

She looked around at the others with her. The elderly couple had come after Alan died. The older woman didn't look strong enough to deal with what was happening to them. Rachael felt shocked that the old lady, Cary Lynn, had not fallen victim to the maniac clown. The woman would serve her purpose, Rachael guessed, when running for their lives, and the old woman was slow to get away. Cary would fall behind and die, allowing the faster, younger of the group to survive.

Gina had confided to Rachael that the clown had killed the man who had brought her to the fair. She had also revealed to Rachael that the man, Larry, had raped her on the Ferris Wheel. Gina only said it shocked her, but Rachael thought maybe Gina was afraid to admit she liked seeing the rapist die. Gina had then met up with the old couple and admitted she felt a little responsible for them, looking out for their wellbeing.

You are responsible for your own wellbeing, Rachael had said to Gina. *Remember that.* Gina had not responded, but the girl had begun following Rachael around like a lost puppy. Rachael didn't mind; Having Gina close at hand prove useful.

Rachael studied the good-looking black guy and his bleach-blond girlfriend, Christopher, and Amber. Rachael hated Amber, the nosy bitch. She sensed Amber looking back at her with a furrowed brow and a frown on her lips. There was no doubting that Amber hated Rachael back.

The new guy and his woman—women? Don't forget about the psychic—couldn't be trusted. He owned the fair. Rachael found it hard to believe someone could own a place and not know about the abomination beneath it, killing people in an underground torture chamber. Also, Rachael thought the psychic knew more than she was letting on.

She stood and walked past the others, walking closer to the corpse manikins. She wasn't afraid of a few dead bodies, and she needed to find a way out. She studied the corpses as she passed them.

"Don't go far," Dashiell said. "We need to stay in sight of each other."

She glanced over her shoulder, but she didn't answer him.

Rachael walked between the displays, marveling at the artistry that went into creating these atrocious attractions. Some seemed to be recently killed and displayed, while still others were mummified and had been there a while.

There was a stink in the place, but it didn't emanate rot. Rachael thought it smelled more like a chemical odor. Not just cleaning supplies, but something medicinal as well. She compared it to the smell of a hospital bathroom.

As Rachael walked among the dead things, Gina came up from behind her. She stared at Gina for a time until the girl explained herself.

"I volunteered to walk with you."

"I don't need a tour guide."

"I know," Gina said. "I don't think we should be walking around alone. Don't you think we're safer as a group?"

"Ask April. She was in a group when he took her. If that asshole wants us, he'll march right into the middle of our group and take us, one by one. Who's going to stop him?"

Rachael could see Gina thinking about this. She had no response, which told Rachael Gina knew this was true.

"Even so, are you saying you don't want company?"

Rachael was silent for a while before answering. "No, you can stay."

They walked in silence for a while.

Finally, Rachael said. "Why aren't we looking for a way out of here? Why are we following the word of the man who probably led us here? I want to get out."

"We all want to get out. But we've also been here long enough to get the gist that we can't just stumble onto a way out. We either have to be shown a way out by the clown — which I don't think he's inclined to do, at least not on purpose — or we have to be rescued by someone from the outside."

"Anyone from the outside is just going to get trapped in here like us. There's no way out, and I'm thinking we are all going to die down here."

Rachael heard Gina swallow hard next to her.

"I'd rather not give up just yet."

There was more silence before Rachael spoke again. "I notice you don't look at the bodies in the displays."

Gina looked at her feet and shook her head. "No, I can't. They make my skin crawl. I can't end up like them, either."

Rachael stopped walking. "Are you thinking that if you don't acknowledge them, you won't end up like them?"

"No." Gina caught Rachael's eyes and held her gaze. "I just don't want to risk losing my mind and end up like April, and I think that's what will happen if I think too hard about where we are."

Rachael looked up at the ceiling, which was about thirty feet above their heads. "I think we're close to a wall, and I want to find a way out. There has to be a way out of here. That's the only thing that's going to save us. I'm not sitting around waiting for that thing to take me, or for a rescue that's never going to come."

"And I agree with you. That's why I'm here and not back there with the others."

Rachael didn't voice her next thought. *When we find a way out, will you go back and tell them, or leave?* Rachael would not go back but thought she *would*, at the very least, tell someone about the others trapped down there, but only after Rachael, herself, had reached safety. Did that make her a terrible person? She didn't think so. It made her smart.

They had moved around the fake rides with the corpse manikin riders until Rachael thought she might not remember how to get back to the others. She found their way out of the maze of oddities to a place where there was nothing for maybe half a football field, and in the distance, she saw a wall.

"Do you remember how to get back?" Rachael asked.

Gina turned and looked back the way they had come. "I think so. If we follow a straight line from there..."

"I'm not going back. You head back. I'm going to follow the wall around and look for a door out of here. They can sit around and wait to die if they want, but I want to live."

"I want to live," Gina said. "Can I come with?"

Rachael shrugged. "Do what you want."

Without another word, Rachael turned and ran.

As she reached the wall, Rachael stopped and looked in both directions, but could see no end in either direction. The sight of the wall going on into the unseen distance caused her vertigo to make her head spin.

Huffing, out of breath, Gina finally caught up to her.

Rachael looked at her but said nothing. She turned to the wall instead and studied it. A mixture of cement blocks, sandstone bricks, and mortar holding the materials together made up the barrier. She looked one way then the other, not sure which way to start.

"It could take us a month and we still might not find a way out," Gina said, having caught her breath.

"Wishing you had stayed behind with the others?"

Gina didn't answer. Rachael took that as a yes.

"It's not as bad as it looks," Rachael said. "The wall curves; it's circular, or oval. We could probably walk all the way around in a few hours."

"What way should we start then?"

"I guess we should head this way." Rachael pointed to her right. "I think this way will lead us back the way we came. Even if we don't find a way out of here, we will at least get out of this huge room of death. What do you say?"

Gina shrugged and gestured for her to lead the way.

They walked for several yards in silence. Gina's pace seemed to slow. Rachael turned to face her.

"What's wrong with you? Are you tired already? You're a pretty girl, but chubby. It's what I expected."

Gina scowled. "It's not that. Let's go back to the others."

"Go back then. I'm not stopping you." Rachael turned and started walking again.

"You don't think we should both go back?"

Rachael didn't answer. Well, she did—the answer was no. After a few seconds, Rachael heard Gina's tennis sneakers slapping at the stone floor coming closer. When Gina caught up, she slowed to Rachael's pace and walked beside her.

"What are the others doing right now? Do you think they are looking for us?" Gina asked.

"No, I think they are still sitting around April's corpse, moaning about how she died, when they should be thinking about how to save themselves." Rachael's pace quickened. "I think I see a doorway up ahead."

Gina saw it, too. They ran ahead, following the curvature of this bizarre, round room. When they reached what they thought was a door, they stopped. What they thought was a door was only a different shade of bricks.

"Well, there's no doorway, so I guess we keep walking until we reach that first door we originally came through."

Gina nodded.

They started walking again.

"Do you think the door is one way, like all the others we came across?" Gina asked.

"I don't know. We'll figure it out then, I guess," Rachael said. She hoped the girl would stop talking now.

Gina continued. "I can't wait to get out of here. Even if it is to go back the way we came. I hate this room. And it's cold in here."

Rachael didn't respond.

Gina said nothing more, and they walked in silence for several minutes.

"The first thing I'm going to do when I get out of here is to take a shower," Gina said, breaking the silence. "I feel grimy from rutting around in this dingy, dirty place. I feel like I have spider webs in my hair and an inch of dirt on my skin." She made a sound with her mouth that suggested she had remembered something else. "I want a bubble bath. I want to soak the dirt off." She giggled.

Rachael said nothing, but the silence didn't deter the girl.

"After that, I'm going to eat until I barf. I'm starving."

They were quiet again for several minutes.

Rachael felt an uneasy twang in her belly. She glanced around; were they still alone? If the clown approached, it would be exposed long enough to allow Rachael time to run. If he came from the back or the front, she would see it coming. The only other direction it could come from was the displays, but it would leave its hiding place and be exposed long enough to give her time to run. Rachael felt confident she could outrun Gina.

As they walked on, Rachael saw a change in the wall up ahead. She believed it was a doorway. She still wasn't sure if it was the same door they had initially come through or another door, but she didn't care.

"Do you see the doorway?" She asked Gina.

The girl squinted in the dim light. "Yeah, I think so."

Their pace quickened as they grew closer to where they believed to be a door.

Rachael glanced back, then looked toward the displays but saw no movement. They would be back in the narrow passageways soon, where the clown could not ambush them. She encouraged Gina to hurry with a touch on the other girl's arm.

They reached the doorway in a matter of minutes, but their hopes came to an end when they could not find a latch for opening the door.

"God damn that freak and these stupid one-way doors, anyhow." Rachael kicked the door.

The door rattled in its frame then slowly creaked forward a few inches.

"It's open." Gina pulled the door the rest of the way open. She peered into the darkness beyond. "There was light when we came through the first time."

"I don't think this is the way we came in." Rachael didn't enter the doorway.

"Then maybe it's the way out." Gina's voice went higher in pitch with her growing excitement.

"Do you have a phone with a charge and a flashlight feature on it? We have to be able to see where we are going. I'm not entering any dark places."

"No, I don't. I dropped my phone when I fell. I never found it."

"Then we should keep going and find the door we came through originally. I don't trust this to be the way out." Rachael took two steps from the door, stopped, and turned to see if Gina was following. Gina hadn't moved.

"I think we should risk it."

Rachael shook her head. "I spent enough time in the dark to know I don't want to do it again. Anyway, even if it is the way out, we'll probably fall into one of those traps before we get to the exit."

After a moment of hesitation, Gina turned away from the darkened doorway and walked toward Rachael. It didn't take them long to reach the door leading back the way they came. There was a handle, and the door opened. The lighting was dim, but they could see beyond the threshold. Rachael recognized the room beyond.

"This is the way we came. Christopher noticed a door we didn't take because of his fear of traps. It could be the way out. Do you want to take it?"

"And possibly get out of here? Of course." Gina didn't hesitate and passed through the doorway. Rachael followed Gina, staying close behind but not getting too close. Rachael continued her survey of the surroundings, expecting the clown to appear at any moment. She considered warning Gina to slow down, but the girl was on a mission.

As they reached the second door, Rachael tried to reach out and stop Gina. "Slow down. Keep in mind that we aren't safe here."

Gina continued. "We're so close. I'm sure the way out is through here."

Gina opened the door and moved forward.

"Hold up, Gina. Isn't this where we saw the—" *trap*. Rachael didn't get to finish her thought.

When Gina stopped, Rachael thought it was because the bars in front of her had blocked her path. When the steel barriers lifted, Gina slowly turned to face Rachael. The blood pouring over Gina's face confused Rachael. As Gina fell forward, Rachael saw the bloody, gaping hole in Gina's head. Realizing the girl had been impaled caused Rachael to slip into hysterics. Rachael screamed and ran back the way she had come, intent on returning to the others. She headed back to the umbrella room and ran headlong for the safety of the displays.

Rachael hit the exhibitions and began weaving through them. She tried to lose herself in the bigger machine parts. A pulse thumped in her neck, feeling like a fist tightening around her throat. Her uncontrollable fear caused a tight pain to seize her back, and she struggled not to cry.

Rachael fell headlong and skidded to a stop. With scraped hands, she crawled toward a nearby hulk of metal. She stood and took account of her injuries. She was hurting, but there was no severe damage. She moved to another display, staying low. She thought she was going toward the others but had no way of knowing for sure. She didn't dare call out to them and risk drawing the clown to her, but it didn't matter. She didn't think she was close enough for them to hear her.

When she heard the sound of something rustling nearby, she froze, staying low. Above her, a male corpse with a smile on its face peered down at her. The sight chilled her to the bone. She willed it to look away.

Rachael moved to the other side of the display and looked around. Still, she did not see anything. She rested with the presentation to her back and thought about her next move. She could move to the left or the right, but there was nothing straight ahead to hide behind. When she looked to the left again, she saw nothing. She ran to the next display, slid behind it, and looked back. There was nothing there.

She searched her surroundings for her next plan of action.

Somewhere far off, she heard the calliope music of the merry-go-round. She thought if she could make it there, the sound could mask her movements. The others couldn't be far from there, either. She would be safe with them.

Rachael looked around, stood, and ran for the next horror display. As she reached it, she dropped to the floor and rolled to hide behind it. She scurried up next to the exhibition and listened. She still heard the tinny, warbling music but nothing else. She peered around the display but could not see the clown.

She stood and turned.

The clown was there, driving a knife into her belly. Rachael looked down. The blade went so deep she could only see the hilt. The clown dragged the knife across the flesh of her stomach. As the weapon came free, a wound seemed to open like a wet, red mouth, and then the ropy organs began to spill out, red and glistening. Rachael caught them with one hand desperately trying to keep her insides in. She glanced up at the clown and saw the eyes peering at her from behind the mask. They were gray eyes, cold eyes, a murderer's eyes. She brought her free hand up with the palm out as if to say stop.

The clown flicked out with the knife. Rachael had a moment of feeling something tug at her throat, and then something hot and sticky and wet was running over her breasts before her world turned black.

Chapter Nineteen: Shaina

She found a dirty, tattered old sheet in the small shack near the stage and covered April with it. She did it for the dignity, but also, she did it because looking at the dead girl was giving her the creeps.

Dashiell had gone to try and find Rachael and Gina, but he hadn't been successful and returned soon after.

Christopher had spent nearly an hour looking for weapons while Clifford, Cary Lynn, and Amber huddled together. Shaina tried to keep up spirits by asking people about themselves. She learned that Clifford and Cary Lynn met in Central Park at a water fountain fifty years ago. He tried to get a drink, and the water shot out over the basin, soaking Cary. They had been inseparable ever since.

"I met Christopher at a Drake concert," Amber said. "I was with a bunch of girlfriends, and he was there with his girlfriend. He said that when he saw me, he broke it off with the girl straight away. I had no idea if it was true or not, but it sounded romantic at the time." Amber released a little giggle. "He asked me out several times, and I responded with a resounding no every time. We became friends first, but one night after losing track of time, we fell asleep on the couch in my parents' basement. When I woke up, he was kissing me. I chased him off, even though I secretly to say yes to his offer to date. " Amber turned her eyes away and spoke in a shy, low voice. "We made love for the first time on that ratty old couch."

"He sounds like a charming guy," Shaina said.

"He'll die to protect me." Amber glanced over at Christopher. He wasn't in earshot of Amber's conversation with Shaina, and he was not paying attention to them anyway. "I don't want him to do that. I can't imagine my life without him."

Shaina had offered her a tissue from her pocket when a tear rolled down Amber's cheek. Amber dabbed at it, but the worn fabric left flecks of fibers on her skin. Shaina brushed them off, and they laughed about it.

When the laughter stopped, Shaina said, "It does no one any good to think bad thoughts. We'll get through this, you'll see."

They hugged, and Shaina moved on.

As Shaina walked around and made sure everyone was comfortable and safe, she noticed that Miss Helen was watching her. Shaina sat down beside the psychic.

"I'm curious to get your take on what's happened. Do you have any insights into what we are going through?"

"The deaths certainly sadden me," Miss Helen said.

"You're a regular chatterbox, aren't you? Don't your ghost friends have any useful information?"

"I'm sorry to say that, for the most part, they are not willing to help us. The dead are suspicious and jealous of our lives."

"So, they will stay quiet and are willing to let us die?"

"They have little interest in us."

Shaina tried to think of a diplomatic way to ask her next question, but nothing seemed quite as useful as the ugly truth. "You're not holding out on us, then?"

Miss Helen sighed. "I promise, I'm not holding out on you. If or when anything occurs to me, I'll let you know. I won't leave you behind."

"I didn't mean—"

"I know you didn't mean it that way. I do have enough insight to know who my friends are. And I do consider you a friend." She smiled. "I only hope you can think of me the same way."

Shaina placed a gentle hand on the other woman's arm. "I do. I never thought I was in any danger from you. Call *me* psychic."

Leaning their heads in, they both laughed a little.

Miss Helen stood and surveyed her surroundings. "So here we are, surrounded by corpses, being hunted by a killer on the loose. Still, there's no need for everyone to be so gloomy. Let's do something fun."

Amber and Christopher scowled at her. Cary Lynn looked at her with a mixture of confusion and concern. Clifford huffed and turned away.

"No takers?" Miss Helen shrugged. "I was going to suggest charades."

"Yeah, I don't think that's going to happen," Dashiell said.

"I keep thinking about those two girls," said Cary Lynn. "Do you think they found a way out?"

No one answered. Shaina thought that maybe they did, just not the way they had hoped.

After a long moment of silence, Cary Lynn spoke again. "A forest of corpses."

The group turned and glared at her.

"What?" Shaina asked.

"That's what I see all around. We are in the center of a forest of corpses."

Clifford tugged at his wife's sleeve. "My dear, people think you're nutty enough. Don't prove them right."

Cary Lynn swatted at him. "Shut your mouth."

Christopher stood and walked over to the stage. He turned around and leaned on it. "I've been thinking about that trap door. I think it might be our way out of here." He turned and hopped up on the stage's platform. "I want to pry it open."

"No, Chris." Amber rushed to him. "If that cage comes down again, you'll be trapped."

"Only if I can't get it open." Christopher pushed off the stage and headed toward one of the displays, searching it by moving parts around. When the corpse attached to it swayed, he fell backward with a yelp.

"Did you think it was coming to life?" Clifford laughed until he coughed.

"You might be onto something, Chris," Dashiell said and strode over to another display to do what Christopher had done. He found a metal bar and broke it off the horse from a junked carousel. He carried it to the stage and tossed it onto the platform. The bar clanged, and the echo carried up, bouncing off the high ceiling. Dashiell jumped up onto the stage and retrieved the bar. Christopher followed him with a similar makeshift weapon.

They worked at the trap door for several long minutes while the others watched. Shaina looked up several times, waiting for the cage to come down.

Christopher's steel bar slipped from his grip and clanged loudly to the platform. "Shit." He placed a hand in his mouth and sucked at the cut he received when the bar slipped. He dropped his hand. "This wood is too damn hard. And the seal is solid. We aren't getting this thing open without an ax."

Dashiell stopped as well. "You're right. But keep your bar. We can defend ourselves with them if the clown shows up."

The men came down off the stage.

Amber wrapped her arms around Christopher's neck and kissed his face. "I was worried about you."

Dashiell approached Shaina.

"And I was worried about you," she said.

"Where's my kiss?"

Shaina smiled and turned away. She wasn't sure why—she certainly wanted to kiss him. Shaina thought her reluctance had to do with the way he asked, almost as if demanding it. She kissed no one on command, not even her husband. Well, no one except her kids.

"I was thinking we should start moving again," Dashiell said. "I wanted to run it by you first before I propose it to the others."

"What about April?"

Dashiell seemed confused. "What about her?"

"We can't just leave her here, can we?"

Dashiell glanced over at the sheet covering the body. He turned back to Shaina. "We have to. We don't know where we're going, and we can't drag her along. When we get out, we can send someone back for her."

She didn't like the idea. She didn't like the idea of leaving their current spot, but she supposed they had to if they wanted to find a way out of there. Reluctantly, she nodded her approval of the idea.

"Okay, great. I'll talk it over with the others." He walked away.

Shaina turned and spotted Miss Helen, leaning over and talking to herself. She walked toward her. When the psychic saw her, she stood up.

"I'm sorry to intrude." Shaina stared at the spot where the psychic had been looking but saw nothing there.

"No, you're not intruding. I've been asking the apparitions that come to me if they know how to get out of here."

"And what do they say?"

"Nothing. Either the dead either don't know what's going on here or don't understand my requests. Maybe they can't hear me and don't understand what I'm trying to say. And there's something else."

Shaina was almost too afraid to ask. "What?"

Miss Helen closed her eyes and sighed. "The others didn't make it. Gina and Rachael are among the dead."

Shaina didn't know how to take that. For some reason, she believed the woman, but she couldn't allow herself to feel anything for the news, not yet. She nodded. Shaina turned to go but stopped. "Oh, Dashiell thinks we should head out and look for an exit. What do you think about that?"

"I'm okay with it," Miss Helen said.

Shaina returned to the rest of the group, where Dashiell had finished telling the others, one by one, about his plan to leave their present position. They stood face to face.

"Everyone is on board," Dashiell said. "Did you talk to our resident soothsayer?"

"She's okay with it, too. She told me something else. She said Gina and Rachael are dead. Should we believe her?"

Dashiell shrugged.

"Should we tell the others?"

"No." He shook his head with his eyes closed. "Definitely not. We don't know for sure it's true, and there's no need to panic everyone over what she said."

"She has no reason to lie that I see. But what if *she* tells the others?"

"I don't care what she does." Dashiell glanced at Miss Helen and then back to Shaina. "I still don't trust her."

Shaina peered around. She still didn't like looking at the corpses, with their fake poses, and their tragic stories, but tried to look between the displays, at places where she could hide.

"Do you have a plan?" She turned to face him. "For getting out?"

"Not really. I don't think to stay here is a very plausible plan of action."

"But is leaving the stage the right decision? Don't you still think the trap door in the stage is the way out?"

"Honestly, I never thought it was. I was supporting Christopher's plan. He seemed to think it would lead us out. I think the answer is going—" Dashiell pointed up. "Going deeper into this place feels more like a trap than a solution to our problem."

"This whole place is a trap. I don't think we are meant to leave." Shaina's voice was a whisper.

Dashiell sighed. "I was hoping you wouldn't pick up on that. But you're too smart not to see it as a possibility."

"I'm sure I'm not the only one to come to that conclusion," she said.

Dashiell shrugged. "Christopher might have come to that conclusion, but Amber looks too naïve to think in such extremes, and he won't tell her. He's too protective to put that kind of burden on her."

Shaina laughed slightly, covering her mouth. "Did you just politely call Amber a dumb blonde?"

Dashiell smiled. "Not at all."

"How about this?" she said. "If we're going to live, we have to kill the clown. I propose that we don't leave here. Instead, we should make a stand. Set a trap for the clown and kill him."

"I second that idea." Christopher came from behind Shaina and now stepped forward.

Dashiell and Shaina shared a look. *Did Christopher hear our conversation?* If he did, he gave no indication.

"Okay," Dashiell said after collecting himself. "How should we go about setting up this trap?"

Shaina looked around. "First of all, we need a weapon: all of us. We'll have to scrounge around for something each of us can use with which to fight back. I, for one, have children I want to see again. I'm not going down without a fight. I want something that will cut. I know where to cut to inflict the most damage. I suggest the rest of you get blunt tools for bludgeoning."

"Okay, but what about the trap?" asked Christopher.

She pointed to the junk surrounding them. "These displays are set up for the clown's convenience. We rearrange them to be a hindrance and optimal for us. We create a perimeter of debris and get him to trip and stumble over the stuff we've placed in his way. When he is off-balance, we attack."

"Kind of a weak plan." Dashiell scratched at his chin.

"Do you have a better one?"

He lowered his head. "No, so I guess your plan is fine."

"I hope you like the next part then. Someone has to move some of the bodies. Will you be willing to do that?"

Dashiell visibly swallowed hard, but he nodded. Christopher also agreed to help move bodies.

"We can put them in that little snack food shack next to the stage."

They started with the displays closest to them. When they had moved several of the bodies, the others came to help disassemble the machine parts and align them, as Shaina suggested.

"The clown has to wade through the junk to get to us. When it's off-kilter, vulnerable, that's when we strike."

Shaina continued to direct the others with tasks, and everyone did as requested of them. She kept her head up and her words firm. By default, the group designated her as the leader. They liked her plan and seemed happy to finally have something to do other than sitting around, waiting to be picked off. This thing—this clown—had been killing for years. She had seen the corpses. Some down to nothing but bones. How presumptuous she felt to think she could beat this thing at its own game? Her biggest fear was that she would tell someone what to do, and they would get killed because of her. She refused to allow her doubts to show on her face or in her actions. As she looked out at the others, she saw smiles. She heard laughter. She saw hope. Only a few short minutes ago, she had been looking at a defeated group of people. They had given up hope of getting out of this. Now, there were limitless possibilities.

"Miss Shaina," Cary Lynn said.

Shaina blinked away her thoughts and glanced at the older woman. "Yes?"

"I'm just wondering about something. Even if we manage to end this sucker..." She balled up her fist and slapped it into the palm of the other hand. "How is that going to help us get out of here?"

Shaina placed her hands gently on the woman's shoulders. She leaned down to look into the woman's rheumy eyes. "Before I came in here, we were looking for that woman over there." She pointed to Miss Helen. "There are cops and fair workers out there now looking for us. And they are going to find us. They will figure out where we are. We have to stay alive until they do. Understand?"

The woman pressed her lips together. Hope shined in her blue eyes like starlight. Cary Lynn took one of Shaina's hands in both her small, frail ones, and lifted it to her lips, kissed it. They hugged, and the woman walked away.

The work went on for another half an hour before Shaina told them to take a break.

"Is that a good idea?" Dashiell said. "That thing could come at us at any minute. Shouldn't we keep going so we're ready?"

"We have a good start on the trap. It won't do us any good if we are exhausted when the attack comes. We have to rest, especially our older folks."

Dashiell nodded.

Shaina felt terrible that she had nothing to give them to drink. They were all thirsty. Hunger was one thing, but thirst sapped your energy.

She walked over to the old couple and sat down next to them. She started with Cary Lynn. "Do you mind if I do a quick little exam on you?"

She shrugged. "Okay."

Shaina took the older woman's wrist in her hand, and with two fingers, felt the pulse. She had no stopwatch or another way to count the seconds visually, so she had to rely on her previous experience. She was looking for a sluggish pulse, a sign of dehydration. Her pulse seemed strong and steady. She was a robust old gal.

When Shaina finished, Cary Lynn placed her hands on her cheeks. She looked like the screamer in that old painting. "What's your diagnosis, doc? Give it to me straight. I can take it."

Shaina smiled. "You are one tough cookie. You're in perfect health."

Cary Lynn reached her hands out and wrapped them around Shaina's waist. She hugged Shaina with her cheek resting on Shaina's chest. When they parted, Shaina examined Clifford. He, too, was in great shape. That put Shaina's mind at ease.

"So, what do you say?" she asked the couple. "Back to work?"

Without another word, they all stood and returned to the task at hand.

She helped Dashiell pull a large sheet of metal into their perimeter when she saw that he was struggling. They laid it over some of the other objects. If the clown came from that direction, he would have to climb over the metal, and with the uneven layer of objects beneath it, this would mimic the unbalanced floor gag in the funhouse. He would have to crawl or get thrown around as the sheet of metal changed position. Dashiell tested it by trying to walk across it, but only managed to fall. He hit the ground and rolled. To get back to his feet, he had to crawl through the debris to a clearing.

"I think this is going to work." Clifford stopped dragging the strongman mallet long enough to watch Dashiell fall. He mimicked holding the hammer over his head and clubbing Dashiell in the head. "You're dead, clown."

Laughing, Clifford set the mallet on its hammer and helped Dashiell to his feet.

Amber and Christopher found some broken benches and placed them in the perimeter upside down, creating little hills and valleys that would be sure to slow anyone down who tried to climb over them.

Miss Helen came over to Shaina and held something out on her open palm. "Can you use this as a weapon?"

Shaina studied the six-inch shard of glass, looked around, and picked up a dirty, threadbare tee shirt. She wrapped one end of the shard in the shirt and held it out as if admiring a sword.

"Thank you," she said. "This might work."

The piece of glass was Miss Helen's only contribution to their little endeavor. Still, Shaina supposed it was enough since everyone else was doing well at turning their location into a hazardous obstacle course.

Shaina studied her team's hard work. A couple of broken-down carousel horses covered a bucket seat from an unknown ride, and a bench seat with its torn leather exhibited rusty springs that jutted out like pubic hairs. A perimeter of haphazard and dangerous objects surrounded them. With the trap set, there was nothing left to do but wait and see if it worked.

God, she hoped it worked.

Cary Lynn collapsed onto the floor, and her husband dropped down next to her. Christopher continued moving objects around, trying to get the most effective positions out of each piece of rubble. At last count, twenty corpses occupied the shack. Amber looked exhausted, disheveled. Amber looked exactly like Shaina felt. As Shaina looked out at the surrounding trap, her first thought was of the rings of Saturn, but then began to wonder if she had trapped them. They must have looked like goldfish in a bowl, and the clown need only reach in and snatch them out, one by one.

Shaina forced the negative thoughts out of her head: the perimeter will work. She believed what she said to Cary Lynn. The authorities were surrounding the fairgrounds and would find them. They had to survive until help arrived.

Dashiell sat to her right, one hand held the metal bar he kept strung across his lap, and his other hand was holding hers. He squeezed her hand, and she looked at him. Dashiell smiled at her, sensing her doubts. He used his eyes to tell her that he believed in her plan — in her.

"You're beautiful," he said in a whisper that only she could hear.

She leaned over and kissed his cheek.

"How long will we have to wait?" Clifford asked.

"Hopefully, we will still be sitting like this when the police come crashing in," Dashiell said. "Maybe the bastard will see what we did and not come back."

Shaina did hope that the deterrent would keep him away. Something told her they were in for a significant fight, however. She glanced down at the shard in her hand not holding Dashiell's hand. She planned to stick it in his femoral artery, or the popliteal, behind the knee, or if she could access his abdomen, she would attack his inferior vena cava. Any one of those locations would give the monster only minutes to live.

Everyone held something with which to fight. The men each had a heavy steel bar, Cary Lynn and Amber both took broken broom handles that could be used to bludgeon, or to stick with at the broken end. Miss Helen wielded a small hammer. She would have to get close with that one, so Shaina told her to hang back and only use it if the clown was brought down. A fatal blow to the head would be the psychic's contribution.

"I feel kind of excited," Cary Lynn said. "Like we're residents in an old western, defending our little town from an adversarial force coming to take away what is ours." She shook her piece of wood.

"Yeah, well, you hang back and let the men deal with this," Clifford said. "I don't want you getting hurt."

Cary Lynn scowled. "I'm in this fight, too. I can hold my own."

"I'm sure you can," Shaina said. "Even still, I think you should hang back, too."

Cary Lynn said nothing.

Shaina was afraid the woman would get in the way, but she didn't want to say that to her. It would surely hurt the old girl's feelings, and she didn't want that.

"Do it for me," Shaina said.

Reluctantly, Cary Lynn nodded.

A moment of silence ticked out the seconds. Shaina almost wanted to scream, to clear the tension. Instead, she looked up at the ceiling, where lights dangled from the trusses. These lights were what lit up the warehouse. She also noted massive stone pillars holding up the roof. She also wondered where the fair was above them. She thought maybe the area around the Ferris Wheel was above them.

Cary Lynn's voice broke the silence. "Oh, goodness gracious me. We're going to die. We're all going to die."

All heads turned to her. She pointed.

The clown stood at the outer perimeter of the clutter. It made no move to enter the ring of debris. Shaina stared at the clown, and it seemed to stare back at her. She waited. The clown moved along the rim of the clutter as if looking for a way in without much struggle. Shaina followed with her shiv gripped tightly in her hand. The clown stopped moving and seemed to study her. She did not flinch back from its gaze. The clown's head tilted to one side as if curiously studying a bug under a glass.

Christopher charged to the edge of the trash. "Come on, asshole."

The clown's gaze shifted from Shaina to Christopher. In a swift, fluid movement, too fast for Shaina to see, the clown produced a throwing dagger and flung it at Christopher.

Shaina screamed. Christopher dodged the knife, and it sailed over his head. The weapon skittered along the cement floor and disappeared into the debris on the opposite side of the ring.

"Oh, God." Amber rushed over to stand next to Christopher and hugged him. "He's throwing knives. April—"

Christopher touched her face. "But we aren't tied to a wooden wheel. We'll be okay. Go over there with the others and stay out of its line of sight."

The clown shot another knife at Shaina this time. She flew to the floor and rolled, and the blade missed her by inches. She scrambled to the edge of the debris field and found a flat piece of metal she used as a shield.

As she stood, Dashiell ran to her and checked her over.

"I'm okay," she said. "It didn't hit me."

"How many fucking knives does this asshole have?" Christopher said.

"We're sitting ducks." Dashiell moved into the junk. "We have to do something." He walked through the trash heap as if wading through waist-deep water.

"No, what are you doing?" Shaina reached out but missed him.

"We have to stop it."

Shaina followed Dashiell into the ring of junk. Christopher followed.

When the clown threw another dagger, Shaina deflected it with her makeshift shield. The clown produced three knives at once and flicked them all in a single motion. One knife missed, and a second bounced harmlessly off Shaina's shield, but the third stuck in Christopher's arm. He cried out in pain.

Amber screamed.

Christopher pulled the knife from his arm and continued charging at the clown. Now he held a pole in one hand and the throwing knife in the other.

The clown charged through the debris. It had very little trouble pushing the heaps of junk aside and moving toward them. It reached Christopher first. The man swung the pole at the clown's head, but it dodged the attack. Next, Christopher attacked with the knife, but the clown swiped an arm out and deflected the weapon. The weapon flew off and disappeared in the trash.

The clown lifted Christopher off the floor and heaved him several yards away. With a crash and clang of metal parts, Christopher disappeared below the surface of the debris. Amber burst out with an anguished cry and ran for him.

Shaina grabbed Dashiell's arm and pulled him back. "This isn't working. We have to go back and try something else."

Dashiell tried to shake off Shaina's grip, but her persistence paid off, and they returned to the group. Christopher made it back to Amber, and she worked on Christopher's wound. Shaina turned and saw that the clown was still moving through their barrier with alarming speed.

"It's not slowing him down at all," Shaina said.

Dashiell and Shaina gripped their weapons and moved to intercept the clown. Clifford joined them as Cary Lynn, and Miss Helen stayed behind to help Christopher and Amber.

As the clown came into range, Dashiell and Clifford beat at it with their metal poles. The clown's eyes focused on Shaina and showed very little interest in the attacks on its body. Shaina held the shard of glass out in front of her. She would gouge out its eyes if it got close enough. She waved the shard around, trying to intimidate the hulk. Her ploy didn't work, and the clown swatted Clifford out of the way and approached Shaina.

Dashiell smashed his metal rod over the back of the clown's head. The strike stopped the clown's forward motion, and it turned. Shaina used the moment to attack, but as she came into striking range of the clown, it backhanded her and sent her sprawling.

"Shaina." Dashiell ran toward her.

The clown lunged for him, but he dipped under the reaching arms and darted away. When the clown turned to follow Dashiell, Clifford was there and smashed his steep pole into the clown's face.

Dashiell helped Shaina to her feet. She glanced over and saw that her shard of glass had shattered into a bunch of useless pieces.

She watched as the clown chased Clifford, heading for the center where the rest of the group shrunk back. She thought she was about to watch as the group was slaughtered, trapped by *her* plan.

"God, no." She ran at the clown and jumped onto his back. "Get away. Save yourselves."

But no one moved.

The clown shrugged Shaina off. She scampered behind the clown and latched herself onto one of its legs. She felt something mushy and unnaturally soft beneath the cloth of the yellow pantleg. She didn't think it felt like flesh, and though the feeling unnerved her, she did not release her hold.

But she didn't hinder the clown as it continued toward the others.

Dashiell retrieved his metal bar and tried to use it like a spear and stab the clown in the back. The clown merely reached around and yanked the bar from Dashiell's grip, flung it away. It lifted the leg to which Shaina clung, and kicked out. Shaina was forced to release her hold and spun like a top into Amber and Clifford, sending them sprawling. Dizzy and disoriented, she tried to stand, but the clown knocked her aside again and picked Amber up from the floor. Christopher threw himself at the clown and Amber. He wrenched Amber from the monster's grip, and she tumbled to the floor. Christopher helped her to stand, and they scrambled out of the clown's reach.

Screaming, Amber ran and didn't stop running. Christopher chased after her. She ran through the debris field, tripping and getting back up and running again. She and Christopher disappeared into the jumble of horror displays beyond the circle of junk.

Dashiell ran at the clown, but with a free hand, it knocked him away. He ran and jumped on the clown's back. It shrugged him off like an overcoat, and Dashiell went down hard on his head. He didn't stand back up. Shaina ran to Dashiell with a sense of dread clutching at her throat.

The clown ignored them and gripped Clifford by the shirt, lifting the older man off the floor. Cary Lynn screamed, but Shaina couldn't help as she tended to Dashiell. She glanced around, searching for Miss Helen, but the psychic had vanished…again.

Just as Dashiell came awake, the clown forced Clifford to the floor on his stomach. As Clifford lay there face down, the clown pressed him into place with a clown shoe. Clifford struggled but could not shake loose of the clown.

Dashiell tried to stand but was unsteady on his feet. When he nearly fell, Shaina caught him.

"You may have a concussion. Take it easy." She let him lean on her.

The clown reached down and picked up Clifford's sledgehammer. Still holding Clifford down with one foot, the clown lifted the hammer over its head, as if playing the strongman game.

Shaina saw the hammer coming down but turned away before the impact. She pressed her face into Dashiell's chest but still heard the crunch of bone as the hammer crushed Clifford's skull. Dashiell held her head in place though Shaina was not trying to look at what was happening. She burst into tears when she heard Cary Lynn's inhuman moan. The older woman screamed, and Shaina turned in time to see the woman run at the clown. Shaina thought: *we have to stop her*, but she knew it was too late. Cary Lynn beat her small, ineffectual fists on the clown. She showed no sign that she knew she was in danger even when the clown lifted her by the throat. Cary continued hitting the clown until it crushed her throat. Her hands fell limp at her sides, and she slipped from the monster's grip, dropping like a pile of rags at its feet.

Then the clown looked at Shaina and Dashiell.

They hobbled away, Shaina still helping Dashiell to stay upright. They scuttled through the debris as the clown followed them, unhurriedly. As they reached the outer edge of the trash, Dashiell felt strong enough to walk alone. They ran for the nearest display, then found a pillar to hide behind. They turned and peered around the support in the direction they had come, but they could not see the clown anymore.

"Where did it go?" Dashiell whispered directly into Shaina's ear.

She didn't know. She tried to control her breathing, but the sound was like a hurricane blowing in her ears. When she got her breath under control, she turned to face Dashiell. Hot, wet tears stung her eyes. "He killed them."

"I know." His voice was thick with emotion and sympathy. His eyes glistened.

"I should go back. I might be able to help someone." When she moved to leave, Dashiell stopped her.

"You can't help them. You know this. Don't expose yourself."

She wanted to fight, to scream. She knew they were dead. She heard Clifford's skull crack. She had listened to the brittle bones in Cary Lynn's neck break. She closed her eyes and took a deep breath. She couldn't help the Javes's, but she might be able to help Amber and Christopher.

"Amber and Christopher ran off. We should try and find them, and..." She stopped because she didn't know what else they could do. Fight it? They had tried that, and it didn't work.

Could they have found a way out? Had they wasted precious minutes not looking for an exit on her recommendation? God, were their deaths her fault?

"I'm sorry."

Dashiell's words shocked her. "Sorry? You? Why?"

"You wanted to go home to your kids. I talked you into staying. Now we're here, and we're..."

"This isn't your fault." Her voice resonated with utter conviction. "You couldn't have known what would happen. I felt an obligation to stay, not because you tried to guilt me into staying, but because I wanted to help Miss Helen clear her name. I knew she had nothing to do with Billy's disappearance."

Dashiell touched Shaina's hand. "Where is she?"

Shaina closed her eyes and shook her head. "I just turned around, and she was gone. I don't know when, and I don't know where. She just vanished."

Dashiell peeked around the pillar and, satisfied they were not in danger, turned back to Shaina. "She's a resourceful lady. She'll take care of herself. If anyone can survive this, my bet is on her."

Shaina agreed Miss Helen was a survivor. The woman proved that time and again, but Shaina wasn't worried about Miss Helen. She wasn't even concerned about Amber and Christopher. As selfish as it sounded, Shaina was concerned for herself and Dashiell. She stood and helped Dashiell to stand.

"We should—" Shaina couldn't complete her thought because the clown was there, and it flung a knife directly at her chest.

Chapter Twenty: Christopher

He caught up to Amber when she tripped and fell. Christopher reached her as she lay on the cold, dirty floor, crying into her hands. He helped her up and used his shirt to wipe the tears from her face. Amber threw herself into his arms and hugged him tightly. They collapsed to the floor, and sat, still hugging one another. He held her until she could cry no more. She glanced up at him, and he smiled at her grimy, tear-streaked face.

"Why did you run, Baby?"

"I didn't mean to leave anyone behind," Amber said. "But I was just so scared. I was scared and didn't want to die."

"I know," Christopher said. "It's okay."

Amber sat up suddenly. "He had his hands on me." She shivered. "It was so disgusting to have that monster's hands on me. He...he..." She dropped back into his lap, sobbing. He leaned down and kissed her head.

"You're okay now."

Amber sat up again. "Did they get him? Did the plan work?"

"I don't know, Babe. When you ran, I ran after you. I couldn't leave you on your own. I didn't see what happened. It wasn't good, though. I don't think the plan worked."

Amber gritted her teeth. "It was a stupid plan anyway."

"Maybe, but it was all we had. It could have worked."

Amber shivered again.

When she had sufficiently recovered from the ordeal, Amber straightened up and sat cross-legged next to Christopher.

He studied her face. Her tears had dried up, and though her eyes were still red and puffy, it didn't diminish her beauty. He couldn't resist. He leaned over and kissed her mouth. She met him, and her lips parted.

They wrapped up in each other's embrace and stayed there for several minutes.

"Don't ever leave me," she said at last.

He pulled away and looked at her with a furrowed brow. "Never, Baby."

"I'm so scared."

He took her hand and pulled her closer. He looked her in the eye. "Me leaving you is not something you have to fear. Do you hear me?"

When she nodded, he took her chin and lifted her face. He kissed her again. She accepted his tongue eagerly. When they parted, he placed his arm around her shoulder and pulled her to him. He smelled her hair and could still detect the scent of her lavender shampoo. He kissed the top of her head.

She pulled away and sat, looking at him. "We shouldn't have abandoned the others. I'm sorry about that."

"It's not your fault. You have nothing to be sorry about."

"Do you think they were able to drive him away?"

He shrugged. "I hope so."

"Do you think she's right?" Amber asked.

"Who? About what?"

"Shaina said we have to hold out until the authorities find us. Was she just wishful thinking? Are we doomed to be trapped here until that thing kills us?"

Christopher took her by the shoulders and shook her lightly. "No. We are not giving up like that. As far as we know, Shaina was telling the truth. I—for one—believe her. The police are looking for the psychic lady. Remember when she told us to get out of line? She ran away, and not long after, the cops came by. She wasn't lying about that."

"We should have done what she said. Why didn't we get out of line?" New tears threatened to flow from her eyes.

"Don't dwell on that. What's done is done. We can't change what we did. All we have to do now is survive."

They hugged again, and Christopher's eyes wandered up to the corpse in the display closest to them. Its head leaned down slightly, and the sightless gaze seemed fixed on him. He gave an involuntary shudder of disgust.

Christopher stood and extended a hand to help Amber up. "We have to get away from here. I want to find someplace where I can't see these horrible exhibitions of dead people. I want open space between the clown and us, so I can see if he's coming for us. I'll look for a weapon, and if he finds us, I'm going to kill him. It's our best chance to stay alive until the cops find us."

"Can we get moving now? I don't want to be around these corpses anymore. I swear that one keeps looking at me." She pointed at the same cadaver Christopher had noticed only moments ago.

They walked in the direction they had been running. Christopher had no idea where they were headed, only that it seemed to be the farthest distance from where they had last seen the clown. He glanced around as they walked, ever vigilant for the rubber-masked stranger. They skirted around a couple more horror displays and found open space. Several hundred yards out, Christopher saw the gray of stone walls. He turned to look at Amber.

"If we make it to the wall, we are home free, right?" Amber's eyes sparkled.

Christopher felt the hope in Amber's eyes radiate like a spark in the night. He smiled his most convincing smile. "Yes."

Amber uttered a giddy laugh. "It's almost over. I can feel it."

She started running, and Christopher followed her. Within minutes, they reached the wall. Amber pressed her body against it, hugging it, her cheek touching it.

She closed her eyes. "It's so cool and hard and reassuring. I never want to leave."

"If we're getting out of here, you'll have to," Christopher said.

He took Amber's hand and pulled her along the wall. They walked his right hand in her left, but Amber refused to take her right hand off the wall. They didn't talk, and Christopher continued to scan their surroundings, but he wasn't just looking for the clown anymore. Christopher also hoped to see others from the group. He worried that they had abandoned the others to a terrible fate. When he thought about them, he heard Cary Lynn telling her husband to shut his mouth. The thought made him laugh. His reverie caused Amber to squeeze his hand and pull him closer to her. She looked into his eyes and smiled. He realized she was mistaking his pleasant mulling as an affirmation that their situation was improving. He did nothing to dissuade her, though he still believed their predicament was as dire as ever.

As Christopher watched Amber walk along the softly curving wall, a finger of her right hand tracing a line in the dust, he couldn't help but recall their day on the beach in Ocean City. She had played a game where she used that same finger to draw a circle around them in the sand. The rules were simple: try and get the other to step out of the ring without touching. The game was stupid, but it was fun. In the end, Christopher had cheated and tickled Amber until she dropped to the sand. Her head had fallen out of the circle. As he recalled, they had yet to play a rematch.

He also recalled the first day he brought Amber home to meet the folks. His mom accepted her with open arms, but his dad, and his sis, Katina, were not so excited that Christopher had brought a white girl home. He had expected Katina's reaction—she had proven herself quite the racist—but his father's response had been unexpected.

Katina had passive-aggressively ignored Amber by not responding when Amber spoke directly to her. Katina never spoke of Amber or even acknowledged her presence. It had bothered Amber, Christopher knew, but she never let the smile on her face falter, or allow Katina's treatment to affect her. Christopher loved his sister and would continue to love her, despite being disappointed by Katina's behavior.

His father, however, was a different story.

Christopher's father had made several derogatory remarks that were purposely intended to insult Amber.

Christopher recalled one of the more distasteful exchanges that had occurred while they sat at the dinner table.

"What's your plan for the future, Chris?" Pop had said. "You planning on marrying this girl?"

"Haven't thought it that far ahead, Pop," Christopher said.

"You were late," Pop said. "Whose fault was that?"

"Mine, Pop," Christopher said, though his dad probably had known it was a lie. Christopher told his mother they were late because Amber couldn't decide on an outfit. If he hadn't heard the conversation, his mother probably told his father about it. Christopher's mother had turned away then, knowing her husband was using her words to prove a negative point.

"I don't believe you," Pop said.

"It's true, Daddy," Katina said. "You know Christopher has always been on BP time."

Christopher turned and looked at his sister. She didn't look back but smiled down at her mashed potatoes, greens, and fried chicken dinner. He loved his sister so much at that moment he could have cried.

After that, the dinner turned to shit.

"I won't approve of this relationship, Chris," Pop said. "I don't want any mulatto grandbabies."

Christopher had stood so abruptly that his chair flipped back with a crash.

"Fredrick," Mom said. Her eyes had gone wide with shock. She turned to Christopher after a moment had passed. "Sit back down and eat."

Christopher ignored his mother.

"Do you know where that horrible word comes from, Pop? Mulatto is the light brown color of a mule. Are you saying our kids would be mules? Is that what you're saying?"

Pop had opened his mouth to speak, but no words came.

"Is that what you're saying? Tell me. Is that what you're saying?"

"Christopher, please." Mom reached over and placed her hand on his hand.

Christopher pulled away from her touch. She gasped.

"Is that what you're saying, old man? I need to know."

Pop had dropped his eyes to his plate and refused to answer.

It had been the last time Christopher had spoken to his father. He had taken Amber out of there, and they hadn't gone back. Christopher still talked to his mother over the phone, but he had no intention of ever setting foot in his father's house again.

The thing of it was, Amber didn't even want kids. Christopher's father had exerted his will over a situation that was never going to happen anyway. As Christopher thought of it now, he couldn't help but laugh. Amber turned back and looked at him, and she giggled as well. Again, he believed she had mistakenly read his expression as one of hope.

Oh, Amber. Honey, I love you.

Her blonde hair sashayed as she turned her head and walked on. He reached around her waist and walked with his arm around her middle. He leaned in and pressed his nose into her hair. "Mmmm, I love how you smell."

"I must smell like shit after being in this hell hole all night."

"No, you smell wonderful," Christopher said.

Christopher stayed beside Amber, holding her hands as they followed the wall. When he spotted a doorway that looked like a dark rectangle in the gray wall, he pointed to it wordlessly, and they broke into a trot.

They stopped before entering the doorway. Christopher thought it was less of a door and more like a hole carved out of the stone. There was no light coming from inside the hole.

Christopher put a hand up, requesting Amber to stay. He stepped closer to the hole and peered into the darkness beyond.

There was nothing directly beyond the hole, but further in, to the left, light shined from another door. Christopher waved Amber forward and took her hand. Very carefully, he led her into the dark space.

Amber's hand tightened on Christopher's, and he had to shake it to make her realize what she was doing.

"Sorry." She stood close enough to whisper into his ear.

Christopher didn't respond but continued toward the lighted doorway ahead of them.

Amber's eyes widened, and she turned to Christopher. "It's the way out."

Chapter Twenty-One: Shaina

The knife seemed to flip through the air in slow motion as Shaina watched it. Dashiell instinctively pulled Shaina toward him, and the blade flew past her, hit the pillar, then skittered away into the distance. Shaina's shock broke when Dashiell kissed her. She met his eyes. *You saved me.*

With the real world returning to her, Shaina turned and searched for the clown, but was unable to find it.

Dashiell shielded Shaina and waited for another attack. After several minutes passed, he stood and stepped away from the protection of the column.

"No." Shaina reached for him.

"It's okay. It's gone."

"Are you sure?"

Dashiell nodded. "For now, I guess."

The place grew eerily quiet, and Shaina watched as Dashiell scanned their surroundings. He walked through the displays, and she followed him. He stopped at the metal pole in the center of the umbrella ceiling.

"Looks like this is the exact center of the room," he said. He wrapped his fingers around the pole and tried to shake it, but it didn't budge.

"Sturdy," Shaina said.

"It is." He placed his foot against the base where the pole met the cement floor. He leaned back, putting all his entire weight on the bar. He jumped up and wrapped his legs around the pole, using the strength of his arms to hold him up. After a few seconds, he dropped back to the floor.

"You're not planning to climb this, are you?" Her voice was thick with surprise and worry. "That's thirty feet up."

"Yeah, but if there's a way out, it's up there. We owe it to ourselves to try."

"If you fall from that height, you'll die."

He kissed her on the nose. "Then, I won't fall."

Dashiell didn't move right away. He stared up at the ceiling for several seconds, scratching his chin. Shaina had a sudden urge to cover his face with kisses. When he turned to look at her, he must have seen something on her face, because his soft features hardened with concern.

"What's wrong?"

I think I'm falling for you.

She shook her head and looked at the floor. "I don't see us getting out of here without falling prey to that maniac. I'm afraid of you falling." She pointed at the pole. "Of not seeing my kids again. Afraid they won't know how much I love them."

He stepped over and pulled her into a hug. She liked having his arms around her. She breathed in his smell—a musky yet pleasant scent—and pressed her lips against his neck.

He whispered into her ear. "You're shaking."

She *was* shaking, and it wasn't from fear. Dashiell's touch caused her to shiver. She didn't want him to release her. She held onto him as tightly as she could and didn't let go until the shaking had begun to subside. She backed away from him cautiously as if he might suddenly go spinning off into space where she would never see him again.

They locked gazes, and Shaina felt a sense of comfort and compassion in his gray eyes. There had always been a sort of playful easiness to his eyes, but now they were sultry and warm...a lover's eyes, or so she thought. Maybe that was reading too much into his look, but Shaina didn't care. When they were safely away from there, she wanted to wrap her legs around him and make love to him.

She turned away before he could read her intentions in the heat of her cheeks. After the moment passed, she turned back to face him.

He was still looking at her, smiling.

He coughed, a nervous little sound, and turned back to the metal pole. "I think I can do this. It's not unlike rope climbing in gym class. I was always good at that in school. My only concern is sweat. Wet hands become slippery, and I'll slide back down if my hands get slick." He glanced around. "Anything here that we can use to keep my hands from slipping?"

She peered around as well. Something dry and absorbent, like baby powder, or...

Or something that will close the pores.

She reached into her pocket to pulled out a handful of singly wrapped hand sanitizer wipes. She ripped one open and handed it to Dashiell. "Wash your hands with this. The alcohol in it will keep your hands from sweating."

He stared at the wet napkin. "You carry hand sanitizers where ever you go?"

"When you have kids, you'll understand."

He shrugged and took the towelette, wiped his hands, then held it out with his finger and thumb. When Shaina didn't take it, he let it drop to the floor.

"Rub your hands together and get them completely dry."

Dashiell did as instructed with a decidedly kid-like enthusiasm. He held them out to show her his progress.

"Good. That should be sufficient to get you to the top. Are you sure you're up for this?"

He nodded. "I have to be. We have to get out of here, and up is our best chance."

He shook his out hands and then did the same with his legs.

"You're stalling," Shaina said. "If you're nervous, you don't have to do this."

"Is it a bad time to tell you I'm afraid of heights?" Dashiell took a deep breath and released it slowly. He closed his eyes for a second as if resting them, then opened them again and gripped the pole. He jumped up and gripped the bar, hanging there for a few seconds.

He dropped back down. "No slip. You know your stuff."

"It's now or never," she said.

He turned back to the steel rod and jumped up again, gripping the bar and then wrapping his legs around it. He moved his hands up higher and dragged the rest of his body after him. He continued to shimmy up the pole.

At first, he seemed to be doing well. But halfway up, his pace slowed. Shaina stared up at him with fear clutching at her throat. He seemed to be struggling, and he still had a good fifteen feet to go before he could pull himself up and through the canvas to whatever awaited him up there.

She bit her lower lip and watched him inch his way up the pole. At one point, he dropped about six feet. Shaina cried out and reached up as if she could catch him. He stopped his fall, however, and continued his upward climb.

When he was nearly at the top, Shaina released a long-held breath with an audible groan of relief.

She watched as he struggled to climb through a tear in the faux ceiling. He snaked through the opening, wiggling his legs like a child trying to climb up to an out of reach cookie jar.

Inside the space and completely out of sight, Dashiell popped his head and one arm from the hole and waved. She waved back and heard him saying something though she couldn't make out the words. After a short hesitation, he disappeared again. She stared up at the place where Dashiell had gone until she realized she had forgotten they were not alone. Her eyes darted around and scanned her surroundings.

In the excitement of Dashiell's climb to possible freedom, she had forgotten to keep a lookout for the clown. She did not see her adversary, and the thudding in her chest returned to a normal rhythm. She remembered to show equal time between watching above and looking around her on the ground.

It seemed like an hour before Dashiell poked his head out of the hole again. He shouted down to her once again, but still, she couldn't hear his words. She placed her hands around her mouth and shouted up.

"I can't hear you."

Her shout caused an alarm to sound in her head, and she scanned the surroundings again for any intruders.

Confident that she was alone, Shaina peered up at Dashiell. She watched as he reached out from the hole and wrapped his hands around the bar. He pulled his legs free, and the momentum caused him to slam against the metal pole. He appeared to lose his grip for an instant and fell several feet.

Shaina screamed.

Dashiell regained his hold and wrapped his legs around the shaft. After a short rest, he shimmied down. She ran to him and threw her arms around him when his feet were again on solid ground. She kissed his cheek, kissed it again. As their eyes met, she leaned in and kissed him on the lips.

It was a long kiss, and when they parted, he smiled. "I'll have to climb up there again if that's going to be my reward."

She ignored him. "What's up there? Is there a way out?"

He shook his head. "I was able to walk around. Steel trusses are crisscrossing the entire upper level. I went over every inch but couldn't find any way to the surface." Steel plates make up the roof. It looks like we're in a humungous underground silo. It's got a concave shape, and I don't recall seeing anything that looks like a steel dome sticking out of the ground, so I'm thinking that there is a layer of dirt covering it. Even if we had a blowtorch, we'd still have to dig our way out."

"Damn it all." Shaina wanted to scream and release her pent-up frustration but had done enough screaming.

Dashiell took her hand and squeezed. "We'll find a way out."

"Don't patronize me. You don't know the way out of here any more than I do. Just face it. We're stuck."

"You're right. I'm sorry. I just…"

She looked into his gray eyes again. "No, I'm sorry. I know you're just trying to keep me from freaking out. Trust me. I'm not a hysterical woman. I'll be okay without your sympathy and condolences."

"So noted." He smiled.

She stared at him for a while longer, and then she smiled, too. "Well at least I don't have to watch you climb that pole again. That was nerve-wracking. If anything turned me into a hysterical woman, that would have done it."

"Aw," Dashiell said, and his eyes got weepy.

"Don't *you* get hysterical either."

They walked away from the metal pole, and she was happy he wouldn't be climbing it again. Shaina didn't know their destination until the stage appeared ahead of them. She turned to Dashiell. "Why did you lead us back here?"

"I don't think I did it on purpose. I was walking, and this is where we ended up. But now that we're here, I can't help but think of that trap door on the stage. Maybe Christopher was onto something there."

Dashiell took her hand and led her to the edge of the stage. He helped her climb up onto the platform then followed her. With his hands, Dashiell instructed her to stay against the wall. He pointed up. She looked to where he was pointing, and she saw the cage hanging above their heads. If the cage came down, where they were standing kept them from being trapped inside. She nodded her understanding.

She followed him, wondering where they were going. They walked into the darkness of the stage toward the back. He led her behind a hidden wall behind the platform, stopping at a ladder. Dashiell placed a hand on one of the rungs.

Shaina placed a hand on the ladder, stopping him. "You're heading up again?"

Dashiell nodded. "No better place to go than up."

After reaching the top, Dashiell turned and helped Shaina through the opening. They stood atop the stage, looking down at the surroundings with high visibility. The umbrella roof hovered ten feet above their heads.

"How did you know this was here?" she asked as she counted the corpses in their displays below her.

"I saw the ladder when I was helping Christopher with the trap door. I was curious to know where it led, but there wasn't an opportunity to explore it until now." Dashiell strode over to the ledge and looked down. "Long way to fall."

Shaina nodded, though she didn't look over the edge. "And you swear you knew nothing of this part of the fair? This stage? None of this?" She didn't mean to sound skeptical, but she needed to voice her concerns.

Dashiell sat with his legs dangling down. "I only became part of all this a couple of years ago. This stuff has been here for years and years. This place is something my Uncle Owen did, I think. And I can also speculate why he did it."

Shaina sat down next to him. She was leery of having her legs hanging over — like dangling her legs in shark-infested water — but she did it anyway. "What do you think this place is?"

"I think my uncle built this for my cousin. He was very sick, and the commotion of the real fair would have been too overwhelming for him. I think he started building this for Owen Jr. but abandoned it when Owen died. The fair closed down after my cousin died. I reopened it because it was part of my uncle's will. I inherited everything — millions of dollars — but the one stipulation was that I had to reopen the fair."

"And in the time the fair has been closed, some lunatic clown took refuge down here, under the fair, killing and stealing spare parts from the unused amusement rides, slowly building this bizarre exhibit?"

Dashiell slapped his hands together. "That's what I think."

Shaina couldn't dispute that. She knew Dashiell didn't know of their current circumstances ahead of time.

Sitting up here is an excellent way to wait for the rescue team. She also hoped more survivors would come along and see them sitting up there and join them. She tried to imagine that kids were playing below her, and parents shouting for them to be careful. Barkers enticed young studs to win a prize for their girlfriends. This scenario was, after all, what the horror displays tried to recreate. Instead of corpses, she let her mind pretend there were living breathing people below her.

When she opened her eyes, she saw that Dashiell was looking at her.

"You were smiling. What were you thinking about?" Dashiell asked.

She leaned closer to him. "I was thinking about being anywhere but here." She paused, then added something else. "But being here with you isn't so bad, either." She smiled shyly and waited to see how he reacted to her last comment.

He smiled. "You're not such bad company, yourself."

It had been two years since her husband died, and she had not been with a man since. But this one made her feel like a teenager again, made her feel like she could love someone again. She surrounded herself with her kids and work and had not entertained the idea of dating till now. There had been men who had asked her out, but no one affected her the way Dashiell did. It was easy to thwart their advances because she had no interest in those men. From the moment Shaina met Dashiell, she had felt an attraction. It was exhilarating to know such feelings hadn't been lost to her.

When she looked over at Dashiell, he was looking at her and smiling. He looked away quickly when he saw that she was looking back at him.

He's acting like a teenager, too. The thought made her smile.

"Dashiell, do you believe in love at first sight?" Shaina asked. She avoided his eyes, but that was alright because he was avoiding hers, too.

He shrugged. "I believe in love."

"I never believed love at first sight was a thing. It took me a few weeks of being chased before I started to feel anything close to love for the man that I married. I didn't believe it could be possible to love someone you just met." She looked into his eyes now.

Dashiell's smiled faltered, and his eyes seemed to be taking in every inch of her face.

"That is until I met you."

They fell into each other, kissing passionately, and tearing at each other's clothing.

Chapter Twenty-Two: Christopher

They entered the lighted area squinting and shielding their eyes. The brightness blinded them. Something caused light to glint and wink as if the flash of a thousand paparazzi cameras going off all at once. Christopher's eyes teared up from the glare.

Amber said, "It's us."

Christopher turned to her, rubbing his eyes. When he was able to keep them open for longer than two seconds, he turned to see what Amber saw.

The room was full of mirrors: rows and rows of them in alternating succession. Christopher stared at himself in an endless kaleidoscope pattern. He took an involuntary step forward.

"Is that what I look like?" She shook her head in defiance. "I'm hideous."

"Nonsense, you're still as beautiful as ever." Christopher wasn't looking at her. He scanned their surroundings to see if they were alone. He urged Amber to come into the lighted mirror room. She stepped forward reluctantly.

"Is it safe?" She asked.

Christopher shrugged. "I don't know, but it's safer in the light. Besides, with all these mirrors, there's no way the clown could sneak up on us."

Amber walked up to a mirror and placed her hand on it. The image in the mirror did the same. She followed the reflective surface until she found a break in the mirrors. Stepping into the gap caused her and her reflections to disappear.

"Amber." He couldn't disguise the panic in his voice.

She popped her head from between the mirror, now looking like a beautiful Cherub. "It's a maze in here. Maybe there is a way out." She disappeared again.

"Amber, wait for me." Christopher followed her.

Christopher followed Amber, not sure if he was seeing her or just a reflection. He thought he had caught up to her, only to find it was a mirror image. She giggled and moved on. He continued, hands out, feeling for open space but finding the hard, glass surfaces of the mirrors.

Christopher listened for her giggles and tried to determine her location with the sound. Echoes and distortion caused this tactic to be just as tricky as visually following her. His patience wore thin.

"Come on, Honey. There's no time for games."

Christopher stopped. He saw only his reflection and no longer heard her voice at all. His throat constricted, and his pulse thudded at his temples. He quickened his pace, bumping into mirrors in his haste to find his way through the hidden gaps in the glass.

He ran forward with his hands outstretched. When he touched a solid surface, he rolled along with the glass until he found an opening. He continued through the mirrors like this, suspecting he was moving in circles.

"Amber." His hoarse whisper reverberated against the mirrors and came back to him, giving the illusion that he was standing behind himself, whispering into his own ears. He whipped around, chilled by the effect. He stopped moving and lifted his head to look up at the ceiling. "Amber."

Her reply was faint. "Christopher, where are you?"

"Follow my voice, Honey. Come back to me."

"Christopher, I can't see you."

"Follow my voice, Baby. Come back. Follow my voice." He continued talking, trying to follow her voice, but sometimes she sounded close and other times farther away. *Damn it, Girl. Why did you go so far ahead?* "Follow my voice, Babe. Can you still hear me? Come to me."

He heard no reply. The silence caused the hairs on his neck to prickle, and he rushed forward in a panic.

"Amber, Honey, I can't hear you."

"Christopher." Her voice was choked with fear but sounded close.

"Amber, stop moving. Call out to me, and I'll come to you."

"Christopher, hurry. I'm scared."

"I'm coming. I can hear you. Keep talking."

"Why did we come in here? I'm so scared, Christopher. Please, get me out of here. I don't want to be here anymore."

"I know, Baby. I'm almost there. Stay put. I'm coming to you."

She stopped talking, and Christopher felt a moment of dread.

"Talk to me, Babe. I'm coming."

"Christopher, I...I..."

"What should we do when we get home? What's the first thing you want to do?"

"I want a hot bubble bath and a big bowl of ice cream. I'm so hungry. I'm going to eat the ice cream in the tub."

Christopher laughed through his tears of fear. "The heat from the bath is going to melt your ice cream, Bae."

"I don't care. I want it all." Her laughter told him her fear was abating. She continued talking about ice cream and baths, and he kept moving through the mirrors toward her voice. He seemed to have struck a nerve. She had begun to talk without stopping. Her words strung together until he could barely understand what she was talking about anymore. He didn't care. As long as she was talking, he was able to track her. After a few more turns, he felt she was on the other side of the glass from him.

She stopped talking again.

"Baby, I'm right here. Do you hear me? I'm like one wall away."

"How do we find each other? I don't want to be alone anymore. Take me home, Chris. Please."

Christopher turned a corner and could see a reflection of her. "I see you, Baby. I'm almost there. Can you see me?"

He watched as ten images of her swiveled their heads, some turned left, and some turned right. Finally, they all seemed to focus on one spot, and she smiled.

"I see you." She took a step.

"Don't move. If you try to come to me, you might make it harder for me to get to you. Wait there, and let me come to you."

She stopped, but her head swiveled and searched, looking for him. He bumped into more mirrors before he was standing in front of Amber once again.

"It's about time," she said. "What took you so long?"

"Well, I had to skirt a few copies of myself and fight off an alter ego, but I made it. I'm here."

She laughed and took a step forward. Before she could take a second step, however, she stopped, and her smile faded.

She screamed.

Christopher turned, following her gaze. The clown stared back at them. But was it an image or the real thing? Christopher couldn't tell. He stumbled backward into Amber, and she clung to him, pinning his arms. He shook loose from her but kept her behind him. Her arms encircled his waist, and she sobbed into his shoulder blades.

The clown took a step to its left, and those dark, bloodshot eyes continued to stare at them, but now there were five identical images of the clown. When one moved, the others moved in the opposite direction until they all melded into one image. The clown — the real clown — moved closer to the couple.

Christopher put out a hand. "No, don't do it, man."

The clown stopped.

"Why are you doing this? Why can't you just let us go? We haven't done anything to deserve this."

The clown studied Christopher, tipping its head, first one way, and then the other. It didn't move forward.

Christopher continued to hold his hand out like a forcefield. Christopher's heart pounded against his breastbone, and his breathing flooded through his ears like a rushing river. Amber continued to cry against Christopher's back, her tears mixing with the sweat dampening his tee-shirt.

The force field broke, and the clown moved forward. Christopher shuffled backward, shoving Amber along with him.

"Don't," he said, and the clown stopped again. "Please, just...don't."

When the clown came at them again, Christopher turned and grabbed Amber by the shoulders, herding her through the mirror maze. In the mirrors around them, he could see the clown following.

He pushed Amber ahead, nearly carrying her when her feet began to drag. She sobbed and screamed at regular intervals, but he didn't let her stop and kept her moving through the pathways between the mirrors, always seeing the clown there with them.

The clown seemed to sidestep and then disappeared view. Christopher stopped and whipped his head around, searching.

Where did it go?

"Christopher." Amber's voice was a moan. "I'm scared."

He shushed her and dragged her by the hand to the left.

"This fucking place can't be this big. We must be running in circles. Why the hell did we ever come here in the first place?" He didn't expect an answer and got none. He tried to think of what to do next.

Amber whimpered.

"He knows this place better than us. We need to keep that in mind." Christopher was talking to her, but mostly he was trying to keep his thoughts in order. He wanted to work through this problem by listing the facts. "We can probably backtrack because the clown is going to pop up in front of us." At the mention of the clown, Amber whimpered again and shivered against him. Christopher rubbed her arm to comfort her.

He changed direction and started heading back where he thought the entrance had been. He would take his chances of hiding in the dark room.

He passed through the original two mirrors, and they were out of the maze. He caught a glimpse of himself, and the look of fright and confusion on his face shocked him. He vowed to never look in another mirror for the rest of his life.

He spotted the darkened doorway and staggered toward it, still clinging to Amber's hand.

"We're almost there." He turned to whisper into Amber's ear.

Christopher turned back to the doorway, but the clown was there, towering in front of him. He glanced up at the masked face, stunned and confused. Stony gray irises peered out at him from the mask's eye holes. The clown lifted Christopher and flung him aside.

Amber screamed. She turned and tried to run, but the clown grabbed her by the hair. Amber struggled to pull free. The clown released her, and the momentum caused her to run headlong into a mirror. It shattered, and reflective glass rained down all around her. She landed in a heap in the center of the broken glass. Her hair covered her face.

Amber pulled herself up on hands and knees, then stood. She turned and looked at Christopher. Blood streaked her face from a cut on her forehead. Christopher picked himself up from the floor as well, but the clown stood between them.

Amber's eyes clouded over with shock and terror. She stared past the clown, ignoring it, and smiled at Christopher. Blood dribbled down the front of her, more blood than he thought should come from a cut on her head. Then Amber moved the hair away from her face, and Christopher saw the shard a glass wedged in her neck. A weak hand fluttered up and touched the thing in her throat.

"Amber, no." Christopher reached out to her, but he would not get to her in time to stop her.

She pulled the splinter from her neck, and it the ground hit with a jingle. Blood jetted from the wound, hitting the mirrors and covering the floor. As the pumping blood slowed, Amber dropped to her knees. She placed a hand to her neck, but the damage was too considerable. She fell on her face without trying to break her fall.

Christopher screamed and rushed the clown, but it turned and met his charge with a knife in its red-gloved hand. The clown drove the blade into Christopher's stomach, stopping the man in his tracks. Christopher staggered back, gripping the wound, and watching blood pump through his fingers.

Christopher's knees buckled, and he fell on his back. Christopher watched as the clown strode past him and disappeared into the void beyond Christopher's vision. He felt hot blood covering his hands and running down his sides to puddle beneath him. After a moment, the bright lights and mirror images faded into blackness.

Chapter Twenty-Three: Shaina

As Dashiell lay on his back, zipping his fly, Shaina buttoned her blouse. She couldn't stop smiling. *He'll probably never want to see me again, but I don't think I care. It was that good.*

Dashiell sat down next to her to put on his shoes. She glanced over at him, and he was staring back at her, smiling.

She opened her mouth to ask him if he would be willing to meet her kids, but when she looked at the expression on his face, the words clogged in her throat. He did not turn in her direction, but looked at something behind her. When he scrambled to his feet, she did, too. Dashiell pulled her behind him.

Shaina looked over at what had worried him.

The clown was there, on the ladder, staring back at them. Only the clown's head had emerged over the threshold. As Shaina watched, the clown pulled itself to full height. She felt a terrible premonition that everyone else was dead. Dashiell and Shaina were all that was left of the group, and now it was their turn to die.

Time was up, and help never came.

"What do we do?" she said in a whisper. Dashiell didn't reply.

The clown-masked thing continued to stare but didn't approach them. Shaina felt a shudder of disgust, and her mind twisted with thoughts of her impending death.

Dashiell kept Shaina behind him when the clown moved forward. Dashiell ushered her backward.

Shaina gripped his shoulders when she felt the precipice looming behind her.

"We're going to fall...or get pushed off." Her voice was barely a whisper in his ear.

Dashiell peered behind her at the edge. Without telling her his plan, he forced her to the ledge. He got down on his stomach, urging her to do likewise. She did, trusting him. He took her by her hands and motioned for her to swing her legs off the edge. With a yip of surprise from her, she slipped off the ledge and dangled down. He continued to hold her by the hands. She tried to look down but couldn't get her head in the right position to see anything.

"You're going to have to trust me. Do you trust me?"

Her voice came out in a breathless rush. "Yes."

Dashiell let her go. She screamed as she dropped the few feet to the stage. The impact of hitting solid ground jarred her legs, but she wasn't injured. She stumbled backward and landed on her butt. She peered up at Dashiell with only his head and dangling arms visible. The clown loomed behind him. She stifled an urge to scream—there was no air in her lungs for that, anyway—so she pointed instead.

Dashiell, without looking behind him, swung his legs off the ledge and hung from the edge by his fingers. He continued to hold on for a few seconds but was too weak to stay there for long. His fingers slipped before he was ready to drop, and he fell at an awkward angle. He landed on one leg and screamed. Shaina watched as his leg bent wrong, and knew he had broken a bone. She thought it might have been his tibia.

Shaina watched in helpless terror as he flopped sideways and tumbled off the stage, continued to the cement floor below. She raced over and jumped down to land beside him. He lay on his side, unmoving.

She rushed to him and began a preliminary check for vitals. He had a heartbeat, and he was breathing but was unconscious. Next, she checked him over for broken bones without touching him. She determined Dashiell's left tibia was fractured. It didn't look too bad, but she knew it would hurt like hell.

Dashiell woke up with a gasp. He grabbed for his leg, but she stopped him. "I have to stabilize it."

Dashiell glanced up. She followed his line of sight.

The clown was no longer up there.

"We don't have time." He struggled to speak through the pain.

Shaina chanced a glance across the length of the stage and saw the shadowy form of their pursuer coming down the stairs. She didn't react, nor did she tell him what she saw. Shaina took Dashiell's left arm and draped it over her shoulder. She lifted him, circling his left calf with her arms to help keep him from putting weight on his broken leg. She ran beside him, and he hopped on one leg into the surrounding horror displays. With something to lean on, Shaina was relieved of some of his weight. They moved deeper into the exhibitions. When they thought they might have bought themselves some time, Shaina forced him to stop. She helped him into a sitting position.

"I have to stabilize that leg."

Dashiell grabbed her hand and pulled her toward his face. "No, you're going to leave me here and save yourself."

She stared at him for a second or two, then shook her head. "I'm not leaving you, so forget it."

"Shaina, he's going to be here soon. Get the fuck out of here."

Ignoring him, she pulled her hand free and searched through the nearest display. She found a two-by-four with a corpse tied to it. She pulled the lines loose, and the body tipped to the side like a wooden cigar store Indian, tumbling off the platform. She took the board and the ropes back to Dashiell. She placed the board against his leg and tied it to his ankle and thigh, up near his crotch. She tied it again, just above the knee. The ropes were secure enough to stabilize the leg, but not so tight to cut off circulation. She helped him to stand.

The board came up under his armpit at just the right height that he could use it almost like a crutch. He wrapped his arms around the two-by-four, and he hobbled away with Shaina staying by his side.

They managed to get a couple of feet, but he had to stop. Wincing in pain, he sat down beside a corpse on the seat of an amusement ride with his leg straight out. The body turned away, then tumbled off the other side.

Dashiell squeezed his lids shut, and he sucked in a breath through clenched teeth. His pale complexion made her worry that he might be going into shock. Dark circles had formed under his eyes.

When he opened his eyes again, Dashiell had to search for her. After he managed to focus on her face, he reached for her, and she took his hand.

"I can't go any further." His voice cracked. "You have to leave me here." He leaned weakly against the back of the seat.

Shaina's head pivoted as she looked for the clown, for a weapon, for a place to hide...anything. She had no intention of leaving Dashiell.

She turned back to look at him and saw that he had closed his eyes.

"Stay awake," she said. "You're in shock."

Dashiell opened his eyes and smiled weakly at her. "You're still here? I told you to go. You never listen." He coughed.

"We are going to share the same fate because I'm not going anywhere."

"No, you have to live for your kids. I'll keep the bastard busy until help arrives."

He looked exhausted.

"You have to live for *me*."

But—"

"You're using up precious energy arguing with me."

He offered a weak little chuckle that must have sent pain through his leg because he sat up with a gasp, eyes wide and full of panic. With a wince, he sat back. He twisted around as far as his board would allow and peered at the spot next to him. He groaned and turned back, nearly falling off the bench. Shaina caught him and helped him to the floor. She glanced at the writhing pile of maggots that had been on the seat next to him, then quickly turned away, her stomach churning.

"Thought I smelled something." He moaned.

They chuckled as they sat next to each other on the floor.

The laughing stopped, and the air around them grew still and quiet.

"I keep waiting for a police force to come barging in at any moment. What are the chances of that happening?"

She leaned her shoulder against his, their heads touched. "Any time now…"

He turned his head and kissed her cheek. He spoke into her ear. "I'm sorry about getting you into this."

"Don't start that again." She turned her head, and their lips touched. She kissed him. He tried to kiss her back.

The sound of something heavy scraping on the cement floor caught their ears, and they both sat up, fully alert.

Shaina thought the scraping sound reminded her of a car dragging its muffler.

The sound grew louder, closer.

Shaina's blood turned cold in her veins when she saw the clown.

She stood and tried to help Dashiell to stand, but he didn't have the strength to help her. After a moment, she had to give up and sat down next to him again. They held each other.

And waited.

The hulking figure of the clown came into view, and within seconds, they saw what made the sound.

The figure dragged the sledgehammer by the handle, the hammer's head lumbering across the cement floor still exhibited remnants of Clifford's brain matter. The clown stopped in front of Shaina and Dashiell.

Shaina clung to Dashiell, shivering and cold, even as sweat stung her eyes. She felt Dashiell stiffen beneath her.

The clown lifted the hammer over its head.

Shaina buried her face in Dashiell's chest, terrified to see what was coming. She heard the clown grunt with tremendous effort. She lifted her head and looked into Dashiell's eyes. He looked back at her. He lifted his eyes to look behind her.

"Dashiell..." Shaina sucked in a breath. "Dashiell Pearson, I think I love you."

Shaina braced against the impact of the hammer blow to her head. She watched as Dashiell's wide eyes flicked, first to her, then to the clown, and then back to her again.

The clown no longer mattered, and Dashiell smiled. "You *think* you love me?"

When she felt no hit to the head, she turned and peered at the clown. It stood unmoving with the hammer handle still clutched in its gloved fists, the head of the hammer hovering a few inches off the floor behind it. The hammer dropped to the floor with a thump. The handle then flopped to the left like a stiff tail. The clown's hands dropped to its sides.

Shaina and Dashiell sat side by side, staring up at the eyes behind the mask. The clown stared back. Shaina thought there was something familiar about those eyes, but couldn't decide why. The clown cocked its head to the side as if hearing a faraway sound then returned to its original position.

Then the thing made a muffled sound behind the mask. Shaina had thought the clown had spoken, but she couldn't make out the words.

Red-gloved hands rose and gripped the edges of the mask. As the disguise came away from the face, infected skin and hardened, pus-filled scabs tore with it. The clown dropped the costume to the floor.

Shaina stared up at the man with the red and festering sores on his face, with bumps that looked like hundreds of warts. She understood right away what the lesions were.

The man had leprosy.

The lips were gone, and bloodied gums extended up to the ruined mass of the man's nose. A staggered row of yellowed, rotted teeth protruded from the jaw in a permanent death sneer. The leprous clown spoke again. Though the words were slurred and distorted, there was no mistaking what it said.

"Dashiell…yuh…ee…" The infected man pointed to Dashiell and then to itself. "Cuz-shins."

Dashiell gaped at the clown, Shaina turned to look at him. Her declaration of love was no longer the most shocking revelation to hit him.

The clown pointed to itself and then to Dashiell. "Cousin." The word came from the ruined mouth as *cuz-shin*.

Dashiell swallowed hard, tried to stand, couldn't, and dropped back down. He stared up at the hulking figure above them.

Dashiell cleared his throat. "Are you telling me you're my cousin, Owen?"

The leprous clown laughed and danced around.

"Yes," said the clown, though the word came out *yesh*. It pointed to Dashiell again. "Cuz-shin, cuz-shin."

Chapter Twenty-Four: Owen

As the small green snake slithered by Owen's foot, he studied it for a moment, then reached down and picked it up. The little mouth latched onto his index finger and he curiously let it suspend from his hand. He carried the reptile this way to the shed behind his house, and entered the tiny building. He looked over the array of garden tools, choosing the hoe. Owen then gripped the snake with his open hand and wrapped his fingers around its tiny cylindrical body, squeezing it until the snake released its hold on his finger. As the snake writhed and fought in his left hand, Owen studied the tiny blood droplets where the snake's teeth had been gripping his hand.

Owen exited the shed and dropped the snake on the cobblestone pathway. As the snake slithered away, Owen trapped it with the blade of the hoe, just below the head. The snake's tail twisted and writhed in an attempt to free itself from the tool. Owen watched it for a few seconds more and then pressed down with the hoe until the head came off. The rest of the snake's body continued to undulate, as if unaware that it had no head.

Owen then used the hoe to chop the snake into several more pieces.

The snake had been Owen's first animal kill. He was twelve years old.

***

At the age of fourteen, Owen learned about his cousin Dashiell.

"Your Uncle George and Aunt Tammy live in Texas. How about we go and meet your newborn cousin?" Owen Sr said.

Owen had no interest in seeing a crummy baby, but it was no matter to him. He went where his father took him. And this time, it was Texas.

Owen lived in a three-story mansion on a hill overlooking the city of Poughkeepsie. His dad owned a lot of lands, including a fair. Owen had been to the fair once and planned to go again. He looked forward to going back so he could see the twinkling lights and go on rides that went around and round.

The house in Texas was a one-story ranch with red brick walls. As Owen and his father headed up the walkway cutting through the trees leading to the front door, Owen glanced around at the other houses on his Uncle's road, but they were all the modest dwellings belonging to poor people like his Uncle.

After being forced to meet his relatives, and checking out the new baby, Owen wandered around the house until he concluded that nothing was exciting to do at his Uncle's house. For no other reason other than boredom, Owen broke a lamp.

When no one could see them, Dad gripped Owen by the collar. "What were you thinking? Get outside and stay out of trouble."

Owen stood in the front yard, looking around, but there was nothing to do outside, either. He found a bike—a girl's bike, but a bike just the same—and rode it up and down the road. An animal entered the road in front of him from the roadside bushes. Owen skidded to a stop and fell off the bike. He brushed the dirt from his pants and looked around for the creature that had caused his spill. Owen forgot about the bike and followed the animal crossing the road in front of him.

It looked like an armored rat.

The animal moved slowly, and when Owen approached, it stopped and turned to face him. He found a stick and poked the animal, making it squeal and back away. When Owen struck it over the head with the rod, it curled into a ball. He reached down and picked it up, tossed it into the air like a football. Owen tried to crush it, but when that didn't work, tried to force it open, but the animal proved to be too strong for Owen. When he dropped it on the ground, it opened and tried to scurry away. Owen caught it, tipped the creature on its back, felt it's soft underbelly. He reached down with one hand to get his stick, but the beast scratched his hand. Owen drew back, started, and the animal shuffled off to the side of the road and disappeared in the tall grass. Owen studied his hand. Deep cuts dribbled blood, and Owen had to hold his hand out away from himself to keep it from dripping onto his clothes. He returned to the bike and peddled back to the house, leaving a trail of blood on the road.

No one was around as he entered the house and headed to the bathroom to clean the wound. He wrapped it with a paper towel and applied pressure to it. When the blood stopped, he crammed the bloodied paper towels deep into the trash can and returned outside.

He told no one of the scratch or the animal that had inflicted it.

***

Owen had a knack for inventing contraptions to catch and, at times, kill small animals. By the time Owen turned nineteen, he had killed more animals than he could count. He also began developing a rash at the spot where the animal had scratched him all those years ago. When his father noticed the outbreak, the man seemed more concerned than the wound warranted. Owen tried to keep his arm covered, always wearing long-sleeved shirts.

The disease continued to get worse because the flesh around the rash began to *liquify*. Owen placed gauze on the oozing flesh to keep it from leaking through his clothes. His father wasn't fooled and knew the blemishes persisted.

"Does it hurt?" His father asked.

"No," Owen replied. "Should I go see a doctor?"

Owen watched as a flicker of anger, skimmed across his father's face. The look passed, but Owen didn't understand what he had done to deserve that look.

"No," his father said. "Forget about it. We'll deal with it ourselves."

Owen shrugged and nodded. After all, his father knew what was best for him.

"I have a task for you." Owen Sr pulled a colorful folded outfit from a bag and placed it on his lap. He removed a mask from the pack as well and set it on the yellow and red suit. Owen recognized it as a clown costume.

"I've begun construction on a new fair," Father said. "I want you to work at this fair wearing this."

Owen Sr held the suit out to him, and with some reluctance, Owen took it.

"Should I get dressed now, or…?"

"No, get dressed when you get there."

Owen followed his father to the car and climbed into the back seat. His dad slipped behind the wheel and started the car. Owen Sr drove the vehicle to the fairgrounds. He instructed Owen to follow him and led the boy to an empty warehouse. They entered a tunnel that led deep into the ground. They passed through a series of halls that brought them to a ladder.

"Go up," his father said.

Owen took the ladder to the hole above them. He climbed out and stood, looking around at the stage. After a moment, his father joined him.

"Follow me," his dad said and led Owen to the edge of the stage where they took a seat with their feet dangling over the side. Owen peered out at the round, ample space around the stage. He looked up at the ceiling.

"This was going to be a type of circus. That's why I had it built to resemble a big-top tent. I had to abandon the project."

"Why?"

"I was forced to close the fair." Owen Sr rubbed the stubble on his cheek. "I guess people aren't into amusement rides anymore. I hope to open it again someday, but for now, I had no reason to continue working on this part of the property. But there is a carrousel down here. That will be fun, right?"

Owen didn't respond.

"This fair is going to be just for you, son," Owen Sr said. "I want you to stay here until I come back to you. Put your costume on and never take it off."

Owen glanced down at the clothes in his lap. He didn't want to wear the stupid costume, but Owen always did as his father commanded. He wore the outfit and stayed hidden in the underground fair. His father visited him regularly, at first. Before long, the visits became less frequent.

"Why do I have to stay here?" Owen asked on a visit with his dad. "Why can't I go home and see Mother?"

"Your mother is dead," His father said. "She was killed in a car crash. The world thinks you died with her, so I need you to stay here, out of sight."

Owen had thrashed and cried at the news that his mother was dead. He refused to speak to his father. It didn't matter. His father rarely visited him anymore.

"Why are you keeping me here, Father?"

"Owen, you contracted a terrible disease, and it's contagious. I'm keeping you here so no one sees what's become of you. You must not come out when there are workers here. Do you hear me? Stay hidden. The costume is important, too. People won't be afraid of you when they see you if you're wearing that mask."

Owen did as instructed, but he got bored. Father did not return for several weeks, and when he did, Owen asked him why he had been away for so long.

"I need something to pass the time down here, father. When are you going to build more rides?"

"I'm afraid that the project is going to have to wait. I think I can arrange something, though."

Owen waited for his father to elaborate, but the man said nothing. Not then. But later, his father showed Owen why when he brought Dashiell for a visit. The boy was only six, but Owen was thrilled for the company. The boy liked the clown and had a great time riding on the carousel. When it was time for Dashiell to leave, Owen grew depressed.

"Will Dashiell come for another visit?" Owen asked.

"We'll have to see," his father said. "I guess that would depend on his parents. If they come to town again, then maybe it could be arranged."

Owen was content with that reply.

Over time, Owen requested materials from his father so that he could return to building traps. There were many rats and other animals down in his fair, and he wanted to trap them. Father agreed and gave Owen everything the boy needed to continue his hobby.

Owen's traps started simple, but over the next few years, they grew more elaborate. Owen also began to develop new entrances and exits, rigging them with traps and making many of them only accessible from one direction. He could go anywhere he wished without being seen. When Owen's father came for what would end up being the last visit, the man seemed distracted. Owen asked what was wrong, but his father only stared at him. It wasn't until his dad decided to leave that the real reason for the visit was made known.

"You are a monster, Owen." The man stared down at the floor. "You kill animals without remorse, and I'm afraid to know what you might do if exposed to the public. That's the real reason I'm keeping you down here. I should destroy you, but you're my son, and I can't harm you. Keeping you here is the only thing I can think of to ensure you're safe, and the rest of the world safe from you. You promised you would never leave here, and I want you to keep that promise. Stay here, or I will kill you, do you understand?"

Owen thought he should be angry with his father, but he did not get mad.

Sometime after that final visit, Owen broke Father's cardinal rule and went topside. He strode through the abandoned park under the majestic glow of the moon. Owen began to disassemble the rides and take them down below. He had intended to rebuild them in his underground fair, but that task proved to be herculean. He found another use for the parts he had "recommissioned."

Intruders regularly broke into the fair, and one night, as Owen strolled among the abandoned rides and game huts, he spotted a couple of teenagers, a boy, and a girl, wandering through the fair. He watched from a hidden location as they undressed and had sex, right there under the Ferris wheel. Owen boiled with rage that they would come here, to his home, and performed such acts. He seethed until he could stand it no more. Owen found a large piece of metal and beat the boy to death. He chased the girl and killed her, too.

This boy and girl were Owen's first human kills. But they wouldn't be his last.

Then, miraculously, and as his father had promised, the fair reopened.

Now, another of Father's promises had come true.

His cousin Dashiell had returned.

Chapter Twenty-Five: Shaina

The infected man danced and capered like a giant in a magical land. Shaina glanced at Dashiell. His color had paled further, and a patina of sweat covered his skin. She needed to get him medical attention.

When the man stopped dancing and returned to stand in front of the two of them, Shaina dared to voice a request.

"Dashiell—your cousin, Dashiell—is injured. He needs medical attention. Will you allow us to leave and get him to help?" She didn't take her eyes off Owen. "We can help you, as well. You have a disease called Leprosy. It's treatable, Owen. With skin grafts, we could even repair the damage already done."

His stony eyes fixed on her with an unblinking stare, and she wondered if she had made a mistake speaking up. After a moment, the eyes turned and studied Dashiell. She hitched her breath and waited to see if she would live to see her kids again. Dashiell had earned his freedom through blood relation, but she could just as quickly end up like all the others around her; she knew she had no such protection.

She voiced her case. "I can help you both, Owen."

"Leg," the lipless man said.

"Yes, he has a broken leg. He's going into shock. I need to get him to someone who can take care of it."

"No." Without lips to form the word, this came out "nuh."

"Owen, buddy, my leg hurts bad. Please let me get help."

A knife appeared in Owen's red fist. Shaina hadn't seen where it came from, but she didn't miss it when light glinted off it. Her mind spun, and again she thought of her kids. Dashiell leaned in front of her protectively.

"Owen, please don't hurt us." He paused. "Don't hurt *her*, please. Don't hurt her."

Owen didn't respond. The man came down with the knife and cut the ropes binding Dashiell to the makeshift splint. He lifted Dashiell off the floor and flung the injured man over his massive shoulder. Owen then turned and strode away.

Shaina scrambled to her feet and followed them. She ran but could not catch up. Owen marched steadily away about twenty paces ahead of her.

As she rounded a horror display, Owen used one hand to vault onto the stage while still holding Dashiell over one shoulder. When she made it onto the platform, Owen and Dashiell had disappeared down the trap door. Shaina cried out in misery and rushed to the doorway. Tears of hope streamed down her cheeks when she saw that the door had remained open. She peered inside and saw the ladder leading into the darkness below.

Shaina heard labored breathing somewhere below her, and she scrambled down the steps, slipping and falling when her feet got tangled in the rungs. She picked herself up and rushed headlong into the darkness around her. Shaina ran with her arms outstretched. She hit a wall and grunted, but recovered quickly then searched for a doorway, a knob, or anything that might open up into a passageway. Where did Owen take Dashiell?

"No." She moaned, and a renewed sense of dread caused her breath to catch in her throat. She nearly vomited but swallowed the hot bile. "No, I can't get lost now. Not now."

She moved to her left until she reached a corner and then felt her way along the next wall. Still, she could not find a way out of the room. She screamed to release the rage inside her but did not give up.

She followed the wall back to the ladder, where the only light was the dim square shining through the opening above her. How could there be no opening? She continued past the ladder, leaving the small patch of light for the darkness once again.

The wall stretched out for what seemed like forever. Shaina would go around again. And again, if need be, until the way out presented itself to her. She felt the wall up as far as she could reach, and down to the floor, probing every inch of the wall for a lever or knob that might let her move out of the room. She found another corner and continued along another wall, but as the minutes passed, Shaina felt a panic rising in her that she might never find a way out.

She moved along the last bit of the wall to the final corner. If she came across another turn without finding a doorway, she would know the truth: she could find no way out.

As Shaina concentrated on the wall, a hand reached out of the darkness and touched her shoulder.

Shaina screamed.

"It's me."

The familiar voice calmed Shaina's racing heart. "Miss Helen?"

The mystic touched Shaina again, questing. When Miss Helen found her hand, she pulled Shaina in another direction. "Come with me."

A rumbling sound echoed through the darkness as a secret door slid open. Beyond the opening, a light shined off in the distance. Miss Helen dragged Shaina down a length of a narrow hallway. The hall opened into another room, and Shaina pulled her hand free of Miss Helen's grasp to walk around, examining the room.

The first thing to assail Shaina's senses was the smell of the room. Half-eaten rats covered one table against a far wall. Shaina shuddered when the implications of this discovery struck her. Miss Helen's touch caused her to turn around.

"Come, we have no time to waste sightseeing."

Shaina bristled but knew the psychic was right.

"How did you know about all this?" Shaina asked but received no reply. She had more questions for the psychic—like how long did she know about this exit—but the myriad queries would have to wait. Shaina needed to find Dashiell.

Miss Helen led Shaina into another tunnel-like hallway with light shining at the end of it. She turned to Miss Helen.

"That's the way out," said the psychic.

Chapter Twenty-Six: Dylan

The sun had gone down twenty minutes ago, and the only illumination lighting the fairgrounds came from lamps, and the strings of lights dangling from various posts adorning the fair. Dylan walked through the midway with only this lighting to guide his way.

He lifted the walkie talkie to his mouth. "Wanda, how are things going with you?"

The radio crackled, and Wanda's tinny, high pitched voice responded over the walkie talkie's speaker. "Lots of police presence here. How about you?"

Dylan pressed the button. "Same. They did a great job of mostly clearing out the grounds. There are a few straggling patrons, mostly gawkers. Smart people have already vacated the premises."

Squelch. "Good to hear. Any luck with finding our wayward friends?"

"Not yet, unfortunately. I'm not giving up that easy, though."

"Keep me posted."

"Will do."

The radio went silent, and Dylan clipped it to his belt. He jogged up to a nearby police officer and tapped him on the shoulder. "Is there any word? I'm still looking for my two people who went missing."

"No word yet on any missing people. We have cops in every nook and cranny of this place; we're turning on the lights in dark rooms. We'll find them…if they are here, that is."

Where would they be? Dylan let the question go unasked. "Thank you."

As Dylan walked away from the officer, he headed toward the orange safety fencing surrounding the damaged part of the grounds and Miss Helen's burned out shack. He couldn't shake the feeling her actions were relevant to what was happening now.

Dylan tore the barrier down and entered the "danger zone."

He remembered when Miss Helen had been staying at the fair. She had a bed in the back of her hut. There had been a beaded curtain separating her work area from her living quarters. She seemed excited to be working at the fair in the beginning. It wasn't until she started talking about having nightmares, and something about a black fog covering the festival—a mist only she could see. Then she began talking about the fair as a "bad place" and started the fire, destroying her place—her belongings with it—and part of the building next to hers.

He had investigated the fire damage before, but something kept turning over in his mind, telling him to come back here. He was missing something, or...

Miss Helen's ruined shed held nothing recognizable, but the adjacent building, the one that survived, and also in this danger zone, drew Dylan's attention. What if this other building had been the original target in Miss Helen's attack?

He stepped out of the ruined shell of Miss Helen's building and turned toward the second building in the area. He had never been inside this building and wasn't even sure why it was there, to be honest. He thought it was a warehouse, but the structure held no commodity, not even an empty box. He walked over to a window and peered inside. The windows were frosted over, but he could see that there was nothing inside.

He strode to the double doors and tried them, but they were locked. He expected nothing less. Dylan glanced around to see if anyone was near. He was going to break in, but it wasn't this that he didn't want anyone to see, but how he *performed* the act.

Convinced he was alone, Dylan gripped the knob and twisted. The metal crushed beneath the strength of his grip. He destroyed the knob and tossed it aside. With the doorknob gone, Dylan kicked the doors in without much effort.

The warehouse seemed unremarkable for the most part, with concrete walls and a floor consisting of crushed gravel. The sound of his footfalls on gravel echoed off the walls of the enormous, empty room. He crossed the long, narrow space to the back, where the unremarkable became downright strange.

In a part of the building blocked from sight on the outside, the floor slanted down, leading underground. Dylan took a few steps down the slant to the narrow tunnel. He paused at the opening and stared in at the darkness filling the passage.

Dylan debated entering the void or going back for the police, but before he made his decision, a door opened, and a shape emerged from the darkness.

Dylan blinked at what he saw.

The shape grew nearer, and Dylan saw a man with something draped on one shoulder. Dylan backed away as the form approached. As it reached the light, Dylan saw an incredibly tall, horribly deformed man carrying someone on his shoulder. The man wore a distinctive clown suit.

The elusive clown.

The clown with the infected face ignored Dylan and walked by him with its load hanging down its back. The man in the clown's grip seemed unconscious, and as Dylan focused on the lifeless man, he recognized it as Dashiell.

"Holy shit." Dylan's deep voice echoed off the walls of the cave-like tunnel.

The man's face was mostly gone. Red gums and grinning teeth were visible where lips should have been. The man stopped and stared at Dylan.

"You have my friend over your shoulder. Is he dead?" Dylan asked.

"Go," the faceless man said.

"Did you kill my friend?" Dylan stepped closer. "Dashiell, are you okay?"

The clown-thing lowered Dashiell to the ground. Dylan heard Dashiell groan—still alive. The deformed thing rushed at Dylan and hit him at a full run. Dylan flew backward and slammed into the ground. He jumped back onto his feet and met the next charge. The clown tried to grab him by the throat, but Dylan deflected the attack. He ducked a swing of the clown man's massive red fist.

Dylan managed a kidney shot that he thought would cripple the man, but the clown turned and hit Dylan, slamming him into the wall. Dylan coughed up blood but continued to press the attack. He caught the clown in the throat, but even this massive blow did nothing to slow the clown's attack.

It lifted Dylan off the ground and threw him several yards. Dylan hit the ground and rolled. He lifted himself onto all fours and stayed there, rasping for breath. Dylan felt broken ribs in his chest and possibly a collapsed lung. He stood back up and turned to face his attacker.

"Going to have to do better than that. I should tell you; I'm hard to kill." Dylan ran forward.

The clown met his charge. They struck each other with all four feet off the ground. Dylan's fists pummeled the clown's chest, but the flesh beneath the clown suit felt like unrisen bread dough. The clown's fist collided with Dylan's jaw and snapped his head back. Dylan spun and landed on his back, knocking the wind out of him. Through all that, the clown had kept its feet.

He's as durable as I am.

The clown stomped toward Dylan. It lifted a fist and swung down. At the last minute, Dylan tried to duck out of the way, but the clown seemed to anticipate his move. The fist hit him in the chest.

The clown's hand was not empty.

The clown pulled the knife free of Dylan's upper chest and struck again, this time in the abdomen. The clown stabbed Dylan four more times before dropping the knife and stepping away.

Dylan dropped to his knees. Blood drizzled through his fingers. He watched helplessly as the victor collected his prize and scooped up Dashiell.

Dylan had mortal wounds, but mortal meant something different to Dylan than to the average man. Even as the clown made his escape, Dylan's injuries healed. Within minutes, he was ready to give chase.

As Dylan lifted himself off the ground, someone else emerged from the tunnel. Dylan turned and faced Miss Helen. His eyes flicked to the second person approaching from the darkness of the tunnel.

"Shaina."

Shaina ran past Miss Helen and threw her arms around Dylan. She kissed him on the cheek. As she pulled away, Dylan wiped the tears from Shaina's face, leaving clean streaks on the dirty skin. They hugged again.

"Dashiell and a giant clown just passed through here."

"I know." Shaina dragged Dylan by the hand and led him toward the opening. "It's Dashiell's cousin, Owen. Owen has leprosy and has been living in the catacombs below this fair for years, killing for years."

Dylan turned and eyed Miss Helen, then the trio ran out of the empty warehouse and entered the warm night air.

Dylan stopped and quickly surveyed their surroundings.

Shaina pointed. "There."

The trio sprinted in the direction of the big man. Dylan charged the clown, but by the time he reached his opponent, a crowd of police had surrounded Owen and Dashiell.

Owen howled and charged at the line of cops. Several guns raised in response.

"No, don't shoot. He has a hostage." Dylan stepped between Owen, still holding Dashiell, and the guns. "Let me try to talk to him."

Dylan turned his back on the line of guns and put his hands out to Owen in a placating stance. Owen stopped charging and stood, pacing, and grunting.

"Please, Owen. Your name is Owen, right? Please, let Dashiell go. He's injured and needs medical attention."

Owen charged at Dylan, but the charge halted when a gunshot echoed through the midway. Owen bucked, and someone screamed. It was Shaina.

Dylan looked Owen over for a wound, first looking to see if Dashiell had been hit.

Dylan saw a drizzle of blood on Owen's left shoulder. Dashiell was draped over the right shoulder.

"Don't shoot, Goddamnit," Dylan said.

Owen spun around and crashed through the line of police, lifting one by the throat with one hand and throwing him into the crowd. Then Owen ran, heading for the part of the park that had been evacuated. The line of cops followed, guns still drawn. Dylan tried to stay between the guns and his friend.

"Move, you fool," the lead cop said to Dylan.

Dylan caught up to Owen and tried to pull Dashiell from his grip. Owen reached around and flung Dylan away then began climbing the framework of the Ferris Wheel. Dylan followed the clown up, trying to latch onto a sleeve or pant cuff. The oversized shoes came off and fell past Dylan. The clown climbed higher, breaking fluorescent lights that threw sparks as they exploded in his grasp. The shattered pieces dropped like glittering diamonds around Dylan's head. The strength to climb one-handed boggled Dylan's mind, but the man rose with little effort. Using both hands, Dylan couldn't keep up with Owen. The big man, Dashiell still dangling from one arm, neared the top. Owen's foot slipped. Dylan, still too far away to do any good, watched in horror as Owen dangled by his free hand. Owen managed to stop his fall by catching a foot on a precariously small ledge. Owen still held the limp and unmoving form of Dashiell around the waist.

The creaking of bending metal caused Dylan's breath to hitch.

"Owen, hold on, I'm coming." Dylan tried to maneuver himself between the ground and Dashiell. If Dashiell fell, Dylan prayed he would be there to catch him. Dylan reached the bar just below Dashiell when Owen's bar bent a little more.

Dashiell slipped from Owen's grasp. Dylan reached out to catch Dashiell as he passed by, but couldn't get into the correct position in time.

The unconscious man continued to fall, even as Dylan stretched out to catch him. A sense of dread pressed on Dylan's chest as he watched his friend spin out of reach. Dashiell hit a bar and spun in another direction. Dylan screamed in rage and pain as Dashiell hit the ground with a hollow thump.

Dylan scrambled back to the ground and dropped into the gravel over his friend's broken body. When the shooting began, Dylan heard it through a haze of grief.

Dashiell's neck had been broken.

The thud of another body hitting the ground caused Dylan to look up. A few feet away from

Dashiell's corpse, a lump of colorful fabric lay unmoving. The clown lay dead.

Shaina dropped into the dirt next to Dylan and cried uncontrollably into his shoulder. They held each other. Dylan's body felt numb, and when the EMTs arrived, he allowed them to take Shaina and himself away in an ambulance.

The technician checked Dylan over, but he had no wounds. Not even a scratch.

Chapter Twenty-Seven: Shaina

After hearing the police found her, Tommy brought the kids to see Shaina at the hospital. She held her kids tightly when she saw them, making them cry and moan that they couldn't breathe. Shaina didn't care. She never wanted to let them go. She thanked Tommy for taking care of her kids.

As the kids hung out in her room, playing with her adjustable bed, and harassing the nurses, Shaina exited the room and strolled down the hall. She spotted Miss Helen and waved. Miss Helen waved Shaina over.

"Will you come with me?" Miss Helen said. "I have someone who wants to see you."

"Lead the way."

Miss Helen turned, and Shaina followed her.

She followed Helen to a room bade Shaina enter. Reluctantly, Shaina pushed through the door. Miss Helen followed her. Shaina met Helen's eye, and the woman smiled, encouraging Shaina to keep going. Shaina turned and moved further into the room. She pulled back the privacy curtain and stepped up to the bed. Shaina stared down at the still form lying under a crisp, white sheet.

"Hello," Shaina said to get the person's attention.

Christopher turned over and lifted his gaze to meet Shaina's eyes. He smiled up at her showing his straight, brilliant row of white teeth. Shaina's eyes widened, and she flung her arms around him. He grunted in pain, and she backed off.

"Sorry," she said.

"I'm okay. Someone stabbed me, that's all."
Christopher uttered a cry that was half a laugh and
half a groan of pain. There was sorrow mixed into the
sound as well. He looked up at Shaina, anxiously.
"Were there any other survivors?"

Miss Helen stepped forward and revealed herself
to Christopher. Her expression was dire. "We three
are the only survivors."

Shaina turned to face her. "Really? No one else?"

"No. The police have completely closed off the
fairgrounds. They are there still looking for all the
secret passages. They've been tearing down walls to
find all the hidden entrances. They removed most of
the corpses, and the process of identifying them has
begun."

"I saw the boy, Billy, when I was down there,"
Shaina said. "Oh, god. Poor Billy. And his family?"

Miss Helen nodded. "The authorities found him;
his family notified."

"Have you been officially cleared of all charges?"
Shaina asked.

Miss Helen nodded again. "They also dropped
the arson charges, since no one was hurt and the
damage I did was minimal. The district attorney
concluded that I was a catalyst for uncovering the
truth behind the fair. There was the talk of giving me
a commendation, but I don't want that."

"I think you should get one," Shaina said.

Miss Helen shrugged. "I can't stick around long
enough for all that. I have places to be. I have a friend
who is asking for my help in Old Forge. I think I'll
head there next."

"You're leaving?" Shaina hadn't expected to hear that. The news stung her.

Miss Helen squeezed Shaina's hand. "There's a whole new adventure for me out there, and I can't keep destiny waiting."

"You'll stick around long enough to meet my kids, at least, won't you? I want you to meet them. You saved my life, after all. If you hadn't found me wandering around down there in the dark, I might still be lost." Shaina allowed herself a little laugh. Dylan had been on the path to finding the passageway, and all the events would have unfolded the same as they had, but still, Shaina felt a kind of gratitude to Miss Helen for helping her get out of that horrible place.

Miss Helen rubbed Shaina's arm. "I can certainly do that."

Shaina directed her gaze at Christopher. "And when you're feeling better, I want you to meet them, too."

"It's a date," Christopher said, smiling.

Shaina turned to Miss Helen. "Where is Dylan? I want to see him again, too. He's still around, isn't he?"

"I'm afraid I saw him heading out of town a couple of hours ago. I told him he should stick around to say goodbye to everyone, but he insisted he wasn't good at goodbyes. He did ask me to give you his condolences."

Shaina lowered herself to the edge of Christopher's bed. She wiped burning tears from her eyes. Dashiell was gone. Dylan had gone away without even a goodbye. Soon Miss Helen would be leaving. Shaina had forged a strong bond in such a short time with this group of strangers, and an ache of loneliness entered her chest, a pain she hadn't felt since her husband died.

She thought of Dashiell. What she felt for him might not have been love, but after what they had been through together, the feeling was intense, and he would hold a special place in her heart. She had often imagined building a life with him during their time together. And when Owen revealed himself, she felt a flicker of hope that they would get out of there alive. How had things gone so wrong?

As her tears returned anew, she felt fingers interlocking with hers. She looked down at Christopher, who had taken her hand. She lifted his hand to her face and kissed it. Looking into his eyes, Shaina understood that Christopher wouldn't be going anywhere. With Christopher, Shaina formed a friendship that would last the rest of her life.

"We should let him rest." Miss Helen directed Shaina away from the bed.

Reluctantly, Shaina turned away from Christopher and followed Miss Helen back into the hallway. Miss Helen caught Shaina's eye and held it. Shaina understood the woman had something to say.

"What is it?" Shaina asked.

"It's Amber. Her ghost is with Christopher. She wants to know he's going to be all right before she moves on."

Shaina didn't question Miss Helen's statement. "She can rest knowing that I will always be there to look after him."

"Good. That's what Amber wanted to hear. I think she'll be at peace now."

Shaina nodded. When Miss Helen turned to go, Shaina stopped her with a hand on her arm. She felt a thickness in her throat that she couldn't swallow away. She feared it would stop her from saying what she wanted to say.

"Dashiell." There it was. It was out. "Have you...seen him?"

Miss Helen stared deeply into Shaina's eyes. Slowly, the psychic shook her head. "I'm sorry.

Epilogue: Dylan

He made it about ten miles out of town when the sun began to rise behind him. He wished he had been heading the other way so he could have watched it come up. He supposed there was another chance to see the sunrise.

When Dylan heard the sound of a car approaching from behind, he turned around and stuck out his thumb. A black Lincoln MKZ pulled up beside him. The windows were tinted, not allowing him to see who was inside the car. The passenger side door lock popped with a metallic clunk, and the door opened a crack. Dylan finished opening the door.

"Going my way, handsome?" The voice inside the car was female.

"Thanks for the ride." Dylan leaned down to see the driver. He rolled his eyes. "It's you."

"I'm happy to see you, too," Miss Helen said. "Do you want a ride or not?"

After a moment of hesitation, Dylan climbed into the passenger seat. Miss Helen threw the car into gear and drove away.

"How did you find me?" Dylan asked.

Miss Helen uttered a disgusted laugh. "Why does everyone ask me that? Does no one have any faith in my ability as a psychic?"

"Okay, okay. We'll concede that you have a knack for knowing things." He shrugged. "When it serves your purposes, anyway."

She glanced at him, and they laughed.

"Okay, fine. I accept your compromise." She was silent for a moment then said something Dylan felt had been plucked directly from his brain. "Shaina was distraught that you didn't say goodbye."

Dylan closed his eyes for a space of a few heartbeats, then opened them again. He stared out the front window. "Leaving her without saying goodbye was hard for me, but I think it was necessary. The longer I stick around, the harder it is to leave. And if you're Psychic, you'll know why I *have* to leave."

"And you always leave."

She hadn't posed the words as a question, but Dylan answered her as if it had been.

"Yes."

"So, where are we headed?"

Dylan shook his head slowly. "Not sure. I plan on going south for a while. I tend to stick to the back roads, avoiding a lot of people."

Miss Helen stared out through the windshield at the morning scenery. They passed a farmhouse that sat back from the road, with a winding driveway leading from the mailbox to the large white house, and a red barn behind it.

After another couple of miles passed them by, Miss Helen turned a glance at Dylan then back at the road.

"I know what happened to you at Yellowstone Park."

Dylan glanced at her, then did a double-take. No one should have known what happened to him there. All the witnesses were dead. "What are you talking about?" His voice was weaker than he had intended.

"What happened there isn't your fault."

"Why would you think that's what I believe? If something even happened there, I mean."

"I speak to the dead, remember? Your friends are always with you. They are here with us now, in this car."

Dylan didn't bother looking around. He knew he couldn't see them, even if he did believe what she was saying. "I carry *them* with me always, as well." He tapped his chest. "In here. I guess they would follow me."

She spared another look at him. "I also know what happened to you there. I know why you heal faster than any mortal man has a right to."

This time he didn't act shocked. "Then you also know why I always have to leave. If I stick around, secrets have a habit of being discovered."

"And you have a lot of secrets to protect."

Dylan nodded vigorously. "I do."

Miss Helen looked at him. She then pulled over to the side of the road, causing a cloud of dust to lift around the car. Dylan stared at her as Miss Helen put the car in park and turned her entire body to face him. She put out her hands.

"Let's do a reading. Come on; it's free."

Dylan doubted anything with Miss Helen was free—including this ride—but she didn't expect payment in money. She would collect payment in the form of the soul. But she seemed harmless enough, so he took her hands. Miss Helen took a deep breath, closed her eyes, and blew out the held breath. He watched as her head lulled back and forth as if in a trance. He smiled, wondering how much of this was for the show.

"I see you settling in with a group of friends who have like-minded secrets like yours. They keep your secrets, and you keep theirs. If you settle down in the New Jersey/Delaware/Philadelphia area, they will seek you out. Your days of wandering will come to an end, and you will live the rest of your days with this group."

Dylan didn't have to accept she was a psychic to believe that what she said could come true. He felt strangely optimistic about what she had said. "Thank you for that."

Miss Helen didn't release Dylan's hands right away. She peered deeply into his eyes. Dylan waited, and soon Miss Helen spoke.

"I lied," she said.

"Lied?" Dylan asked.

"I've never lied before, Dylan. I may stretch the truth or withhold it entirely, but I never lied. Until now."

"What was the lie?" Dylan asked.

"I told Shaina I didn't see Dashiell at the hospital—his spirit—but I did. He is there with her. He's looking over her, following her."

"Why did you lie about it? She probably wouldn't believe you, anyway. She is a pragmatic woman. She doesn't go in for that voodoo."

"That's exactly why I lied about it. If Shaina could find comfort in the knowledge Dashiell was there with her, I would have told her. If I told her and she didn't believe she might feel conflicted. I didn't want to burden her with a truth she couldn't comprehend. I did it so Shaina could go on with her life. But the truth of the matter is she and Dashiell forged a bond that followed him into death. He will be there, watching over her for the rest of her life."

Miss Helen released his hands and placed them back on the wheel. She drove away, and they spoke very little for the rest of their journey.

When they passed through Pennsylvania, Dylan sensed their time together was drawing to a close, and he turned to the psychic. "I'm in a unique position to believe that you do have the ability to see the future. I've got to know—did you foresee the events that unfolded at the fair yesterday? And more importantly, could you have prevented it?"

Miss Helen drove on as if she hadn't heard him. After a time, she responded. "Let me ask this: why do you think that just by seeing an event before it occurs, you have the power to prevent it—or change the course of the event in any way?"

Dylan hated when people answered a question with a question, but he knew he wouldn't get a more straightforward answer from her, and Dylan didn't have an answer to the question she posed, so he dropped the subject.

They stayed together for another few days, but eventually, they parted ways. Dylan headed to New Jersey, and Miss Helen went off to find her adventures in places unknown.

Except Dylan somehow believed these places were known to Miss Helen.

Afterward

I hope you enjoyed reading Black Fair as much as I enjoyed writing it. Some people might be wondering what secrets Dylan Moyer is hiding. My reasons for keeping his secret out of this book aren't so much for suspense as for other reasons. The truth is if you want to know more about Dylan's secret, and why he has an uncanny ability to heal, all these details are revealed in my first novel Immortal Coil. I invite you to read Immortal Coil to learn of these secrets, as well as to read the rest of the trilogy, which includes the books Immortal Clash and Immortal Conquest.

Acknowledgements:

At this time, I would like to take the opportunity to thank a few people, without whom, this book would not exist in its present form.

Thank you to early readers Lisa Streeter, Millie Gawarecki, Jennifer Francisco, and Theresa DeVaul (my sister). Their contributions made this book better than it has a right to be. Although their help made this book better, any mistakes lie solely on the Author's shoulders.

Made in the USA
Middletown, DE
12 April 2021